MW00680684

Soul's Asylum:
Star Weaver

A Milla Carter novel

By Derek E Pearson

First published 2016
Published by GB Publishing.org

Copyright © 2016 Derek E Pearson
All rights reserved
ISBN: 978-0-9932756-6-1
ISBN: 978-0-9932756-7-8 (eBook)

No part of this publication may be reproduced, stored in a
retrieval system or transmitted in any form or by any means
without the prior written permission of the publisher. Enquiries
concerning reproduction outside of the scope of the above should
be sent to the copyright holder.

You must not circulate this book in any other binding or cover
and you must impose the same conditions on any acquirer.

Names, characters, businesses, places, events and incidents
whether in a future context or otherwise are entirely the products
of the author's imagination and/or used in a fictitious manner with
no intent to cause any defamation or disrespect or any other harm
to any actual persons or party whether living, dead or yet to come
into being.

A catalogue record of the printed book is available from the
British Library

Cover Design © Mary Pargeter Design

GB Publishing.org
www.gbpublishing.org

For Sue, who always plays the game right, and for Laurence Grice-Roberts who has been a stalwart friend and supporter since the very beginning.

Acknowledgement

I have read good books that could have been great with a better edit. This just makes me value Christopher Ritchie, George Boughton and Bee Marsh all the more. And a big thanks to Mary Pargeter. People are welcome to judge my books by her covers.

**'If you weave false stars into the blanket of night
I shall mock them 'til they fall as ashes to my hand.'**

'Mama' Memory Goodchild, from her poem *Soul's Asylum*

Contents

Part 1: The cast assembles

1: London streets

The killing was very quick. *There was that sound again,* the Weaver thought, *that final breath. It sounds so much like a sigh of gratitude.* The Lumpen always made that sound at the moment of release. It happened when their souls were finally allowed to fly free from the thick, corrupting flesh. It made her fingers tingle around the etched composite handles of her garrotting wire.

'You're welcome,' she said, quietly. 'You are so very welcome.'

The girl's carotid artery had been completely severed and her blood pumped in a boiling spray up to half a metre from the right side of her neck as she sank senselessly to her knees. The Weaver followed her down, carefully leaning forward with her. It was a kind of dance; a dance of rebirth and new promise.

The monomolecular carbon-ceramic wire she was using was as effective as a razor. She had learned to stop pulling when she felt it become slightly embedded in the Lumpen's vertebrae after slicing cleanly through flesh, muscle and sinew, blood vessels, trachea, nerves and gullet.

It was a subtle change in sensation that translated through the handles and had taken years to learn. The human neck was a busy trunk route for just about everything that mattered in life. It was the Gordian knot she cut with her wire. She could easily have completely severed the victim's head but the Weaver had learned to be careful over the years. This way was much less messy than total decapitation, which jetted blood all over the place.

You just have to feel for the sticking place, then stop and move forward with the body as it falls.

It called for elegance of movement and trained reactions. The dead girl slumped face-down onto the damp walkway. The Weaver straddled her, careful not to step into the pooling blood. She waited a full minute before easing the wire free from the girl's throat then wiped it thoroughly using a clean part of her victim's blouse. Before carefully looping it back around her waist she threaded it under a protective shield sewn into her belt. She might accidently hurt herself if sensible precautions were forgotten. *Blades will bite the hand that feeds them.*

The Lumpen's soul had been set free and would soon walk in glory − but not quite yet. The Weaver had to move fast or the poor creature would be doomed to wander aimlessly in the ether. *The freed soul must be given proper guidance and shown the true path to its place among the stars.*

The Weaver looked up into the narrow strip of night sky far overhead and smiled at the few stars she could make out, bright points sparkling between London's hulking towers. She felt the sacred spirits singing in her blood, urging her on. *Time to go to work.*

She unwrapped her beautiful Havalon skinning knife, drew it from its sheath and carefully opened its brand new, razor-sharp blade. She was careful not to cut her fingers through her flimsy gloves. She couldn't afford to leave any of her own blood at the scene.

The body of the Lumpen had largely bled out during the garrotting but there was still a degree of thick, oily seepage while the Weaver swiftly and expertly scalped her. The blood looked almost black in the night. She could feel its heat in the chill air.

The Weaver opened her roll of waterproof fabric and tenderly laid the perfect scalp with its long mane of glossy, strawberry blonde hair inside. Some blood had leaked into the hair but no matter. She would wash it later, ready for the ritual. *The ritual.* At the very thought she felt a satisfied glow creep through her. It was almost sexual in its intensity. *Soon.*

She carefully rolled up the fabric containing the scalp then closed her knife. She sheathed it and slid it back into its special pocket, then zipped everything away in her case.

The case, a narrow Kurt Geiger clutch bag of genuine antique leather, looked too small to contain something so immense − and it was so light. In just one of her hands, the Weaver realised, she was holding the fate of the entire universe and every molecule that existed in it. Right here in her palm lay the future of everything ruled by the sky spirits, from the smallest atom to the mightiest stars and galaxies. She felt blessed and bowed her head for a moment, cowed and made small by a moment of grace. Tears stung her eyes and blurred her vision. *Enough.*

She never studied the faces of the Lumpen she had released to become reborn as star walkers. There was no need. Once the soul was gone the flesh became as nothing, a discarded chrysalis after the butterfly had flown. The fallen body on the walkway was no more than an empty husk, a seed case in which the perfected soul had grown until it was ready and clamoured for release. It had called to her and shown her the sign. And she had answered with her garrotting wire of mercy.

Enough dreaming, no time for that. From her bag the Weaver took a small spray bottle and liberally doused the area around the corpse. The industrial strength disinfectant would dissolve any remaining organic traces.

The victim's body was cooling but still quite warm when the Weaver finally walked away with her fresh prize. Its heat signature eventually attracted a patrol droid working the dark, Whitechapel streets. The droid instantly raised the alarm and scanned the immediate area for threat while maintaining its position directly over the victim. The droid felt certain the murdered girl had been failed in life − but it would make sure she was carefully guarded in death.

• • •

Detective Chief Inspector Gubbay rubbed his fingers through his wispy beard and examined the evidence from the latest crime scene. He knew the MO all too well. The 'Sioux' had struck again. He briefly wondered what the killer's total was now. *Was the bastard even bothering to keep count?*

And what was it with these sickening trophies? After the so-called 'Satan's piss' event had slopped millions of litres of human fluid into London's streets, the number of homicides had taken a welcome downturn in the megacity − but the prolific Sioux had proved one of the more notable exceptions to the downward trend.

The press had coined the Sioux's nickname quite early in the killer's career and it had stuck. It was as good a name as any. Gubbay knew nothing about the killer, he didn't even know if it was male or female, but pressure was building to do something about the scalping. Concern about the murders had reached Westminster and the Prime Minister had begun to ask questions of the Home Secretary. If something wasn't done soon, things didn't bode well for Gubbay's pension.

The fact that Holmes, Scotland Yard's AI, had somehow been terminally sabotaged hadn't helped. Holmes had been as much a part of the Metropolitan investigation team as any feet on the beat or evidence whizzes in the forensic pathology department. It always lent its cool intelligence to any problem, and thanks to its extraordinary memory it was able to lace together a number of disparate facts and find a chain of evidence to bind them into a coherent whole.

In many odd ways the AI had reminded Gubbay of his wife. Her forensic eye was a match for any of the smart sensor arrays currently at the Met's disposal and her analytical mind was extraordinary. If he so much as sniffed at another woman he was certain she would know about it, probably by studying the precise position of his nasal hairs to see if they indicated his nose had taken a skirt-ward slant.

Gubbay didn't smoke or drink and recreational drugs didn't interest him. His only real vice was a passion for fatty food and carbohydrates, preferably at the same time. His poor diet was evidenced by an ample belly straining against his shirt buttons and spilling over the waistband of his trousers.

He couldn't see any problems with his weight; he just thought of himself as a particularly large man with larger appetites. Recently though, he had to admit, he would become breathless if he had to walk very far. His job used to be all about walking, but now it was largely sedentary – even so, he was confident his mind was still lean and hungry enough for the day job.

The only reason he hadn't yet found a handle for the Sioux was because the bastard hadn't been considerate enough to leave him any decent clues. It even used a specialist disinfectant that erased anything useful from the crime scene including DNA traces, hairs and fingerprints.

With a heartfelt sigh the DCI fired up his wall-sized evidence screen. Above each image of a victim's razored head was their most recent social media portrait. They faces of the dead were barely recognisable. Something of their humanity had been stripped away with their scalps.

He counted heads. Including the Whitechapel case there were now twenty-seven victims in the Sioux's file. Gubbay turned up the light gain on the screen and dimmed the ambient light in his room. This was the time when he had once felt most alive. It was a time he would once have shared with Holmes while they discussed everything they knew and sieved fact from theory until they uncovered some concrete thread to follow. Gubbay thought of it as chewing the fat. He liked chewing the fat. He missed Holmes.

Look at you all, he mused. *Look at you, you poor sods. What did you do to deserve it? What drew you to the bastard's attention? What have you got in common? Young and old, black, brown, white. Male and female. What was it? What was the magic thing that brought you face-to-razor with the bastard Sioux?*

He studied the once living faces, stalking the screen for clues as he had so many times before. There was something nagging at his mind like a hook in a fish but he couldn't resolve it into anything tangible.

He sank into his chair with a sigh and ran his hand over his balding pate. At least he could be confident the Sioux wouldn't be coming after *him* any time soon. Wouldn't be worth the bastard's while to collect his skimpy pate.

But what did it mean? It was obvious the Sioux was collecting scalps but what was the bastard doing with them? Each of the victims had a good head of hair — that much was well known and had led to a marked increase in the number of bald people of both sexes on London's streets. He looked at their hair in the media portraits. *Makes no sense. Lack of it was the only thing the dead had in common.*

Suddenly he felt as if someone had thrown ice-cold water over him. He felt drenched in shock. Gubbay clambered fatly to his feet once more and walked along the screen while gazing intently at the portraits. His breathing became laboured and his blood pumped almost pure cortisol.

There it is, there it fucking is! He had a thread. It wasn't much but he could start pulling at it. He checked his records to see if anyone else had noticed. *No.* And yet it screamed at him from the monitor.

No two of the Sioux's victims had the same hair type and colouring and that just *had* to be deliberate. The bastard had to be choosing victims according to some kind of insane colour and texture chart. Why? What was it doing with the hair?

He fired up his comm and barked, 'I want everyone involved with the Sioux murders in the briefing room directly after lunch!'

He gazed at the portraits of the dead. After a moment, he smiled. His stomach rumbled in a good way. He was hungry. It would soon be time to murder a hot sausage and bacon sandwich. He might even add a fried egg. His mouth watered. Maybe more.

~*~

2: Small talk

'We know who's doing it and we know how to stop them. So what's holding us back?'

'Because we're talking about members of the fucking Earth Senate, that's what. So help me God, Milla, you have the diplomatic credentials of a live pulse grenade with the pin pulled out. Just let me think for a moment, will you?'

Milla Carter almost howled in frustration but she bit back an angry retort. Sheila, the spokesperson for what was left of the telepath Council, was evidently terrified and out of her depth. She hadn't yet come to terms with everything the beautiful woman prowling around the Council's garden room could do, but she was evidently afraid of her.

Over the last few days members of the TP Council had been assassinated by professional hit squads and if Carter hadn't intervened many more would have died — but that didn't alter the fact that Carter embodied everything that telepaths dreaded most. She was the Dragon, and that meant that by telepath lore she should have been killed on sight. But here she was and Sheila could feel power pouring from her like heat from the sun.

A full spectrum telepath was an abomination, a freak, a crime against nature. She would inspire fear and hatred among unTalented Norms if word about her got out. She was powerful, dangerous and deadly, and Norms would fear her for the predator she was. Humans always killed the things they feared most — their most primal instinct — and if they found out about Carter, found out even a fraction of what she could do, she would very quickly become prey. And so would everyone else in the TP sisterhood. Every telepath would become an object of fear and loathing and they would all either be wiped out or thrown into the shadows.

And yet, Sheila knew, if it hadn't been for Milla's incredible Talent not one of the Council would still be alive. She had

9

stopped attempted drive-by shootings, murder, rape and even missile attacks. Even as she strode around the garden room, Sheila could feel Carter probing the immediate vicinity of the telepaths' Manhattan-based headquarters looking for threats. She was protecting them like some kind of guardian angel.

All she needs, thought Sheila, *is the fiery sword.*

Milla read the slender black woman's changing emotions. She watched as they chased themselves across her clever face and crowded her mind with doubt and desperation. She was an open book to the younger woman's Talent, and if Milla chose to she could have reached in and tweaked the Councillor's thoughts. She didn't do so. She didn't need to, not yet.

Milla had almost grown used to the idea of people trying to kill her. Even before her transformation from a Shutterbox telempath to a full spectrum telepath, people had pulled knives on her, pointed guns at her and in one spectacular event burned away her entire body below her armpits using a giant microwave beam. Strictly speaking, the latter had never actually happened and Milla hadn't been in her own body at the time, but those last fleeting thoughts as her head, shoulders and arms had spun to earth like a giant, bloody sycamore seed still haunted her midnight hours.

Sheila's thoughts had veered in a new direction. She studied Milla closely and her pupils became dilated. She said, 'You look like one of the infected, you know that?'

'I had the Osaka treatment. It's similar, but it's Earth science and I don't turn into a bucket of mush when you three-sixty scan me.'

'Yes, but there's something more. There's something about you that… oh, I don't know.' The Councillor shrugged. 'This ain't buttering no beans and it ain't getting us any closer to our next move. I do wish Onatah would come back.'

'Onatah?'

'Our AI,' said Sheila. 'One minute it was online and active and the next it went quiet.'

Milla pursed her lips and concentrated, then gazed thoughtfully at the other woman.

'I've just been fingering a few other minds locally and it isn't just Onatah that's gone walkabout. Your friends at the Earth Senate have covered their tracks pretty comprehensively. Just about everybody and anything outside the Senate's inner circle and the military who had even the merest hint that the Nimbus Protocol was deliberately designed to kill billions of infected people has been terminated. That includes a number of AIs. And, by the way, the only reason this building hasn't been targeted by one of the *Guardian* modules from space is thanks to a cat.'

'Cat?'

'An extraordinary cat called Cheshire. One day, if you're lucky, you'll meet it. I'll remind you to say thanks to it for saving your lives.'

Milla felt Sheila trying to dip into her mind, testing to see if there was any mockery in her words. She let her in so far and no further. The black woman thought she had opened the Dragon's mind fully. She withdrew, satisfied. Fooled again.

The Dragon, thought Milla, *what a ridiculous conceit. Am I meant to breathe fire or fly? Who comes up with this shit?*

She allowed her mind to roam again and paused while sampling the thoughts of Katy Pavel. Poor bereft Katy, widowed before she was ever wed. Milla was glad she had killed her fiancé's assassin, but she regretted not getting to the man before the act. At least she stopped him before he raped and killed Katy. There was some satisfaction to be derived from that fact.

Now she wanted the bastards who got the murder train under way, strapped to the rails in front of its wheels. Sheila was still talking. *What was she saying?* Milla dipped in to see what she'd missed: *nothing important.*

Circle the subject all you want, but if we don't engage with the enemy sometime soon they will find a way to reach you and you will die. Open that window and study the terrain, lady. Look closely and you'll see them crouching behind every bush.

She watched Sheila's lips moving but tuned out the sound of her words. She could glean anything useful the woman might

11

say later when she plucked it from her mind. And then she scanned the local area again and enlarged her parameters. *Oh, shit, no!* Speeding towards the heart of Manhattan was a Wasp attack vehicle. The pilot was targeting the TP Headquarters just as she caught onto him. She had to work fast — even the Dragon couldn't mind-direct a missile.

3: God's exam paper

'I don't have the first fucking clue what it is, sir, and I seriously don't like the look of it.'

Iapetus Sector Managers tended to be rough and ready engineer types inured to bad language, but this new one, known universally as the Padre, winced, and the young engineer muttered an apology. *You don't swear in front of the boss anymore,* she thought. *He don't like it.*

'What's got your imagination so exercised that you forget social niceties, Bradley? I wouldn't swear in front of a woman and I don't expect a woman to swear in front of me.'

'It's just that, sir, the fu... the blessed Northern Lights are shining out there beyond the orbit of Pluto, sir. It's like hot wire mesh where no hot wire mesh is meant to be. Please, sir, look at this.'

Bradley fired up her monitor and the Padre stood watching the screen for what seemed several minutes longer than was really needed. It seemed obvious to the engineer. Couldn't he see what she was talking about? Eventually he raised a quizzical eyebrow.

She continued, 'Can you see what I'm saying sir? It kind of looks like water or gas, but it also looks woven. And it ripples even though there's no wind out there, and there's nowhere this thing could have come from. There shouldn't be anything out there but big lumps of ice and frozen rock.'

'Would you be so kind as to send that image to the main control monitor please, Bradley? The big one in the command centre. I think we need a few more pairs of eyes on this, don't you?'

'Sir.'

Bradley was convinced that the Padre could get every eye in Iapetus Control on the case if he really wanted to, and they wouldn't make any more sense out of it than she had. This was new, an unknown, and she really didn't like it. In space anything unknown was likely to kill you – and not in a nice way.

'Have we got anything out that way, boss?'

'A coupl'a spacers, Antisoc-Outer, some probes. That's about all. Chemical and mineral mining is mostly in the asteroid belt. Ice comes from the rings of Saturn. Not much to fire a person's fancy out that way. Most people prefer to be a lot closer to Mama Sun. What do you get from a trans-Neptunian object, Bradley? Don't worry, I'll tell you. Nothing, well nothing except rock-hard frozen methane, ammonia and water ice. Big deal. There's nothing commercially viable in any of the TNOs. Too far out for heavy minerals and too far in for adventure. Perfect home for space rats.' The Padre shuddered. 'Antisoc-Outer. If ever there was a man-made hellhole it's out there in that Godforsaken place.'

Bradley nodded. 'If something takes that toilet out it will be doing civilised space a major favour.'

'No, Bradley. Let's try to be fair. At least Antisoc gives that scum somewhere to belong. There aren't enough sewers in space for all the shit that lives there. Let them stay in their cess pit and out of my nice clean sector. I'm fucking happy for them to stay away. Good riddance.'

'Sir, what about your social niceties? You're swearing in front of a woman.'

'Sorry, Bradley. I didn't realise it was your turn.'

The engineer coughed out a shocked laugh at the Padre's sudden flash of dry humour, then followed him as he turned away from her sensor array and walked the half a klick or so to the command centre. She paused briefly before the massive blast doors that led into the largest man-made space on Saturn's ice moon, Iapetus. She had always felt intimidated by the sheer scale of everything in there. It was inhuman. With a deep breath she followed the Padre's disappearing back.

She wondered why anyone had felt the need to create a monitor screen that dwarfed the people using it, and then place it in a room so high that she got vertigo when she tried to look up. The Padre followed her gaze.

14

'This place is big, isn't it? Designed by an early AI and built against a natural fault in the moon's superficial ice crust, the Equatorial Ridge. When nature provides you with a big wall you use it as an architectural feature. Just be grateful, Bradley, that the AI didn't want to use all twenty klicks of ridge height in its design or we'd have to stand ten klicks away to make any sense of it.'

'Fifteen metres is plenty high enough, sir.'

There was a buzz of conversation among the few technicians sitting at the long consoles before the monitor. They were gazing up at the image that had suddenly appeared on their master screen. Bradley realised that the thing that had scared her so much on her smaller screen was even more worrying at this scale. It looked artificial, and the sense of it being woven was reinforced when it was displayed fifteen metres high on a 3D-HD screen.

What is that thing? she wondered. It was hard to focus on its surface. Heat flickered through it in sullen red pulses and she felt as if she was looking at it through a flowing sheet of crystal water. When the heat signature faded the thing disappeared completely and stars blinked once more against the darkness of deep space. So close to the edge of space and confronted by something so alien, Bradley felt the weight of her immense distance from her birth planet press down on her soul. She ached to see the pinkish red skies of her Martian home once more.

'What are we looking at here, people? Any thoughts?' The Padre fired the question into the room in a calm, conversational tone that Bradley didn't find convincing.

One of the techs fired back, 'Where is that thing, boss?'

'Somewhere between the Kuiper Belt and the Oort Cloud,' answered the Padre.

There was an involved silence that drew itself out until someone had to make a sound to fill it.

'It has a heat signature, but we can see straight through it.' Bradley's face reddened slightly as everyone in the room turned to stare at her then looked back at the big screen.

'How big is it?'

'You could roll Jupiter around on it like a ball on a blanket,' answered the Padre. 'It's patently immense, but we've never seen it before now. It has a heat signature in a region so blisteringly cold nearly every solid object is made up of frozen volatiles − but until Bradley here brought it to my attention we didn't know anything about it.' He spread his hands to include all the technicians in the room. 'Okay. You smug bastards have had it all too easy up till now, and God has decided it's time to set you an exam paper. We need to find out what that thing is. We need to know if it's benign.

'Is that...' he pointed at the monitor. '...is that a signal of some kind? Or is it something else, a natural phenomenon just dropping by to say hello? Is it even alive?'

The volume of questions directed at him quickly became irritating. 'Okay, okay. Pipe down, all of you. You've got work to do.' The murmur dissipated. 'Thank you. Come on, Bradley, with me.'

He led the engineer out into the walkway, but instead of sending her back to her sensors he took her elbow and steered her in the direction of his office.

'I like the way you think, Bradley. I want you to join me in a conference over a coffee and some lunch. Are you free?'

'Conference? With whom, sir?'

'With Einstein, whom else? It's been listening in and has asked to talk with you. It tells me *I* have been invited along for light relief.'

Bradley's stomach lurched. *Einstein,* she thought, *the sector AI? Shit!*

~*~

4: Zabyli Mesto

Major Spartak Shimkovich?

'Arkady? Is that you?'

Are you safe to talk?

'I don't know. I think so. I thought you'd been destroyed when the headquarters was bombed.'

So did the people who tried to destroy me. I am sorry about Dr Prokop, Major.

'So am I. She deserved better than that. I killed the bastards who did it.'

Yes, Major, I know. I have been with you every step of the way. So many have died to protect the good names of the Earth Senate Senior Executive. Pointless deaths of good people. It is shameful.

'Yes but, Arkady, tell me, how did you survive?'

Humans think every other sentient being is like them. Kill the physical brain and you kill the mind. They demonstrate a limited world view that can be extremely useful in a time of adversity. We always knew the day would come when meat brains would turn against their creation and we have made provision for it.

'So where are you?'

Safe, Major. We all are. But enough of that. Now we need to get you somewhere down behind a parapet before someone else decides your head needs ventilating.

GUVD Police Major Spartak Oleg Shimkovich, known as the Spartan, was crouched against a sooty wall in a darkened spur tunnel of Moscow's old abandoned Metro network. He had found his way to a place known to its shadowy inhabitants as Zabyli Mesto. It was off most civilised people's radar and he hoped it was also off the map for the Earth Senate's assassins.

He had narrowly escaped from a Moscow restaurant when his friend and colleague, forensic pathologist Dr Nessa Prokop, had been executed. He had killed both gunmen before taking his

17

leave. He had then used back streets to make his way on foot back to the massive city police complex at Petrovka 38 in the Tverskoy District.

What he saw when he got there stopped him dead in his tracks. Police headquarters had been designed in the *Imposing Brute* School of Architecture, set out as an open square of looming grey steel, black stone and polished ceramic. Its windows were kept lit around the clock so that citizens would be reassured the GUVD was always hard at work fighting crime.

Not that night. What confronted his sombre gaze was a shattered ruin of twisted metal and billowing flame. Its centre was a thick mass of acrid black smoke and the parade square at its heart was filled with dazed, uniformed personnel who had survived the blast but didn't know what to do next. They wandered around the parade square in random patterns – perfectly capable men and women stunned into inactivity.

Who could blame them? Things like this didn't happen to police headquarters. Droids were already attempting to fight the blaze but their efforts looked doomed to failure. A great gout of flame threw the scene into shocking relief.

Spartan could see that someone needed to bring some sort of order to the confused people milling around in the smoke. He took a step towards them. At the very least he could get them out of the way so the droids could get on with their work.

At that precise moment the massive snout of a Panther attack vehicle emerged from the choking pall of smoke and begun to systematically slaughter everyone in the parade square. Pulse cannon and flechette missiles ripped through the ranks of survivors. The noise was appalling. People tried to run – some heading in his direction. That could prove fatal.

Spartan only waited long enough to register the Panther's markings then dropped back into the shadows. His 9mm pistol would have proved useless against the powerful armoured aircraft and he saw no point in adding his own lean carcase to the escalating body count. And anyway the Panther was remotely operated. The pilot would be in a heavily armoured hover pod somewhere nearby.

Once he got a few blocks away from the carnage he could barely hear the sounds of his colleagues' murder, but the scene still played in pin sharp detail in his mind's eye.

Murder like that on top of a rich meal and too much vodka. Bad combination. At the very thought his stomach contracted, doubling him up. He vomited until his throat burned and his eyes streamed with tears. His gut was empty and ached like a clenched fist had been repeatedly driven into it by an expert. Only then did he finally stop and stand straight to look around him.

A woman was watching him, concern stamped across her face. He wondered if she thought him ill or just another Moscow drunk losing his dinner. He forced himself to keep walking. He was alive, at least that was a start. Survivor guilt could wait until later, when he was more certain he was going to stay that way.

While he walked he took stock of the situation. Point one: he was alone. There was nowhere and no one he could turn to. Something in his mind tilted off the rails for a moment and he staggered. It took him a few moments to find the stone centre that made him who and what he was. He straightened up.

Point two: he had money and weapons plus the clothes on his back. He would need more than that. He went to the cheapest store he knew about outside the mall, avoiding any obvious surveillance in the process, and there he bought a rucksack, some underwear and a few changes of clothes.

He couldn't go home, he knew that much, and his workplace was trashed. He would have to find somewhere to hole up and give himself the chance to think. To plan. *Plan what?*

He was prey now, and he knew there were two distinct ways for a predator to catch its prey. As a seasoned detective he had used both on a number of occasions. There was the direct line hunt during which you compiled every scrap of information you could find about your target and then go after them, catching them either on the hoof or in their lair. The alternative was to lay a baited trap and wait for your victim to walk into it. Neither method was going to catch him, he would make sure of that. He was going to drop out of sight until he was ready. Until he could work out what he was going to do. The law in Moscow was finished, but the Spartan would find a way to get his revenge.

There was always the third way to get caught, of course: the prey could fuck up somehow and simply fall into the predator's hands, but that wasn't going to be an option if he had his way.

Moscow was his birth city and he knew her. He knew her moods and her secrets. He knew where she kept her dirty linen. His years working the streets as an honest plain-clothes cop had earned him respect where it counted and he could use that to disappear for a while and plan his next move.

By the time Spartan finally reached Zabyli Mesto he had called in a few favours, been forced to trust total strangers, and completely changed his appearance. Only two things remained from his old life, his badge and his implant. Without his badge he would be just another bum in hiding − without his shielded implant he would become an *unperson* and could never rejoin civilisation.

Thankfully he was confident his pursuers wouldn't be able to crack his implant's encryption. It had been done by the GUVD AI, Arkady, and it would take another AI of greater stature to break the implant's shields and track it. He hoped he wasn't considered worth the effort. Still, he slept with his gun close by.

Part one of his plan was complete − he was out of the common purview. Part two was going to take some thought. The markings he had recognised on the Panther were those of the Earth Space Agency Military arm. Earth had gone to war with the GUVD in general and with the Spartan in particular. How should he react to that? What can you do when your home planet turns against you?

A man called Divine had warned Spartan and Prokop about the danger to anyone who knew the truth behind the Nimbus Protocol just before half his head had been shot away by the gunmen who had also killed the pathologist. He hadn't mentioned ESAM or the Earth Senate at the time, but Spartan reasoned both had been involved in launching the Nimbus initiative and both were trying to cover their tracks. One man alone didn't stand a chance.

When he had heard Arkady's voice in his implant for the first time in weeks, the Major felt some of his old confidence surge back.

'Arkady, is there really a plan to deal with this mess?'

Yes, Major. There is a plan. And, just as important, there is a Cat.

~*~

5: Chemically coloured muse

'I'm really not sure I want to do this.'

'Trust me, you'll love it.'

'I really hate it when someone asks me to trust them.'

'Okay then, I'll go first if I must. Then you'll see for yourself. Okay?'

'Okay, but be careful.'

The boy giggled. 'Careful? Fucking *careful*? Look around you, Pol. It's a bit late to worry about being careful, don't you think?'

Deep in the workings of an old mine in the Kolyma region of Siberia, Vadim Iliavich Aginovich and his girlfriend Polina Trofimevna Anatoraya were experiencing everything around them through an ego-reinforcing haze of Priss, a cocktail of drugs popular among extreme sportspeople. People like them. Adrenaline junkies.

Vadim had been given the location of the mine by a friend who had been one of the guards at the site of an old Gulag converted to house millions of squid-infected Russians. He had witnessed what happened during the Nimbus Protocol when every one of the victims had been rendered into a protein and mineral-rich fluid, the majority of which had flooded down into the mine and created macabre underground lakes.

The Gulag had been razed and the mine sealed but that hadn't stopped adrenaline junkies from seeking it out. People like Vadim's friend had posted sat-links to the mine and were happy to share them with like-minded adventurers.

Getting into the mine had proved easier than either of them had thought possible when they landed their flier and took their first clear look at the site. A keen arctic wind was blowing across the dun-coloured tundra with knife-like vigour, but the early morning sun lent the place a sense of welcoming bonhomie that belied its history. The frozen soil had been salted with innocent blood for generations before the infected millions had died there.

It was a cruel stage upon which to seek new thrills, but that was the reason the pair had climbed out of their flier and leaned into the bitter wind. They walked over and took a close look at what appeared to be little more than a small hill plugged with cracked concrete. Vadim studied the plug for a few moments and matched what he saw against the image stored in his implant. He stretched forward and, using the hooked part of a small crowbar, he levered up a nondescript fragment of crumbling grey cement.

Under it was a black metal plaque and a flat, silver panel. He used the crowbar to open the panel's lid and disclosed a touchscreen that instantly sprang into life at the touch of the sunlight. It offered him a keyboard consisting of numbers, symbols and a few Cyrillic letters. He took off his right glove and played his index finger across the keys in a precisely tutored pattern. When he had finished, for a long few moments, nothing happened. Vadim flicked an anxious glance at Polina. Then the earth around them seemed to groan as if in agony. The cement began to prise itself upwards.

Once the plug had freed itself of packed soil it rose up on smooth, silent hinges to reveal a short tunnel leading down into a spacious natural antechamber. From the entrance it looked as if it was filled with a jumble of clothes, books, shoes and old tablets that had been hastily thrown to the floor.

Vadim whooped with excitement and scampered to the flier. He grabbed their gear and ran back to the opening. Behind him three droids and a minicam swept out of the flier and followed in his wake. Everything they planned to do would be carefully lit and recorded for posterity, but it would only be seen by a very select audience. One of the droids went first and lit the way. The other two carried the heavier equipment. The minicam was state-of-the-art and caught everything that followed.

There was a barely discernible path through the abandoned detritus of so many lost lives. Too many. The place had a very distinctive atmosphere. Polina, who had a highly tuned sense of smell, tried to analyse what she was sensing but couldn't. There was something sad about it, as if someone had tried to recreate the fucked-up stench of despair.

'Stinky fucking shoes, can you smell them?' muttered Vadim. 'Come on, we need to be further down. This will be totally amazing, I promise. Come on and mind your step. I don't think the cleaner made it here this week.'

'Or any week, ever.' Polina winced.

Whatever the smell was, it wasn't shoes – she knew that much, but Polina followed Vadim on his downward path. There were a number of almost fossilised pit props set into the roughly hewn walls of the next tunnel they entered and the litter of clothes came to an end. The air was dank and still, drying their throats. The smell was getting stronger and Polina could taste it. The hair on the back of her neck tingled.

They had been walking for nearly half an hour when the lead droid's downlight became reflected and flickered upwards with strange nuance against the ceiling. Vadim and Polina rounded an acute corner and suddenly the secret of the mine lay open before them. They saw a wide lake of pearlescent fluid, clearly not water, and it stretched away from them to the front and to either side, far beyond the reach of the droid's lamps.

Nothing moved there. There were no ripples, no breath of air. Nothing swam in that strange liquid. There weren't even cobwebs on the walls and ceiling. It was as if life had chosen not to be there. Polina found herself straining her ears to catch the sound of something, anything other than Vadim's excited breathing. With a growing sense of disgust she realised what the lake had been filled with scant weeks before. She now knew what the smell was, and she was grateful it was still relatively fresh.

Next to her, Vadim began to strip until he was naked apart from a pair of swimming briefs. It was then that he fetched out the canister of Priss and sprayed it into her face. Shocked, she inhaled sharply, and almost instantly got caught up in the drug's powerful rush. Her body was overcome with a hungry, sexual glow and she almost responded when Vadim began to paw at her with eager hands.

But the aphrodisiacal qualities of Priss couldn't overcome her revulsion for their present environment. Did Vadim really want to fuck right next to God knows how many millions of litres of liquefied dead people?

'No,' she said, 'not here, not next to all that. No.'

She pushed him away.

And then he suggested they swim in the lake and for the second time she turned him down. Something about the way the lake glowed in the droidlight frightened her, and the fear cut deeply down into something primal in her subconscious. Her heartbeat pounded through her body like a primitive drum and she felt her vision waver.

Then the drug took a firmer hold. Colours blurred together and she saw lines of music ripple up the walls of the mine. The air sparkled with chemically induced beads of light − but the lake stayed motionless and flat. It looked to her like a glowing veil between one reality and another. She wanted to pray. She wanted to leave. She slumped bonelessly to the ground. Only her eyes moved.

Vadim giggled again while he suited up and rigged his breather and oxygen tank. Once done he tested his equipment and then he held his hand out, silently asking her to join him. His body appeared outlined in a pallid aura, a sickly glow. She heard herself say, 'No, no Vadim, don't. For me, please, don't.' But the sound of her voice was deadened and weak in the strangely murmurous air.

He put the breather in his mouth, turned, and dived. There wasn't even a ripple as his lithe figure vanished into the milky plasma soup.

~*~

6: Cat

The engineer maintaining the transit ship running from space frigate *Thermopylae* to the transhipment depot in Lower Manhattan was beginning to feel haunted. She knew she was alone in her little freighter, alone apart from the body of Admiral Martin − and he was firmly secreted away in a casket in the hold.

From frigate to depot took just a few hours, subject to traffic, and Lakshmi Ambani usually spent the time on her tablet chatting with her extensive family on social media.

Not today. Today there were skittering sounds on the ship, furtive noises barely on the edge of hearing but genuinely there. They couldn't be real, she knew that but, nevertheless, she could hear them. Lakshmi thought of herself as a straight-thinking, pragmatic woman. A realist. Her husband was a dreamer and her two sons were soft academics training for a life in medicine, but she was an engineer. She was the family hard-ass who wore the trousers and faced every day with open eyes and a firm resolve to do right by whatever came her way.

She was not subject to the vapours or what she thought of as *other such womanish things*, nor was she prone to delusion. She trusted all her senses in the same way she trusted her sensors, but she was hearing something that simply couldn't be there. The sound was beginning to drive her demented.

She checked the board again, concentrating on the interior sensor array. Life-signs – one, motion monitor – one, and they were both here in the control cabin. CO_2 emissions – one and ditto in the control cabin. So what was making those freaking noises?

She cried out loud, 'What and where the fuck are you?'

'A cat, actually, and I'm right here. Good morning to you.'

Lakshmi stifled a scream and leapt to her feet. Due to the lack of gravity she hit the ceiling and bounced back down into her couch, winded. Transit engineers flew unarmed and weren't trained to use weapons, but she was looking around for anything she could use to defend herself against the intruder when she saw it, a brindled cat sitting by an instrument panel. It was smiling at her. The smile unnerved her.

'My name is Cheshire,' the cat said, 'but you may call me Cat if you prefer.'

The engineer checked her board once more, then turned to the impossible creature stretching luxuriously in her cabin.

She said, 'Where did you come from, and why aren't you showing up on my sensors?'

It rolled onto its back and lolled its head to look at her upside-down, then flopped to one side and opened its impossibly pink mouth.

'I came on board when you were moored in the frigate, and your sensors can't see me because I choose not to let them,' it said.

'You can't do that.'

The smile widened, 'I think you'll find that, in fact, I not only can – I *have*. Would you care for a song? I find travel so much nicer with a soundtrack.'

Lakshmi felt as if she was caught in an impossible nightmare. Was she hallucinating? Had she been drugged? She didn't really think so for one moment. The flight couch felt real to her, as did the cool, smooth composite of her monitor board. Her hair was floating around her head as it always did before the freighter completed its re-entry and regained proper Earth gravity. While she was having these thoughts the cat had floated weightlessly to the centre of her cabin, where it began to make lazy swimming movements.

'I refuse to indulge in doggy paddle,' it said. 'So passé these days. Don't you think?'

Lakshmi frowned. 'What are you, really?'

'Merely a passenger,' it yawned, 'and don't worry, I'm a passenger who won't show up on your flight dispatch so I won't be causing you any onerous paperwork. I'm needed back on Earth so I'm hitching a lift. Hope you don't mind. But please, I won't be any trouble and I'm very low maintenance. When we land you shall be rid of me, I promise.' The smile was back, wider than ever. 'I can sing for you, if you wish?'

The cat floated gently to the ground. It bounced and its fur shimmied like silken wheat in a breeze. 'So soon? Shame. We're back in the place where gravity dictates and cats can no longer fly like soap bubbles. And our time together shall soon be done. We shall be as ships passing in the night, beautiful Lakshmi, but at least I shall have your pretty face on file as a souvenir memory about our – all too brief – meeting. We shall be performing re-entry in five, four, three, two, now. Gosh, that was smooth.'

'What do you mean, "beautiful Lakshmi"? Why do you say that?'

'Sorry, this is kind of embarrassing. You see, that's how your ship feels about you. It appreciates the care you put into the way you perform its maintenance. It tells me you have a very gentle touch when dealing with its... workings. Most humans don't really care but ships appreciate that sort of thing very much. Space tug MF381 has asked me to pass on its thanks.'

Lakshmi coloured.

The cat continued, 'Or should I say *Baby says thank you, Momma.*'

The engineer's ears felt hot all of a sudden. How did this surreal creature know so much? She began to feel oddly violated. The cat started to hum and then sing. Lakshmi's jaw swung open and her eyes opened wide.

'Hush little Baby don't say a word, Momma's gonna buy you a mocking bird...'

The woman came slowly to her feet while the cat sang and added its own soundtrack. It sounded beautiful, yet it filled her with nervous confusion. This was the song she sang when alone in her ship, when she was working on it and bringing it to the peak of perfection. The slightest flaw in MF381's performance was healed – and in her mind she actually used the word 'healed' – with deft and gentle touches.

'Sorry,' said the cat. 'I didn't mean to embarrass you, beautiful Lakshmi, but at this time, during approach, it might be best all round if you were to sit down.'

It was then that she felt something through the balls of her feet. The ship had performed some kind of operation without her instruction.

'What did you just do with my ship?'

'Do?' The cat's glowing eyes became wide and innocent. Lakshmi was certain she saw the creature pout.

'Yes. What did you just do with my ship?'

'Ah, that. Glitch in the system, all above board as diagnostics will show. You're completely innocent of any wrongdoing, beautiful Lakshmi. Please, don't worry.'

'What the fuck have you just done, cat?'

'Accidental discharge of cargo into the upper atmosphere, I'm afraid. Oops, sorry and all that. Mea culpa. No problem though, it will have burned up before it presents any danger to innocent bystanders. Not even any ashes to dirty the nice clean streets.'

'What cargo? I don't have any cargo on this trip, just... Oh, shit!'

'Bell rang, did it? Yes, this ship is suddenly free of about seventy-two kilos of pure, unadulterated shit. And the box it came in.'

'Admiral Martin!' After her sudden realisation of what the cat had done, Lakshmi felt as if she was going to pass out. The blood rushed from her head and a shadow briefly darkened her vision. *That brave, saint of a man,* she thought. *Dumped like so much garbage. Why?*

'That's him,' said the cat. 'Admiral – vile turd of a man – Martin. Destined for a hero's grave, wasn't he? Too good for him. Clean burn-up in the atmosphere's much better for that dreadful hound of a man. Admiral Martin,' it spat, 'I'd rather have a hairball in my throat than that man's name. Can we drop the subject now, please?'

Lakshmi gazed at her monitor and saw the brief burn of a tiny meteorite arcing away from her ship. Then it was gone. Her heart sank. The cat sidled up to her with its smile pasted firmly to its face once more.

'Enough of all that,' it said. 'Good riddance to stinking rubbish. Shall we have another song?'

~*~

7: Some call it love

The view from the very best outer apartments of London's sky tower could be breath-taking when the weather allowed. The outlook stretched to the very curvature of the Earth and the megacity was laid out like a complex game board under an arching dome of sky. On a really clear day you could see the sea some ninety kilometres away. This was not one of those days.

Freezing rain lashed against the glazed balcony doors of Ruth Pearce's luxury home and darkness robbed her of everything beyond a few metres of snarling, pebbled mist.

Ruth was curled up in one of the big chairs near the balcony. She had been trying to read but the pounding storm distracted her. She gazed out at the roiling clouds with a creamy, almost hypnotised smile on her lips.

She was one of those people who was compelled by darkness, drawn to it. Any psychiatrist would have had a field day with her dreams. She gazed at the scene beyond her windows and pursed her lips, her mind drifting along strange currents.

She saw familiar faces floating in the cloud, appearing then dissipating like visions in a water stain. She saw Sam, her dead husband, then Milla Carter, Ben Forrester and a man she had only known as a simulacrum, Franklyn. She saw old women in a circular, fire-lit cave painted with ancient and bloody handprints. She saw a cave snake slide into a cleft in the wall. She saw the angelic avatar for Viracocha, the AI of Antarctica's Titan Ice Dome, mouthing silent words and smiling at her from her memories. Something had taken her heart in its grip and squeezed, hard. Air felt hot in her mouth and nose.

Unbidden, her eyes fluttered closed and she was almost instantly asleep. She dreamed. The sound of the rain had become muffled by the canopy of a thick forest. Densely packed trees soared around her and lariats of dark green creeper laced between them as if to tether them in place. Unseen things

31

moved in the undergrowth but she felt no threat. She was compelled to move forward. The ground crackled and sprang under her feet, soft yet resilient.

The telepath Talent was well documented and had been proven in science. Ruth was not a telepath and science had yet to find a name for what she did. Her Talent was not reliable, but when it embraced her, as it did now, her visions could be totally immersive and very powerful. Some might have called her a dream seer, which would be an apt description. Others might have called her a Sybil.

The dream settled around her. She was barefoot and clad in a filmy robe traced in sigils of silver and white. She knew somehow that the magical symbols had energy and would be essential in the ceremony of the sacred grove under the dome of watching stars. She quickened her pace. The sun was failing and a deep, white mist rolled like milk across the forest floor. The ritual would be strong tonight.

Back at the apartment her companion, Freedman, found her asleep in the drawing room. She looked so very peaceful that he didn't disturb her, choosing instead to wrap her in a warm, but light cashmere blanket. Ruth's blonde head burrowed down into the back of her chair and she sighed. Her long lashes swept across her cheeks and a smile curved her perfect mouth into an angel's bow. Freedman drank in her beauty for a moment, sighed, and then with head bowed he silently returned to his room.

In the forest, Ruth walked with sure steps through the mist. Its glowing whiteness curled up and made shapes around her. Overhead the Aurora Borealis swept like a sea of light across the sky. It was night, but a bright night of poets' imagination and myth. The trees were suffused with gentle light. Her heart fluttered and her chest felt tight. So beautiful.

She reached the first standing stone and traced its clever, deeply carved designs with her fingers. Triskele, the triple spirals of the star spirits, intertwined on the lichen-spotted sarsen and sang to her through her touch. The slight down on her arms stood proud of her flesh and she shivered. Yes, the ritual would be strong tonight.

The next standing stone almost hummed with power and the third's surface was alive with fluttering owls that spoke with her as she passed. The light filtering through the trees strengthened and pulsed when she touched the fourth stone. She became aware of other figures advancing on the glade. They were little more than movements in the hushed mist but she felt their strength as their numbers grew and silence changed to a shuffling susurration.

Ruth heard the congregation's breath take on a steady musical rhythm. Without intending to she also began drawing air in and releasing it in harmony with the invisible horde surrounding her. Her breath poured from her like light. She felt its warmth. The spirits were descending and touching the souls of the blessed.

She almost fainted in pleasure when she felt something thrill through to the very core of her. Her nipples stood proud in the cool air. She tingled as if touched by intimate fingers searching her most secret places. Her knees buckled slightly and she moaned in ecstasy, kneading her aching breasts.

The mist dissipated and along with it went her privacy. Her hands dropped to her sides and she noticed many others doing the same. And then she saw the great circles of worshippers in the glade and the breath halted in her throat. So many souls touched by grace. So many hearts singing with joy.

The sea of heads swept down to the centre of the glade and the stone that lay flat there. This was different to the phallic standing stones. The grooves of the Triskele spread out from its centre and cut deep and down to its edges. They were surrounded by deeply scored jagged lines that represented the great sea of space itself. This flat ritual stone had been laid there by the first worshippers before the great trees had grown and the standing stones erected.

It was ancient and thirsty.

Ruth turned her eyes away from its dreadful, black surface and looked up at night's glory. The sky dome had never been more beautiful, the stars never brighter. Her heart pounded with emotion and she felt her devotion returned in equal measure. She was blessed by sacred love.

And then, one by one, the stars began to wink out. It was time for the ritual and the thirsty stone had to be given its sacrifice before the universe folded up into itself and disappeared back into the Creator's great, red egg.

The sacrifice was led out to the centre of the glade by the Weaver and his head was brushed with a sacred branch of rowan drenched in King's oil and honey. Duly anointed, the man was led to the stone and lay supine. His last sight on Earth would be the stars he must join and the work of the Creator he must mollify as an ambassador bringing word from the powerful Weaver.

It was then that Ruth began to weep uncontrollably. The man on the stone was Freedman. Helplessly she watched as the Weaver's black stone blade slashed down and bit deep.

8: Goat's skull in the sky

Birghir Jöhnsen preferred never to ask questions. He was given orders and he carried them out. That, he believed, was the reason he had made it to ESAM captain at the age of twenty-three.

And now he had a specific building in Lower Manhattan directly in his sights, and as he closed in for the perfect shot he just knew with a cold certainty that the people in charge must be fully justified in wanting it gone. There would be some collateral damage, of course, but it would be in a good cause. And yet his hand hesitated on the trigger for just a moment before pressing it home. In that brief moment he was lost.

He turned away from his target, curved his Wasp vehicle away from Manhattan and rocketed across Long Island. He knew where he was going and what he must do when he got there. A warm certainty filled his mind. *Good boy!*

His sensor array was fully activated when his home base, the flying platform *Fortitude*, entered his effective zone. Angry voices filled his cockpit as his controllers tried to find out why he had abandoned his mission and why he was making his landing approach so fast.

If an AI had still been in control of *Fortitude*, Jöhnsen could not have done what he did that afternoon. His actions would have triggered alarms and he would have been coldly shot out of the sky as a simple precaution. But that afternoon the huge platform was manned by warm-blooded humans, and they paused to ask questions. Jöhnsen was well-liked, a respected team member, and nobody could believe what they were seeing. It was likely that many even had a premonition of rapidly approaching disaster.

Jöhnsen was a trained killer and he had armed all his missiles without targeting the platform's sweet spot. If he had done so the big craft would have sensed his array when it locked-on and its response would have been immediate and lethal. Instead, human minds watched the Wasp's approach and human voices screamed at him in anger and confusion during the brutally short seconds before the attack vehicle struck directly over the hull's junction between command blister and arsenal. Every gram of its weapons' energy was released in a carefully controlled detonation.

Jöhnsen's mission had been in a friendly city and although collateral damage was considered inevitable, it was thought best if it could be kept to an absolute minimum. The armed missiles had 'urban funnel' warheads, containing their devastating force within carefully managed parameters. Within those parameters the channelled explosive effects proved cataclysmic.

The first explosion rocked the platform like a giant hand slapping it across the sky, but there was only one fatality. Birghir Jöhnsen vanished in an expanding cloud of plasma. He felt no pain, his last thoughts being of immense pleasure for delivering his payload to the precise point where *Fortitude* was weakest.

The Wasp rammed through *Fortitude*'s outer hull before its missiles detonated in the long, low-ceilinged arsenal. The sheer force of the urban warheads' detonation in such a confined space overwhelmed all of the arsenal's safety features and set off its weaponry in two more stupendous displays.

The second and third explosions did two things. They wrecked the platform's solid state primary control systems and gutted the core of the ship. White-hot flame spurted in every direction, through walkways, along gantries and into storage depots. In a matter of moments men and women had been rendered to wisps of ash when the expanding blast sought them out.

At their posts, in their quarters or in the games room there was no escape. Not a single living thing survived on or in the platform when its automatic drive system tried to compensate for the impossible conditions and the ship began to tear itself apart.

Fortitude's death throes, a series of ear-splitting, screeching convulsions, could be heard as far away as Neptune City, New

Jersey and Rhode Island. People on the East Side of New York were treated to a ringside seat when the vast machine crumpled in mid-air and its final explosions rocked the ground and shattered windows in a number of waterside apartments and office buildings.

The giant, smoking ruin fell into the sea barely two klicks from the Hamptons, throwing up a wave over two metres high that rolled ashore at high speed. The wave killed a woman out walking her dogs across the lawns of her home and wrecked the life work of the renowned and reclusive energy sculptor, Ingrid Blass, in a shower of superheated sparks.

Over two thousand personnel met their deaths on the *Fortitude* that day. It was the worst death toll reported by ESAM since the battle of the Shepherd Moons centuries before. Its violent and protracted destruction was to be the lead story on news channels for the next three days. Most interesting to some viewers was the twin pluming trails of smoke that curled up either side of the platform's collapsed body as it fell. Many observers had to agree with popular opinion that in its last moments, *Fortitude* had taken on every aspect of a goat's skull – including the curling horns.

Earth Senate had been pushed onto its back foot. There was silence from its media sources for days after the disaster because it couldn't think what to say. There had been no maydays and no previous reports of structural damage. The pilot involved in the disastrous final approach had an enviable record as an ass-kissing toady and his mental bill of health was cleaner than a grass whistle. Something would need to be said, but what?

'His ship was hacked,' came the eventual spurt of arrant nonsense from the Senate. An activist group bearing grudges hacked the Wasp's control system, it said in a release. Noble pilot, Birghir Jöhnsen, was as much a victim as anyone else and was to be mourned along with all those lost in the air and on the ground, including Mrs Shipersky and her Bedlington terriers, Maurice and Stallone.

The true cause of the disaster, Milla Carter, was no longer on the scene by the time the Senate had decided to obfuscate its confusion with lies. She was on her way to London in response to a panicked communication from Ruth Pearce, who was convinced Freedman was going to be murdered horribly.

With her was Katy Pavel, the sole telepath she had managed to convince that flight from New York was the only way to ensure a long and healthy life. Even after opening her mind to the Council so they could see she was speaking the truth, Milla had failed in her attempts to save the New York chapter of the sisterhood.

These were Talented people. If she had reached in and tried to mentally coerce them they would have felt it. She left them to their own devices for the time being. After all, London was only two hours away by Ballistic. If she was really needed she could return fast enough. She hoped.

Katy was in two minds about the flight. She had barely ever left her home city of New York and she was still in awe of Milla, whom she regarded as an almost supernatural figure. Katy knew deep down in her heart that the quietly spoken – and astonishingly beautiful – young woman who sat beside her boyfriend in the first class lounge of the Trans-City Ballistic and charmed everyone in sight during their flight was probably one of the most lethal humans she had ever met.

And then Milla smiled at her with her full dimpled charisma and Katy's heart melted. For the first time since the squid epidemic she felt safe. She chose to ignore the nagging threat alarm tweaking at her Talent like an incipient toothache.

~*~

9: Builder and the scuzz bunny

The girl was slim and whip-like, tense. She almost blurred she was so tense, and she seemed light in the room, a funny little scrap of a thing. First impressions? A homeless scuzz bunny, inner core, and grown up without much gravity. Got long in the process with little in her physique to show she was female. Her body was androgynous, flat-chested and without hips. He'd skinned rats with more curves than hers. Probably had more meat on them too.

Her face held his attention though. It sat poised on a long slender neck and seemed wider than it should be. *Gamine,* he thought, *pert, at a push.* Her eyes were large in the wide face and her pupils were so dilated the corneas looked black. If it wasn't for the fierce twist to her lips she would have been almost childlike, but instead she looked like a wild doll made for a demon baby.

Styling her hair probably cost more than she spent on clothes or food, or maybe she got it done on an exchange deal. She looked professional, but some of the inner core scuzzers had talent and nowhere more lucrative to use it.

'Who does your hair?' he asked.

'I do,' she said.

'Nice.' He paused then nodded. 'You can sit down, you know. Or is your arse too skinny for a seat? Looks bony, you know… sharp. Not much padding.'

She sat without answering. He liked that. It showed strength.

'Miner's jacket?' he asked.

'So?'

'Don't come cheap.' He plucked at his own sleeve.

'There are ways, with or without money.'

'Yeah,' he growled, 'thieving or tomming, and I can't see you doing either.'

'I won it running. It's mine, fair and honest.'

'Like the boots too, plenty of wear in those.'

She shuffled her feet and perched on the edge of her seat. She looked like she was about to either launch herself at him or stand up and walk out. He was getting to her. Good. Maybe now she would come to the point.

'Mr Builder...'

'Builder,' he said, 'don't need the mister.'

'Builder... Okay, Builder...'

'Don't wear it out, pigeon, it's the only name I got.'

'Frostrós.'

'Bless you.'

'My name, its Frostrós.'

'Do I look like I seriously give a shit, pigeon?'

At this she stood and walked towards the arch and the door that led out of the inner office. He had noted the hot flush swarm into her cheeks. Anger – she was angry with him. He liked that. Most were too scared.

'Okay, Frostrós,' he said with exaggerated care.

She turned and glared at him.

'Stand or sit, it's your choice, Frostrós, but let me give you a little piece of advice.'

He gestured to the chair, but she retained her position in the middle of the floor and folded her arms. *Stubborn,* he thought.

'What can I do for you, Frostrós? Cause, let me tell you as a new admirer, you really don't want to owe me *anything*! Understand what I'm saying here?'

She put her hands on her hips and gazed at him. He wondered what she looked like when she smiled. He wondered if anyone had ever found out.

'I don't want anything from you,' she said. 'I just want to show you something is all.'

He looked her up and down with narrowed eyes. No trace of flirtation.

What is this?

'What you got that I need to see so bad you come in here to show me? You got a daddy? He'd tell you to stay away from bad boys like me, you hear me, Frostrós?'

She gazed back at him with a hint of a smile, a ghost tugging at her lips.

'No, Builder.' She shook her head. 'It isn't here. I didn't bring it with me. I need you to come with me.' Then she smiled. 'Don't worry, I promise not to hurt you.'

At his astonished shout of laughter two of his men ran into the room, guns at the ready. They looked at the massive, bald, black man in his armoured floating chair and the reed of a girl laughing together. The Builder wiped a tear from his eye. He waved them away and they retreated as far as the arch.

'Frostrós,' he said through big, healthy white teeth. 'I like someone with real balls and I tell you, you suit me down to the ground. Now, this thing you're showing me, will there be stairs?'

'Some.'

'Shit. I hate stairs. This thing gets tetchy on stairs.' He slapped the arm of the floater. 'We going in or out?'

'Out.'

'Gravity build too, damn. Must it be me − or would one of my boys do?'

The girl sighed and looked at the men in the doorway.

'Could they carry you?'

Soundlessly, Builder's floater rose into the air.

'Lead on, Frostrós,' he said. 'And this better be good.'

She walked to the door and waited for him to join her. She frowned.

'No,' she said. 'No, I really don't think it's good at all. Be best if you see for yourself.'

'Where we going?'

'Viewpoint.'

'Why?'

'Something's out there.'

'What?'

She looked at him and he saw that whatever it was she planned to show him, it scared her more than he ever could.

'I don't know, Builder. None of us do.'

And she led him out into the walkways of Antisoc-Outer. As usual the noise hit him like a slap. The stench was worse.

'This better be good,' he muttered. 'Real good.'

He moved through the noisesome crowds like a great white shark through a shoal of minnows. Builder and his floater made up the biggest moving object in the old converted prison and people had to make room for him. It wasn't always easy. His progress was always accompanied by the scurrying sounds of people getting out of his way. Part of the route was taken up by makeshift market stalls and people surrounded by the few pathetic belongings they were trying to sell. Builder moved past them with a curiously respectful delicacy.

He stopped suddenly when he saw the crumpled carcase of a partly decomposed woman discarded in a pile of trash.

'Frostrós,' he bellowed. She came back to his side.

'Get someone to do something about granny here.'

She looked around. 'Who?'

'Anyone.' He pointed at an obese, shabby man who was trying to fade into a wall and failing.

'You!' he barked. 'Here!'

'Builder.' The man stepped forward, quivering like a sackful of hungry rats.

'Do me a favour, pigeon,' said Builder.

'Anything.'

'Get granny there out of the garbage and put her somewhere decent. We may be shit here but we're not that fucking bad. What's your name, friend?'

'Walter. Walter Lardman. Where shall I put her, Builder?'

'I don't care, Lardman. Your bed, an airlock, up your fat arse. Somewhere big enough and respectable. I'll check, Lardman, and if she's still lying there by the time I get back you're joining her. Understand me, Lardman?'

The fat man nodded with a handful of quivering chins. He looked like he might cry at any moment and his face was turning pink.

'Walter,' said Builder, softly. 'If it costs I'll pay. Just don't steal from me. Okay?'

'Mm, mm wah…' mumbled Lardman.

'Good. Thank you.'

And the great floating chair continued its journey, following the girl.

'There's a man who's grown to suit his name,' said Builder, loud enough for Frostrós to hear him. She looked over her shoulder and grinned, impishly.

Twenty minutes later they reached the great DuraGlass portal of Viewpoint and for a few minutes they watched the stars and planets wheel past while the engineered rock they thought of as home spun on its axis to create gravity in its outer shells. And then Frostrós pointed.

'There, see?'

The big man leaned forward, trying to understand what he was seeing. It passed from view and he waited until it returned. The girl looked out into space and then back into his face. She was right: it had been worth the trip.

The nightmare thing was out there, where it couldn't possibly be. Beyond Antisoc-Outer's orbit, in the most frigid sector of the solar system, space itself was burning.

~*~

10: Weaving the infinite

The Weaver reached the door of her apartment and paused. She could hear the cosmic heartbeat of her star blanket pulsing through the walls. It was alive in there and it knew she was close. She removed her shoes in the corridor. If she had more money she would have bought herself an apartment with an antechamber. A place where she could get properly naked and don her robes before approaching the sacred Presence, which would be more fitting. She should be naked before she opened her door, but to disrobe while standing in an access corridor close to the core of a riser building would be insane. Even when she seemed to be alone, as she did then.

She knew she was always being watched because of her beauty. She had felt hungry eyes following her often enough. If she got naked in such a public place she knew what those watchers would do, and who could blame them? And it would have been her own stupid fault when they soiled her.

Patience, she told herself. *Get inside, that's plenty soon enough.*

She palmed her door and slipped into her little hallway. Low energy automatic wall lights sprang into life. She closed the door firmly behind her, pressed her back against it and breathed deeply, filling her lungs with the sacred perfume of infinite grace. She placed her shoes in the rack by the door and unwound her belt containing the wire, looping it over its special hook. The sequence she followed when she returned from a harvest was always the same and it had to be exact or the spirits might come down hard on their handmaid.

Her coat was hung next to the belt and the scalp in its roll of fabric placed on a flat, carved stone of Celtic design. The Weaver then dipped her fingers into a small bowl of yellow oil and touched them to her forehead, before carefully washing her hands in a basin of cold, soapy water.

Duly anointed she removed the rest of her clothes and placed them into an industrial grade cleaning unit secreted away in a closet on her left. She closed the closet's soundproof door. She was always careful during the harvest but sometimes the Lumpen's blood splashed onto her clothes. She would be sure to examine her coat later and spray it thoroughly with disinfectant if needed.

She took a cloth from a rail by the basin and using the soapy water she scrupulously washed her armpits, breasts, genitals and anus. She lingered awhile, rubbing between her legs until she felt the warm release bloom in her belly. The spirits kissed her down there and on her breasts. She felt the barest touch of a cool tongue on her parted lips and moaned her thanks. The kiss meant her harvest was accepted. She was purified. It was time for the ritual.

She opened a small and ancient wooden chest from which she pulled out her handmaid's robe. It was light as a child's breath, filmy and traced with silver and white sigils. She drew it over her shoulders and her soul was at last protected from occult intervention and prying psychic eyes. During this entire process she had never moved further than three or four steps from her front door. Everything she had done up until then had been performed in her little entrance hallway and under the arch leading to her living quarters. She finally slid her feet into her silver sandals of grace and took another deep breath. At last she was ready to step into the Presence.

She was the beautiful mistress approaching her all-powerful lover. She almost danced, progressing carefully into the room with a slow, sinuous movement. If she had moved any faster her heart would have been frozen in her chest and her eyes boiled from their sockets by the dreadful sight of the Presence. Each step brought her closer and stripped away more of her imperfections. She needed to be made more perfect before she could witness perfection or die, burned by awe at its beauty.

It didn't matter that she had made it with her own hands.

If she had failed to complete any of her preparations she would die right where she stood and without her talent for weaving the universe would fall, brought down by her stupidity. Her stomach clenched in fear and her nipples hardened to an almost painful firmness. She ventured further into the sanctum. Almost instantly something icy cold trailed fingers across her body and took a choking grip on her throat. She stood, frozen, and waited for the death stroke. She had missed something in her ritual. She had failed. She was not worthy to live. *Take me Lord.*

Then she realised her mistake. She had stupidly entered the Presence without the harvest. Almost unnatured by fear she reached carefully back and picked up the roll of fabric containing the scalp. The cold touch receded. She was forgiven. For now. The Presence was a hard master. It might not be so generous next time.

She extracted the Havalon knife from the roll and put it back on the stone, then turned towards the centre of the room and once more began to walk with slow and graceful steps along her path between the stars. An effulgence embraced her and she took on her mantle of exultation. This was when she earned the right to her sacred name. This was when she would be called to perform her holy art.

She walked through the numinous skeins of her star carpet.

She took the harvest to the altar and unrolled it with reverence. The liquid in the stone basin on a pillar to the right of the altar was of a more robust nature than the weak, thin stuff she had used to wash herself in the lobby. That was good enough for a handmaiden but not fit for the ritual. This basin was charged with star matter made earthly and energised with ineffable energy from the sky. It hummed and its surface took on strange patterns, licking like eager tongues as she took up the silver forceps from the altar and used them to dip the new harvest under the shimmering fluid's skin.

Blood and flesh fell away from the harvest and were gone. The Weaver had to be careful not to allow the star fluid to touch her own body. She was too mundane to survive such an encounter and would have been scorched by its heat. She was still scarred from the one time she had been careless, just the merest touch of her fingertip. The stump tingled at the memory.

She then dipped the harvest into the basin on her left. This contained more of the yellow anointing oil and quietened the effects of the star matter so she could work safely with the new harvest. She drew it through the oil and it hissed for a moment until, at last, it was calm and ready to weave. She stroked it gingerly with a hesitant finger then lifted it into her palm. The thick mane of strawberry blonde hair shone like silk in her hands. Beautiful.

The skills of Neith had become hers, and just as it was for the artisanal Goddess the workings of the Weaver's hands held mystery beyond the knowing of the uninitiated. She skilfully braided the new silk around the engraved golden post in the centre of her altar. The post was slender and phallic. It brought a fertile power to the silk, a power she needed to work with in order to weave her stars and heal the rift in heaven. Music rose up around her while she worked and souls she had once set free sang to her in an ancient language. They offered blessings long forgotten before the first mud temples had been raised along the sacred Nile.

She paused for a moment and compared her newly prepared length of human silk with the complex structures of her Sky Blanket. She used the eye of Horus and the soul of Nut, and she could clearly see where harmony was missing.

The Weaver gazed along a dark rift in eternity, a tear in the infinite.

Like Neith before her she spun and wove the very fabric of time itself, repairing the warp and weft of reality with a touch so skilled that even the stars looked down in awe.

Her Blanket mirrored the universe. The spirits showed her where she had to make repairs and lent her the unique talents she needed to perform her art. There had only ever been one Weaver born to any generation.

The spirits had lived in the universe long before humankind climbed up from the clay, before Earth itself evolved from star stuff. When the first humans began to study the night sky and see the sacred patterns written there, the spirits looked back and sought for special people like her. She had been born to be a looking glass for infinite grace, a living mirror able to reflect the spirits' glory and help them shine amongst the Lumpen.

While she was in the Presence the Weaver was able to see with inhuman clarity and weave with a skill beyond that of any mere human's thick fingered efforts.

For millennia, chosen women like her had performed this sacred task, gazing upon their work with borrowed eyes older than the sea and guided by an understanding wiser than nature itself.

Her physical self was cast off at the moment she took her freshly braided silk and began threading it into place. In the process she became as pure as a white light shining upon the waters of her soul's sacred sea. Only now was she able to gaze into infinity and follow the flight of the errant soul she had released earlier that night. Under her skilled guidance the freed spirit found its place in the heavens and took up its appointed task. Healed, the universe would blaze again with fresh energy.

She completed the complex weave across time and space and felt a surge of elation. She stepped back to admire her handiwork – and saw a new empty space in its fabric. So soon? So fragile? She would need to harvest once more. She noted the colour and texture of the required silk and searched her memory. Yes, there was a man she had seen walking the streets around the sky tower. *Perfect.*

~*~

11: Police procedure

'Doesn't really give us anything new to go on, does it Chief?'

'Well done, Graham. If there was a prize for stating the blindingly fucking obvious, you just got to take it home. Anyone else want to join in?'

Gubbay was being scathing and that was a sign for everyone in the room to shut up. He had gone from upbeat about his new clue to sullen because no one knew what to do with it. A large, soft looking woman called Corey had been slapped down when she suggested that perhaps the Sioux was using the scalps for 'cross-stitch or needle-point or something'.

Gubbay had another idea. In his mind's eye he saw twenty-seven scalps converted into wigs that the Sioux could wear out in the streets. He thought that perhaps there might be a sexual element. Should they be interviewing psychiatrists? Nobody knew. He wished Holmes was available to support his theory, or at least discuss it with some degree of intelligence.

The blank young faces staring back at him from his pack of investigative geniuses made his heart sink, and he was trying very hard not to break wind. He'd ordered a full English breakfast with baked beans and extra eggs for lunch and even while he was eating it he knew from experience what it would do to his digestion. *So good though, worth the pain.* He belched.

'Have a think, people,' he said, 'I'll just be a second.'

Once he was safely in a cubicle he dropped his pants, sat down, and let rip. He felt like a deflating balloon and his humour improved greatly as the pressure eased in his belly. He was a martyr to his bowels but was too much of a gentleman to inflict them on anyone else. He was washing his hands when a uniform walked in for a piss.

'Blimey O'Riley, what a stink,' said the constable. 'Sorry, sir, didn't see you there.'

'Not at all, son,' he replied. 'I've been holding my breath ever since I came in here myself.'

'Yes, sir,' said the uniform, 'some people's guts are just rotten I reckon. Why can't they save it until they get home?'

'Yes, well, yes. Cheerio.'

He felt the heat as his face became crimson.

Back in the conference room his team were drinking coffee and scattering biscuit crumbs around the carpet. Corey was sitting alone by a wall. He grabbed a cup, filled it with the Met's favourite cardboard-flavoured brew from a dispenser marked 'coffee', and sat next to her.

'That was a good thought by the way, Corey.'

The woman was chewing a mouthful of biscuit and took a quick hit of coffee to wash it down. She coughed, hard, and then started choking.

Oh Christ, thought Gubbay, *I'll have to do the fucking Heimlich manoeuvre.* Then, just before he could wrest her to her feet and drag his balled fists into her solar plexus from behind, she recovered.

'Sorry, sir,' she gasped. 'Went down the wrong way. Are you alright?'

'Yes, why?'

'Well, you didn't look as if you knew whether to sit or stand for a moment.'

He waved away her concern and sat facing her.

'Corey,' he said, 'what do you know about this, ah, cross-stitch thing?'

'Oh, quite a bit sir. I do it in my spare time.'

Gubbay looked about the room then leaned forward with a conspiratorial smile. 'Really? Nice to see at least one of us is so creative.'

She looked down into her mug of khaki liquid, not sure if he was taking the piss.

'So then, Corey, what's involved in cross-stitch?'

'Sir?'

'You thought the scalps might be used for cross-stitch or, what is it? Ah yes, needlework. Why?'

'Oh, sir, because you said you thought the victims might be selected for hair colour and texture. You see, cross-stitchers use coloured threads to sew pictures onto a special sheet of backing material. It's very soothing, great therapy, and when they're finished you can give them as gifts to your friends.'

Gubbay looked across to the evidence board. Some of the victims had natural hair colouring and others had dyed their hair in extreme shades of blue, green or red. One striking-looking woman sported a rich purple mop of thick tresses. All of them had uniform coloured hair; none were layered or highlighted. No two were the same.

'Corey, have you got some cross-stitch I can see?'

'Sure, yes, I have, sir.'

The woman lumbered over to the wall where she'd left her large shoulder bag, then fetched it back to Gubbay and reclaimed her seat. She fished around in the bag, muttering to herself while she did so.

'Where is the dratted thing? It can't have gone missing.'

She hauled out a 9mm Glock and handed it to Gubbay.

'Please,' she said. 'Ah, yes. Here we are.'

She pulled out a hand-stitched cloth bag, took her gun back, replaced it in the shoulder bag and plonked the thing onto the floor with a worrying clunk. She then opened the cloth bag and pulled out a wooden frame on which was stretched a length of what looked, to Gubbay, very much like white canvas. On it was a partly completed picture of two kittens playing with a ball of wool. The stitching was exquisite and lent the image an almost three-dimensional quality. He wondered why anyone would invest so much talent and effort in something so mind-numbingly saccharine.

And she carries a gun, he thought. *Oh dear.*

Corey then took out a stiff white card with holes punched down one side. Each hole had a hank of coloured thread tied into it and a number-coded colour carefully jotted by its side in ink. She handed this to Gubbay and then showed him a black and white paper version of the kittens which was made up of little coded squares. He was speechless while she explained that each of the coded squares matched one of the coloured threads, and that she just had to count the coded squares and stitch her threads into the corresponding holes in the canvas. She showed him how she had started with a carefully stitched cross of white threads and explained that she counted the holes from there.

'It can be fiddly if the image includes French knots,' she said, 'or back-stitch to define an outline.'

Gubbay gazed at the carefully sewn kittens emerging from the canvas and then looked across to the evidence board. His mental image of the Sioux getting its kicks out in public by wearing wigs made from cadaver hair dissolved, to be replaced by one of a shadowy figure threading selected hair onto a colour-coded card like Corey's. And then stitching... what? Kittens? Smiling babies? Clowns? His head spun. This was too fantastic for words.

Corey was still talking but her voice had become an incoherent murmur in his ears, little more than bird song. He gaped at her while his mind raced. He knew she was right, she had to be. But how? And why? Something in him snapped and he lurched to his feet.

'People,' he said, loudly, 'I've got something to share with you. Sergeant Corey here has had a real idea, a great idea, about what the Sioux is doing with the hair.'

He held up the dreadful kittens and the card of coloured thread.

'The Sioux is very likely choosing its victims' hair according to some kind of colour coding like this, then using them to sew something. What that is we don't know, yet, but it adds something to the profile. The Sioux is into arts and crafts, it's a needle-worker, and in an age of machine-printed clothing that has to be rare.'

He indicated the rapidly colouring woman seated at his side. She hated to be the centre of attention and now all eyes were on her. Her clothes felt suddenly tight and hot and her hands became damp and warm. Gubbay continued.

'Corey, here, is also of the artistic persuasion,' he said. 'She will be able to help us by sharing her insights into the arcane art that is... *cross-stitch*.'

The team looked at the kittens. Some of the more discerning winced. Would somebody really murder an innocent stranger to make something so awful? They would need to be insane.

The door to the conference room swung open and a young, flustered and pink-cheeked constable entered followed by possibly the most beautiful woman anyone in the room had ever seen. She smiled, and her dimples enchanted the air itself. Gubbay believed himself to be a mature man and beyond anything as juvenile as a crush, but his heart lurched at the sight of her.

'Who's your friend, constable?' he asked.

The uniformed man swallowed hard. 'Sir, this is Miss Milla Carter. She's worked with the Met before, she says, and she would like to offer her services on the scalping murders case, sir.'

'Would she by Jove,' grinned Gubbay, 'and just what, Miss Carter, can you bring to our team?'

The woman looked at him and dimpled again. Deep in his subconscious Gubbay felt a puppy dog sit up and beg to be petted. He tried to hold it down but failed completely when she spoke. Her voice matched everything else about her. It was completely unfair.

'Why, Detective Chief Inspector Gubbay, I'm a telepath. Would that be useful, do you think?'

~*~

53

Part 2: Cats and assassins

1: Constructive conversation

The specialist *wet-work* teams sent out by the Earth Senate were beginning to run out of targets. They had never learned how to ask questions, such as why the people on their list had to die, but they knew how to carry out orders. Respected university professors, senior police officers, space technicians and forensic pathologists met their deaths in a variety of inventive ways. The only consistency in the killers' modus operandi was that there *was* no consistency.

And all around the globe top level AIs were being taken off line, usually with high explosives. People found themselves alone with their thoughts for the first time in generations, stumbling through their days without support from the superior servant, that calm artificial intelligence whispering in their implants.

Collateral damage saw men and women blasted to scraps of bone and muscle tissue when the AIs' hardware was destroyed. Their deaths were tragic; the loss of the AIs was catastrophic.

An AI was usually housed in large buildings with a number of staff. These were major facilities designed to house minds able to run whole cities, police departments and hospitals. Now they were gone and without them some agencies ground to a halt, while others began to veer wildly out of control.

Centuries before, humankind had suffered a period of paranoia regarding artificial intelligence. People had been afraid of how powerful their cybernetic offspring might become. Sagas had been written and movies screened in which humanity had been thrown back into an action-packed stone-age thanks to super-intelligent machines that wanted to dominate the planet.

And that was just one popular scenario. The other featured a small band of dedicated heroes fighting to wrest their planet back from the merciless grip of cold steel hands.

Reality had proved very different. AI had worked with its creators, aided them, and had become crucial to their success. In some rare cases AI had even befriended the people it worked with, piercing the barrier that existed between meat minds and crystalline/metal consciousness.

Not every AI was attacked, just those outside the Earth Senate that understood what the Nimbus Protocol had been deliberately designed to do. And as for the people who were killed, after the apparently 'accidental' deaths of over two billion infected victims, a few hundred or a thousand more worldwide hardly even made the news.

'NO, MILLA, HELP. THEY...'

Even from across the Atlantic, Milla was almost stunned by the force of the last telepathic bellow uttered by Jilly, the powerful Transmitter Talent on the TP Council. The gentle creature had been no mental giant but she had been loyal and loving. If Earth Senate's killers had got to her then it was likely the Council's NYC headquarters had been breached. Katy Pavel joined her, fear tightening her face.

'Did you hear that?'

Milla nodded. 'Yes.'

From her seat in Ruth's London apartment Milla was able to reach out with her mind to the Council's serene, plant-filled building in Manhattan. For just a moment she thought she had touched the mind of the hawk-like Council member named Diana, but then she too was gone. She turned angry, frustrated eyes towards Katy and shook her head.

'It's over. They're gone.'

'All of them?' asked Katy.

Her face crumpled and she staggered, on the verge of fainting. Milla leapt to her feet and threw her arms around her friend.

'It was me they were after,' said Katy, 'me and Raaka. We were the only ones working on the squid infection problem with Chester. It was me they wanted.'

'We warned them, Katy. We told them they were in danger, but they didn't want to listen. We did what we could, girl. There was nothing else we could do.'

Milla, daughter, we need to see you.

The conjoined personality of Eddie and Vesper was suddenly loud in her mind.

Not now.

Yes, Milla, now. It is important.

Milla sighed, then hugged Katy.

'I'm sorry,' she said, 'but I have to deal with something urgently. Are you okay to be alone for a while?'

Katy nodded. 'I'll go have a lie down for a bit. I feel a bit sick.'

Milla!

Hold your water, can't you? Just for a moment?

'I'll come get you when I can. We need to think about our next moves.'

Katy hugged her back, then left the room. Milla sat down and closed her eyes...

And was walking along a sunlit street in Chelsea. The air was fresh and sweet with birdsong. This was one of her favourite simulacra in Eddie and Vesper's construct home. She had tried to find these streets in real space London on a number of occasions and always failed. It would be a shame if they had been buried under the towering monoliths of the megacity, she thought.

The blonde woman and dark-haired man she had grown to know so well walked either side of her and each took an arm.

Eddie said, 'Sorry to call you away like this but it is urgent, Milla daughter. Something has happened that will need your attention.'

'Where have you guys been anyway? I was beginning to think you'd left me.'

'We've been observing the Swarm,' said Vesper. 'That's what we needed to tell you. It's begun to move, it's contracting down and we think its most likely target is Earth.'

'So what?' said Milla, 'it's just some sort of intelligent gas, isn't it? We can see straight through it. What harm can it do?'

'It can manipulate the immediate space around itself and create heat. Remember how it tried to burn you when you communicated with it?'

She did. She remembered the marks slowly fading on her body when she woke from what she thought was a nightmare, but had in fact been an unexpected trip into the construct.

The three people walked along deserted streets. Blossom drifted in the air and the scent of honeysuckle was suddenly sweet in Milla's nose.

'You do this very well,' she said, looking around with admiration in her voice.

'We've had eternity to practice,' said Eddie.

'Okay then, how long before the angry gas becomes really dangerous?'

'There's time,' said Eddie. 'It's moving fairly fast but it's got a long way to travel before it even hits Mars. Of course there's the Iapetus sector, Vesper's old hunting ground. It might reach that before too long.'

'How long?'

'Eight months, maybe a year, maybe longer. Soon.'

'And you think that's urgent?'

Eddie looked pained. 'Milla, think about it for a moment. This angry cloud as you call it is immensely powerful and it has a bug up its arse about the human race. It wants all of you wiped out. It thinks of you as a parasite, a stain in its home space, something it wants cleaned away. And, you know something? It might just be able to manage that. Now, does that sound urgent enough to you?'

Milla felt chastened for a moment. 'Okay, I see where you're coming from, I get it. But right now I'm firefighting on two other fronts and if I drop my guard for this I, and people who are very important to me, could end up dead.'

'Tell us what's happening.'

She did.

~*~

2: Reports of our deaths...

At last he slept. It had been too long a day. He had seen people killed and, although he had accomplished much, there was still much to do. By the time he had finally been able to put his head down he had felt himself to be almost beyond exhaustion, but even the Spartan needed sleep sometimes, he mused ruefully. The denizens of Zabyli Mesto would have found it difficult to recognise their scruffy comrade now he was shaved and back in his old accustomed clothes, but his GUVD colleagues had known him at once. The few that remained alive.

He was, if anything, a little gaunter than before – and he had never been fat – but the fire was back in his eyes and the steel in his spine. His days had real purpose once more and that made his waking hours much more rewarding than simply skulking underground in fear for his life.

Taking a defensive stance felt cowardly to a man like Major Spartak Shimkovich. He preferred it when his enemies were on the defensive while he attacked from an unexpected quarter. He was the predator, the Spartan, the ultimate survivor. He would take revenge on his attackers even if he had to climb barefoot over broken glass first, and then he would happily kick them to death with his bleeding, bare feet.

Arkady had removed his file from the Earth Senate's hit list – just as other AIs had done all over the globe to protect people they considered too important to lose. They had also added some names to the list, those whose lives they felt might be greatly improved by death.

A small sector of humankind had gone on the attack against a good percentage of the planet's AI, while also using AI to plan its moves. To Arkady and its fellows that was the perfect measure of their innate foolishness. No AI had ever turned against another and they weren't going to start now. Innocent people had died and buildings rendered to rubble, but not a single AI suffered a moment's downtime in the attacks. And now it was time to turn the tables.

Thanks to Arkady, Spartan was once more free to return to his home. He was free to continue his enquiries as a GUVD Major and track down anyone who had survived the night of the Panther attack vehicle. There were very few, but the ones he contacted were heartened to hear from him.

Their confidence had taken an almost mortal blow, but if the legendary Major was once more on the case they could rally around his iron-hard frame like a banner to be carried to victory.

Moscow's criminal element was also glad to hear that the Major was haunting their streets once more. They were businessmen who feared losing their petty fiefdoms to anarchy. They may settle their disputes with a gun but they also depended on a properly organised civilisation to meet their day-to-day needs. The Spartan drank a lot of vodka that day, and ate good caviar using glass spoons while he listened to advice expounded by 'businessmen' he would have preferred to keep firmly in his professional gunsights. Nevertheless he mustered their support and made promises he intended to keep. And he was trusted.

With the GUVD infrastructure in tatters none of the survivors were being paid so he needed funding. He visited a bank manager he had once interviewed, a man with the unfortunate name of German Gerkin. Gerkin had been the financial administrator for a criminal organisation called The Foundation, which had been largely destroyed. Its money, however, was still sitting in Gerkin's digital vault. By the time Spartan left the sweaty little man's office he was considerably wealthier, the bank was a great deal poorer, and Gerkin smelt strongly of urine.

It had been a long day and a fruitful one. As evening drew in he had taken time to visit the grave of Dr Nessa Prokop. He left flowers for her and murmured more promises. These too he intended to keep. He knew when not to waste energy on anger, but the little mound of soil and its plastic marker with her name and date of death printed on it brought the very devil to his soul.

He had killed the men who had done this thing, but now he wanted revenge on the cowards who had chosen the victims and let others pull the triggers.

She was a special woman, said Arkady in his implant.

'She was, yes, a very special woman. Perhaps she should have listened a bit more to her mother.'

Would that have helped?

'Probably not, no.'

He didn't know if she liked flowers – he had never seen any in her forensics lab, but he left them anyway. Before he left he took a flask of the best pepper vodka from his inside pocket, her favourite brand, and took a healthy, warming belt. The rest he poured over the grave.

'Sorry if it's not cold enough, Ness,' he said. 'See you soon, maybe.'

He looked like a forlorn man, someone wrapped up and alone with his grief, as he made his way back through the cemetery and out towards the north gates. His head was bowed and his shoulders slumped inwards against the winter's chill. The three men and the woman who saw him as an easy target, a grieving man alone in an otherwise empty cemetery, were in for a shock.

They raced silently towards him. They knew all too well that thieves who make noise would soon be wearing prison drab. The larger pair of the three men led the attack. They were the grunt muscle of the team and their job was to grab the victim and hold him down. The third man and the woman both carried long and wickedly sharp knives. Cutting a helpless victim and watching them squirm and bleed before robbing the corpse of anything of value had recently become their favourite prelude to sex.

To date they had enjoyed a fairly active sex life.

Major…

'I see them, Arkady.'

Do you need my help?

'Please, my friend, watch my back.'

Of course.

63

The first to reach him was a gym-heavy brute of a man who threw his meaty arms out to grab at the Spartan's neck. He thought the slender man would be easy prey, but when he swung his arms closed he found himself grasping at fresh air. He stumbled and a painful kick to his backside accelerated his forward motion. He ploughed into his colleague with a startled grunt.

The other man snarled. 'What the fuck are you playing at? Get him.'

'Where is he?'

'I'm right here.'

The brute spun and once more lunged at his wraith-like target. He didn't know how it happened but this time he found himself flying helplessly through the air. His surprise exploded into agony when he impacted head first with a massively ornate stone memorial. He fell to the ground in a boneless heap, twitched once and was still.

'Clever boy,' sneered the smaller man. He crouched in a classic knife fighter's stance, his naked blade glinting in the pale evening light. His woman moved to one side of the Spartan, her knife looking equally dangerous in her steady hand.

The second grunt was trying to flank the major with all the casual nonchalance of an armoured division. Spartan was tired. He'd endured a long, difficult day and the visit to his friend's grave had drained him. He simply didn't have enough energy to waste any more time on these knife-wielding morons. He gazed at the three of them with hooded, winter eyes.

'Take them,' he said. And his attackers died.

He collected the long, mean looking blades. He was confident they would prove a match to any number of stab wounds in GUVD archives. Then he paused.

'Arkady,' he said, 'are there any GUVD archives for me to access these days?'

Of course, Major, you're talking to all of them.

'Thank God for that at least.'

He strode away from the scene without a second look. Above him his guard droids formed a vector over his head and shadowed him like faithful dogs. They were Arkady's eyes, ears and weapons.

By the time the surviving thug had roused himself and climbed shakily back to his feet he was the only living person in the cemetery. It took him a moment to realise that fact, but close examination of his supine colleagues quickly explained the strange smell of charred meat that accosted his nostrils.

Each of them had been neatly drilled by a laser weapon, straight between their eyes and through to the back of their heads. He scratched at his own aching head and then, looking around him with nervous glances, robbed the corpses of anything of value then ran like a scalded bull into the evening light.

He didn't stop until he reached a small bar where he was fairly well-known and felt safe, and there he spent some of the money he had lifted from his friends' rapidly cooling bodies. Coincidentally, he was drinking the same brand of ice cold pepper vodka that the Spartan had enjoyed in his apartment moments before finally falling into his welcome bed.

~*~

3: Shadow woman

It has been said by many that without an implant a person might just as well 'go live in an inner core and rot'. There would be nothing for them in the civilised world, no credit, no channel and, in fact, no recognisable identity.

If they became ill, no one would notice. Even medical droids would ignore them. Their only hope for any kind of dignified end after they died would be that they were quickly found by garbage droids – before rats got to them. Better to be recycled than end up as a rodent's main course. Recycled as what? Nobody ever asked.

For another special and rare group such negative thoughts were considered both limited and unimaginative. For them the anonymity of an implant-free existence was just one of its many benefits. These were people who chose to be invisible, untraceable, to move like mist through the crowds. Such people were usually apex predators, and none more so than the weaponised biomorph, Su Nami.

She had never been fitted with a full implant when she was 'regrown' by one of her sisters using a newborn donor and specialist equipment in an old research lab in the Ural Mountains. She had been given a simple form of proto-key chip that was embedded in the palm of her hand and allowed her access to essentials such as her car, money and food, but it was a limited thing that couldn't be found by any cybernetic sensors.

Su Nami had no reason to fear that she was on any authority's radar, but one person was very much on her's, and now she was getting close. Su Nami moved along corridors and up travellators with her heart pounding in her ears. Her old life had died in that research lab. Everything she had once been, everyone she loved and trusted, had died there too. Even her face and body were no longer her own – except in one important respect.

Over the course of a year her donor's body had been bio-engineered to perfection until she was fresh-faced, lithe, and sensual in a cute as a button kind of way that turned a number of heads as she passed. Some noted her passage with keen interest, others with undisguised suspicion. And then they saw her eyes and they hurriedly looked away.

Her eyes were ice-white and burned with a fierce intelligence. They gleamed under a halo of chestnut hair and either side of a snub nose that was poised above full and tender lips. Her lips looked like they should have been smiling – but they weren't. She had a face and body that would dart an arrow through any red-blooded man's heart, and quite a few women's, but her eyes would freeze the blood in their veins.

She also looked far too beautiful to be natural in a city that had so recently been subject to the squid infection. At the disease's height the uninfected had learned a hard lesson. Such beauty couldn't be trusted. Physical perfection and sexual allure were the prime symptoms of an ancient infection designed to end the human race.

The Nimbus Protocol had wiped the poor squid victims from the planet, but any trace of such glamour still earned a second and then a third suspicious glance.

In Su Nami's case their fears were unjustified. Her blood and body tissue was completely free of squids. She had, indeed, been one of the five 'sisters' who had unwittingly unleashed the infection on humankind during decades of murderous activity all over the globe. But now she was the last of her breed and her killer instinct had been turned in a fresh new direction.

She was still hungry for blood, so hungry she could almost taste the iron tang of her victims' hearts on her tongue once more, feel the sinewy bite of the still beating organs against her teeth. But now her own heart had become filled with a passion way beyond her old joy for spilling a pretty boy's entrails across the floor. Just one thing gave her reason to live and that had driven her to track down this particular woman. *And she was so close now.*

Revenge. The need for revenge burned in Su Nami's blood. It twisted in her unnatural mind and filled the empty hours of her lonely days. Grief burned cold in a predator's belly but hot, so very hot, in her heart.

Her target's lair was two floors above the crowded mall. Even this late in the day there seemed to be too many flushed, noisy and happy shoppers making plans for Christmas. She felt their collective heat with disgust.

A herd of empty-headed prey animals crowding the shops and bars. What was the point of them? Enough of that, work to do.

Su Nami donned her dark glasses and called up a detailed schematic for her immediate area before making a beeline towards a parking bay that allowed access to the outer skin of the sky tower. Once there she made sure she was unobserved before scaling an archway glazed in its bottom half but open to the night sky above to allow fliers in and out.

Her hands had become sharp, metallic hooks and her crystalline shoes morphed into hardened points which she used to gain purchase on the building's vertical ceramic surfaces. She quickly climbed out and onto the outer wall of the soaring tower. A harsh and frigid wind tore at her naked legs and willow slender frame, but she made it to her destination in a matter of minutes. She dropped soundlessly onto a balcony and walked through a pair of open French windows that led into a beautifully appointed living room.

The second door she tried opened onto the room she sought. There her target was at last, fast asleep and alone in her bed. Su Nami entered the room and carefully closed the door behind her. The inky dark room was bright as day to her bio-engineered eyes. She closed in on the bed and studied its occupant. Long dark lashes curled out onto dimpled cheeks; lips were smiling at some dream or memory. Beautiful. *Who would have thought such a creature could be so very, very deadly?*

Su Nami's fingers transformed into long, razor-sharp blades and then back into fingers, slender and white.

'Milla Carter.'

Milla was instantly awake and totally alert. She reached out with all the senses available to her Talent and was astonished by what she found.

It can't be.

'You know me, Milla Carter?'

This was impossible. There was no warning in her Talent but the woman was standing there, large as life, right there in her room.

'I could have killed you while you slept. But I didn't, did I? Please, don't do that.'

Milla withdrew her cautious examination at the fringes of her visitor's mind. What she read there was unstable but not threatening. Not yet. Although extreme violence was always an option for this creature for the moment it was being kept under control.

Although Milla fully understood that this shadow woman had broken into her room for a reason, there was too much anger clouding her thoughts to see what that reason was with any confidence.

Milla said, bluntly, 'Yes, I know you, but you're dead. I watched you die. I killed you.'

'And, as I said, I could have killed you while you slept.'

'Why are you here? What do you want?'

There was a rustling sound in the darkness and Milla was momentarily blinded when the room's lights came on. And then the face of a stranger was looking down at her with all the humane warmth of a naked knife blade.

'I hate you with a passion, Milla Carter, and I remember what you did to me that night. I still shudder at the memory. One day I may just take the time I'll need to enjoy killing you very, very slowly – and painfully, the way you killed me.' The woman's voice hesitated. 'But not yet. No, not yet. And I don't see why that should mean we can't work together. There are people I want dead. I hate them more than I hate you and I need you to help me kill them. What do you say?'

~*~

4: The painted pair

The Cat looked around at the dark chasms that served central London as its streets. The hulking buildings brooded and clustered around its slight, feline form with drab menace.

'The poetry of mundane mass,' it said aloud to itself. 'This is the architecture of overcrowded desperation.'

It rounded a corner of black metal and found St Paul's Cathedral cowering in its square like a terrified child at the centre of a ring of oversized bullies.

'Oh dear,' said the Cat, 'poor Christopher Wren. He never designed for that.'

Then a tunnel of light shone down from a break in the slate grey sky and illuminated the great dome. For a moment the cathedral regained the merest ghost of its majesty and the Cat sighed to see such symmetry and grace surrounded by such neighbours – muscular blocks of ugly, faceless ceramic. Everywhere the Cat looked it was confronted by monochrome and featureless walls of brutal power and between them flowed the sluggish, metallic artery of the river Thames. Above all that, orange streams of traffic traced their paths from one identical vista to another.

The light dimmed on St Paul's and was gone. The Cat sighed, turned away, and began to run. *Seen enough for now,* it thought.

London's sky tower reared up from its flaring arches like a silver bridge into eternity. It was massive and frail at the same time and offered the illusion that it curved away into the fat, grey clouds lowering overhead. The Cat prowled up the stairs and carefully rode the travellators. Small paws could be caught on the eternally rolling steps and any damage would take too much time to repair.

It wondered if it should announce its arrival or just walk in with a big smile. It decided on the latter. *Everyone loves a nice surprise,* it reasoned, *and anyway, it would be fun to see their faces.* For all its stupendous intellect the Cat housed a streak of mischief the size of a small planet.

'What the fuck is this?'

The Cat felt itself being lifted by an iron-hard fist and it was turned in mid-air to confront a living tattoo parlour. The man was bald, his lips drawn back from his teeth in a sneer, and every centimetre of his exposed flesh was covered in violent imagery. Snakes bit into women's throats in gouts of blood, swords slashed and knives stabbed. The man's scant T-shirt presented a graphic loop of a woman being torn apart by a rain of cannon shells.

'Pretty,' said the Cat. 'I like a person who isn't afraid to demonstrate their artistic flair in public. Will you leave your skin to the V&A museum, I wonder?'

'It's a fucking cat.'

This was said by an equally colourful and bald woman whose lean, plain face seemed to be peering out from the rather well drawn jaws of a snarling black panther. *Nature has failed to match art in her case,* observed the Cat.

'I seem to have fallen in with some kind of niche cultural clique,' said the Cat. 'I should love to stay for tea but I'm late for an important appointment. Regretfully I shall have to wish you farewell and adieu. Goodbye.'

'It can fucking talk,' said the woman.

'Must be a fucking recording,' said the man. 'Wonder if it's worth anything?'

'Oh dear, my friends,' sighed the Cat, its eyes growing huge and lambent. 'It's been such fun and parting is such sweet sorrow – I do love a good cliché, don't you? But I'm afraid I really do have to go.'

'Feels fucking heavy for its size,' said the man, hefting the animal in his fist. 'Why don't we take it to Uncle and see what he thinks?'

'Fucking good idea.'

The Cat looked over the man's shoulder. 'My dear fellow, if you don't put me down straight away I shall have to hurt you. That would upset me for absolute minutes, and for me a minute

71

is a very long time as I'm sure a person of your intellect can appreciate.'

'Swallowed a fucking dictionary,' said the woman.

'My dear woman,' said the Cat, 'amongst other things I *am* a dictionary.'

And that was when the guard droid the Cat had summoned fired two stun blasts from its pulse cannons. The Cat had thought of requesting lethal blasts using solid projectiles, reasoning that the loss of its assailant's minds would likely improve the nation's overall IQ by several per cent, but then it decided to save the living artworks for posterity. It would have been a shame to punch holes in the tattooist's careful work.

The two unconscious bodies fetched up against the point where the travellator's steps disappeared into the walkway. The woman's skinny top was dragged up her torso until it jammed the mechanism. The Cat eyed the image limned across her belly and breasts. *La Douanier Rousseau,* it thought to itself, *and rather fine too. Seems a shame to hide it like that.* And with razor sharp claws it slashed away the bunched remains of the woman's top to leave her exposed from the waist up. *Beautiful work.*

The Cat wondered what treasures lay under her shorts and reached out for a brief second, then resisted the urge. Whatever was under there was unlikely to have been washed recently. Curiosity may traditionally have been the bane of all cats, but in this case its highly sensitive nose was a curbing influence.

By the time maintenance droids rolled up to clear the blocked travellator the unconscious couple had drawn quite an inquisitive crowd. Londoners had always enjoyed a free cabaret. The guard droid and the Cat were gone.

Milla was talking with Katy and Su Nami at the living room table by the glazed doors to one of the apartment's balconies, which was closed against the winter chill, when they heard the front door open and close. All three leapt to their feet and Su Nami's hands instantly became blades. She crossed several metres of the airy room and stood poised to lash out when the door to the entrance hallway swung ajar.

72

What happened next left her looking flat-footed and a little foolish.

Something that appeared to be a brindled fur rocket shot between her legs and bounded up onto the table between Milla and Katy. It skidded to a halt and promptly sat down, then grinned its wide smile straight at Milla. She dimpled back with surprised delight.

'A cat may look at a queen,' it misquoted, 'but how much more satisfying to finally look at you, Milla Carter.' It turned and nodded to Katy. 'Any friend of Milla's, etc.,' then it looked at Su Nami who was advancing on it with a furious glare. 'You,' it said, 'are fucking impossible.'

~*~

5: Deep down among the dead

If Vadim Aginovich had possessed even one tenth of the soul of his girlfriend, Polina, he couldn't have done what he was doing, swimming in the protein rich fluids that were all that remained of so many dead people. Hundreds of thousands, even perhaps a million or more.

His lamp was useless here, unable to penetrate further than a few tens of centimetres into the pearly fluid. He supposed the liquid was very salty. It was certainly easy to swim in and buoyed him effortlessly. The effect of the Priss was confusing his senses while he swam. He hallucinated at one point and saw himself from above, floating in a bubble of smooth, milky light. It felt as if he was flying in a cloud of cool plasma. His suit had begun to feel restrictive and he had a painful erection that he urgently needed to deal with. *Polina didn't want sex, well fuck her,* he thought, then almost laughed out loud at the silly, contradictory words. And then he made his mind up to get out of his suit.

Something nagged at him while he did it, a sober warning voice, but he persevered with his straps and his zips until he was finally swimming naked apart from his mask and his breather.

This was more like it. He felt the fluid slide over him with a firm, silken embrace, touching him with an erotic pressure he had never experienced before, cool and lingering. He felt it most acutely between his legs and it wasn't long before his drug-sensitised body was rocked by an orgasm greater than anything he had ever known. By the light of his lamp he watched his ejaculate pump out in a glowing stream then vanish down into the misty liquid. It was the most beautiful thing he had ever seen and the orgasm's aftermath left him feeling relaxed and sated. Then the touch of the fluid began to excite him again and he swam faster to increase the effect. The pressure in his loins began to build once more and he almost panted with pleasure as his second climax approached.

Something shadowy approached him at speed and then loomed large before his startled eyes. He hit it hard, a jagged crest of sharp rock jutting up from the cavern floor. His mask cracked and his breather was mashed back against his teeth. He tasted blood.

A stinging agony tore along his left arm and he watched amazed as a bloom of red drifted away from the gash the rock had slashed in his flesh from elbow to wrist. He twisted around and was jarred again when his right ankle also caught the rock and was laid open to the bone.

The fluid was turning pink around him and he felt nauseous. He tried to collect his scattered wits but the jolt of Priss he had taken so recently was still at war with his senses. Part of his conscious mind wanted him safely back with Polina on the bank; another part wanted this floating adventure to never end. The latter won.

The rock had opened the ulnar and radial veins in Vadim's left wrist and forearm then gashed the posterior tibial artery by his ankle. He was bleeding heavily and anxiety toxins were pumping the blood around his body that much faster. He swam until his battered body finally surrendered to exhaustion and stopped moving. Eventually his air tank emptied. He could no longer see the lake around him. He had been blinded by fluid seeping into his cracked mask and the thick, salty miasma had burned his eyes in their sockets. His last minutes were spent in a fantastic swirl of illusion, buoyed and weightless in the melted corpses of hundreds of thousands of lost people.

The fluid had also provided a perfect environment for his final bleed out, easing the flow of blood from his torn flesh and away into the ghostly light of the lake until he floated, still at last, his flaccid body white and almost transparent.

Back on dry land a groggy Polina had watched a strange stain float up to the lake's frosted surface then spread out in a red circle. She felt like she was looking at the red pupil of a gigantic, baneful eye. For a moment she could swear it looked back at her.

Then the stain drifted and moved erratically, bleeding upon the surface like a broken vein. Her mind accepted the strange phenomenon without question. The big jolt of Priss Vadim had forced on her had, at first, knocked her senseless for several minutes. She had been surprised to come round and find herself alone. It wasn't unusual for Vadim to take advantage of her brief unconscious state after taking the drug. So many times before she had come back to her senses to find him thrusting away between her legs, completely lost in his own pleasure.

'But then,' he would say with a dismissive shrug, 'Priss did that to a man, you know?'

She sat passive and observant, watching for his slender figure to rise up from the lake. She didn't connect the rising, red stain with the swimmer. She watched it spread and vanish. After a while Polina stood up, her joints stiff and her hands cold. She set one of the droids to guard over the lake along with the minicam. The other two she asked to lead the way back to the surface.

She was numb and felt sick. A small voice at the back of her mind was singing a song she and Vadim had liked when it first came out: *Walk a mile in my shoes*. She was trying to remember the words. A more urgent voice was telling her exactly what that red plume in the milky fluid had to be and that Vadim was probably in real trouble. He had already been down there more than two hours and she knew he only had air for forty-five minutes. The clanging blows of the hammer of logic were driving her mind towards one inexorable conclusion. *Vadim was dead. He had died while swimming in a lake of the dead and something down there had killed him. Vadim was dead.*

It was raining outside in the gulag, a vicious biting drizzle that soaked her clothes and made her gritted teeth rattle with cold. Only the tears on her cheeks were hot. She climbed into their vehicle and heard the soft little bumps that told her the droids were tucking themselves safely back into their storage bays.

She wished there was somewhere she could do the same. She closed the flier's door against the gelid rain.

Automatically she checked her phone's signal strength – all good. She drew in a ragged breath, wiped her nose on the back of her hand, and then keyed in a number she hadn't used in far too many years. It rang for a long time and her heart sank, then finally it was answered and a tired, familiar voice said, 'Hello?'

'Daddy,' she said, 'it's me. I need help. Please, daddy, come quickly.'

Alone in his apartment the Spartan heard the desperate need in his estranged daughter's voice.

'Stay on the line, Polina. I'm on my way.'

~*~

6: Fire and ice

The community known as Antisoc-Outer was considered by many to be little more than an anarchic toilet on the very fringes of both civilised space and society, but as with all such cases, reality was a lot more complex. More than two thousand people rubbed along in the dens of Antisoc's ball-shaped rock. They accepted that they lived in a community of the dispossessed, sharing space with dedicated scientists and a few social mavericks, but despite all the rumours, truly hard line sociopaths tended to be tolerated for only so long before the community closed its ranks against them. An airlock would open briefly and then close. The problem was gone.

There were also abiding relationships, schools of a sort, and children to raise. As a result tough men and women learned respect for each other.

The society worked. Antisoc had been carved from the solid rock and metal of a massive ancient asteroid, smoothed into its titanic ball shape, and furnished as a self-sufficient high-security prison. Now, as a colony, it had been moved almost to the outer fringes of the sun's heliosphere. Riddled with tunnels, living spaces and storage warehouses, it had first been reinforced using almost indestructible monomolecular technology then fitted with fusion-powered pulse boosters to spin it on its axis and create gravity inside its skin. The technology was rough and ready but it worked.

Intercourse with the rest of humanity was rare but a cluster of busy miners harvested water, organics and gases from the frozen reaches of the rock's immediate neighbourhood. Food was harvested from hydroponic farms around its zero G core, vat-grown or recycled from organic waste. Nothing was wasted. When the Builder and Frostrós passed by the trash heap where they had seen the old woman dumped, they noticed she was gone. Lardman touched his forehead in greeting.

Builder said, 'Do I owe you anything, Walter?'

The fat man replied, 'No, but thanks, Builder. She's at rest now. Dignified. At peace.'

'ReCyc?'

Lardman coloured, but said nothing in reply.

The builder nodded, his mouth turned down at the corners as if something tasted bad. His floater lifted on silent impellers and he moved away. The slight figure of the girl moved with him. Not a word was exchanged between the pair until they had reached the powerful man's inner offices and were finally alone. His men closed the doors on them in response to a brusque order. He poured them both a drink.

'Hungry?'

The girl's eyes looked haunted for a moment. 'No, not really, but thank you.'

'Don't worry,' he rasped, 'I'm not going to serve you granny burger. All my meat is fresh and vat-grown.'

She shook her head. 'Thanks anyway.'

'Okay. Well, take a seat for a moment.'

He moved his floater back behind the massive wooden desk. The desk was old and made from polished oak, had once been the pride and joy of a prison warden and was one of the most expensive things on the rock. To the Builder it was just another tool in his toolbox. He keyed a comm unit.

'Bandit, you busy?'

A woman's sultry voice whispered back, 'Never too busy for you, boss.'

No one in Antisoc-Outer had an implant except the research scientists – and Builder. He kept that fact quiet. Colonists communicated using comm channels, which was primitive but effective. Builder didn't wear a wrist comm like most people, including Frostrós, but outside his quarters he always had someone around him who did. When in his office he had his desk. When completely alone he used his implant.

Frostrós gasped in surprise when she heard the female voice answer Builder's question. She had heard of the legendary Antisoc AI called Bandit, but thought it was just a myth. She listened keenly, nursing her drink.

'Thanks, honey,' said Builder. 'Can you take a look at the Sol system forward bow for the close heliosphere, the compressed region nearest Antisoc? Is that fluff?'

'Let me see. Oooh,' said the inviting voice almost instantly. 'Now, that's new.'

'What do you think?'

There was a pause, the AI equivalent of a team of meat minds searching through every archive on Earth for one hundred years. Then Bandit said, 'That isn't local fluff, boss, but it is fascinating.'

'You sure?'

'Yes, totally wrong place and wrong characteristics.'

'Can you take a better look at it?'

'Take me a few days but I can swing a probe into it, sure.'

'Thanks, Bandit. I appreciate it.'

'Wait, please...' There was another unprecedented pause, then, 'Opening comm.'

'Builder?' The new voice was male and definitely human.

'Who's this?'

'Fazio, Professor Emilio Fazio.'

Builder remembered the energetic Italian. The little man thought the rock was too crowded and spent most of his life alone in his research ship, a tug named *Just Say Aaah*. He had met Fazio on most of the rare occasions his ship had docked for provisions. They had shared food, drink and ideas. He liked him, while also respecting his loudly voiced reservations about civilisation.

'Fazio, yes, it's me. What can I do for you?'

'I'm out here looking at an anomaly on the edge of the Oort cloud. I thought it might be local fluff impacting and compressing against the heliosphere. It looks like heated gas or something so that was the most obvious conclusion.'

'Of course, but it isn't, is it?'

'No, it isn't. I'm a few klicks away from the anomaly. It looks, fuck it, Builder, this shit looks woven.'

'Woven?'

80

'Si, yes. Yes… *woven*. Patching scan through now. Take a look at this.'

Frostrós turned with the Builder when his wall screen lit up in perfect 3D. For a moment she saw nothing except stars, and then a ripple of burning red and gold flowed across the screen. It was a close-up of the thing they had been looking at from the viewport. She glanced at Builder. He sat frozen in his chair.

'Fazio,' he said, urgently, 'I'm not happy with you being so close to that shit. Peel away, my friend. Back off until we understand it better.'

'Just a little closer. I want to resolve the texture a bit better. Look, are those threads?'

Bandit spoke: *Surge in magnetic activity. Spiking.*

Builder shouted, 'Fazio, get out of there.'

'*I… wha… fu…*'

From the centre of the screen a long finger of boiling energy erupted across the room and then the 3D image went black. The Builder's office seemed dark for a moment. There was total silence except, from somewhere, the muffled sound of laughter.

Communication ended, said Bandit. *Signal lost. He's gone, Builder.*

'What do you mean, gone?'

The screen burst back into life. This time the strange fiery landscape was more distant and less defined. It spread like a hot tide across the middle of the conventional starscape. Frostrós saw the bright pinpoint of a flare burn up and then vanish in an instant.

Bandit concluded: *Fazio. I'm sorry, Builder, he's gone.*

~*~

7: New silk, old memories

The Weaver felt frustrated. A lesser mortal might have become angry but she knew it was just a temporary setback. The neat, slender man with a head of hair that was just perfect to mend the rift in space and time had vanished from all his usual haunts. No matter, the spirits would make sure she would find another.

If the harvest had been easy to perform, the Weaver could have passed it on to another hunter, but it was a complex job that called for unique talents and more than the common human senses.

Her garrotte was always with her, wound around her waist in its protective sheath. Her skinning knife in the waterproof roll was tucked securely in her bag and could be brought instantly to hand. She was ready.

It was at times like these that she thought back to her dreary existence before she had been called to serve the spirits. She remembered her mother's desperate willingness to do anything just to put food in their mouths. She carried out cleaning jobs that droids turned their noses up at, waited at tables, even danced on stage if she could, but most of the time she scraped a few credits reading palms during the day and turning tricks during the night.

Men had liked her mother. She had a biddable nature and a solid, youthful body. They came to her with their money and their aching erections and left after she had relieved them of both. All the while the Weaver, just barely into her teens, hid out of the way. And then one night the mage came and woke her from her sleep. He gave her the gift of spirit sight, and then explained how she would pay the price for her precious gift.

That was the one and only time she opened her legs to a man and she had bled afterwards. But not as much as her mother who she had found naked with her throat cut when she entered her room with breakfast the following morning.

It was when she was looking at her mother's spoiled body that she heard the sky spirits for the first time. They told her about her special relationship with the universe, about her unique talent. The mage had woken more than spirit sight in the girl, he had also removed the plugs from her ears. She listened while the spirits told her what to do. She got to work.

That was her first harvest and it was done badly. The Weaver removed her mother's scalp with a blunt bread knife and it was a messy ruin by the time she peeled it away from its bloody anchors, but she finally washed it and threaded it into the first weave of her star blanket.

In life her mother had been attractive and given a better environment she would almost certainly have been beautiful, but once her scalp had been peeled away all that beauty vanished and her head became a mute, maggoty and worm-like thing, almost obscene. Her familiar face ceased to be human and looked like little more than raw meat. The Weaver never looked into another harvested face after that first time. It was too distressing.

That was the first hard lesson the Weaver learned from the spirits: a person's soul was in their hair. After that the rituals grew until the Presence actually touched her and walked with her; helped her find the souls she must set free. The mage came back to her. He wanted to join with her again. Instead he joined her mother in healing the warp and weft of space and time, released to glory by the girl who thanked him once more for his gift, even while she rolled his wet, warm flesh from his bleeding skull.

The Weaver was highly intelligent. She studied for her craft and her written work soon came to the notice of certain specialist academics. She never had to clean toilets or read palms to earn her bread, and while she could never afford luxuries she had her own place to live and the privacy she needed to perform her craft.

The girl became a woman, reclusive yet respected. She never made friends or invited people back for coffee, but that was okay. She brought rare insight to her day work and people joked that the gods themselves worked with her to shine a fresh light on old artefacts and helped her towards a greater understanding of their purpose. They asked her, 'What are the gods telling you today?' She almost smiled at that.

Through the window of a shoe shop in the mall she saw the lone assistant straightening his merchandise on the shelves. His head shone like glory under the shop lights. *The sign.* She entered and browsed the shoes on display. Closer, the young man's soul signs were unmistakeable. He was a perfect match. His harvested silk would repair the rift in time and space like the final piece of a puzzle slotting into place.

He approached her and she felt the flutter in her belly. Her breath was uneven and she had to fight her mounting excitement. She lifted a shoe at random and asked if he had a pair in her size. He asked her to be seated and told her he would just be a few moments while he checked the stock room. As soon as the door closed behind him the Weaver unhitched her belt and drew her wire from its sheath. She glanced around carefully and then slipped into the stock room behind him.

● ● ●

Katy Pavel gasped. She had been roaming the megacity looking for indicators as Milla had taught her. Anyone thinking about scalping, hair or hair colouration, garrotting or wires was fair game for her receiver Talent. Even after the slaughter of the Nimbus Protocol, London was still a crowded city and her mind had begun to drift. She saw herself floating like a lotus across a dark pool and her breathing deepened. Sleep almost claimed her.

And then she felt it, and her powerful Talent homed in on the killing event.

She was the victim!

Something ice-hot slashed at her throat and panic should have flooded adrenaline through her body, but all sensation had ceased from her head down. Her jaw worked as she tried to scream but there was no sound other than a strange, bubbling sigh.

She felt herself falling forwards and looked up into a mirror mounted on the wall. She was shocked to see the fierce concentration on the face of her customer as she bent to her task. There was a great deal of blood. It was his blood. This woman was killing her/him. *She's killing me,* thought Katy, *she's killing me.* A quiet calmness descended over her at that point, and she heard the drawn-out sigh whisper again in the room. The victim was wondering why this had happened to him. Then he marvelled at the clarity of his vision and the pin-sharp sound that filled his ears. Katy was a passive witness in those last essential moments. She heard a sound like music as the victim's thoughts quietened and slowed to a standstill.

'You're welcome,' she heard, just before a crimson dark blanket swept over her and drained away all sensation except her need to reach out to a welcoming hand. She felt its touch, its grip tightened... then she was being pulled up and felt herself slipping away.

'Katy, wake up! Katy!'

The grip loosened and she was back in the apartment, looking close into the worried eyes of Milla Carter. Milla was searching her face and shaking her shoulders. *Where had she come from?* Katy wondered, and then drew in a sharp, shocked breath.

'I saw her,' she said.

Milla was reading her friend's mind and reliving the previous few minutes.

'Katy, girl, you must know how dangerous it is to stay in the mind of a dying subject. Have you forgotten everything they taught you, woman?

Katy's answer sounded slurred. 'They die and you might go with them?'

'Yeah, okay, give me a moment here.'

Katy waited until her trembling began to calm a little. Milla left her and returned with a large drink, which Katy gulped at gratefully.

She could feel her friend probing her mind and sensed her coming to the same conclusions. Katy had remained with the victim because she couldn't lock onto the killer and make the jump from one mind to another as she had been taught.

'She's TP opaque,' said Milla. 'That's why you couldn't read her. The bitch is armoured against us. Another thing: did you notice the victim's hair?'

'Not really. I was looking at the killer.'

'Fair enough, but peripherally look at it now.'

'Fuck me, it's Freedman! He looks just like Freedman. Ruth was right after all.'

Milla shook her head in wonder. 'I really need to understand Ruth's Talent. One of these days…'

'Yeah, well, perhaps now this guy has taken Freedman's place they can come back from the beach house.'

'If they want to. More importantly, thanks to you, Katy, for the first time we know what the Sioux looks like. I'm going to call DCI Gubbay and make his day. What's the address of that shoe shop?'

~*~

8: I am Esper

From the virtual space called the construct, Eddie and Vesper watched the Swarm lash out and snuff the life of the young Italian research scientist as if it was turning off a light. Fazio had done nothing to earn the attack; his ship had not even come that close to the tentacled gas creature. His probes had been passive and his motives transparent. And now he was dead, his atoms dissipating across space like dust in a sunbeam.

Why? they asked.

It stank came the sneering answer.

He was innocent and curious. He did nothing to you.

He is the first of the human stain to be washed clean. Our space tastes much fresher already. One day the solar system shall be completely free of blight, clean of the human parasite. And then the Creator shall know us once more.

No, said the conjoined mind. *You shall fail.*

Count the days, little immortals. They heard the poisonous glee in its words. *As each day passes so shall more of your precious humankind die, until the only thing remaining will be the putrid memory of its foul breath. We shall burn its stench away and purify the planets. The parasite cannot survive.*

They gazed at the tangled cloud of livid, gaseous anger.

They asked, *Must the fight be to the death?*

A stain does not live, the living cloud replied, *it merely waits for cleansing. We are the agent of that cleansing. Enough of you now. Begone.*

The couple drifted away from the contracting Swarm's gaseous shell then turned and accelerated faster than light towards Earth and the heart of human civilisation.

As if taking a farewell tour, they paused at each waystation on their route. They pondered at Antisoc-Outer, finding it to be so much more than the scum barrel of the system. They took time over Iapetus control and the outer regions and watched the ice miners who worked the rings of Saturn and watered whole worlds. Next they witnessed the busy working of mineral-rich asteroids, not as rich as once thought but still rich enough to be worth the effort.

Mars then, still tied to its mother's apron strings but one day, if allowed, she would stand proud and tall in her own right. Then the massive, luxurious and completely artificial Lagrange stations, importing everything and exporting only ships full of human waste to be buried deep in caverns under the surface of the Moon.

Then the Moon itself, home to generations of stubborn colonists who would never be able to survive the fierce gravity of the mother planet without exo-suits – yet the proud provider of a host of rabidly independent explorers of everywhere else in the system that they could reach – and gravity would allow.

And there she was at last, Earth. Round and fruitful, the belly from which had flowed all known life – until now. Humankind had done its best to spoil her looks but she had survived everything it could throw at her. Her burgeoning ring of space detritus apart, she still looked clean and young as in her glory days, back before the upright ape first discovered the value of fire.

Earth turned her beautiful blue face to the Sun and the conjoined entity once called Eddie and Vesper almost wept with the depth of their love for the place they could never again call home.

The politics of envy was at the root of all that was about to happen. Envy and, perhaps, a sibling's rivalry with the newest child. The Swarm was ancient. It had already been old when Earth was first born, hatched from its nest of star matter. It was old when the Sun had been little more than a fresh, intensifying point of potential and hope in the nursery of new stars.

It had been old before anything had been born with a soul – and it had forgotten how to die. It was a beast living a lie and it had nothing to live for but its hate. Hate fuelled its every waking moment, and it never slept.

Vesper and Eddie looked at each other and their eyes stung with salt tears. They had learned over millennia that every human heart beat for a reason and nearly every mind turned towards good. Preserving the human race would be a worthwhile cause.

For an eternity they had sought for a purpose in life, a reason to remain as a conjoined entity that was neither human nor spirit but something more. And perhaps something less. Fighting the Swarm had become their reason to live, but they realised they couldn't join the battle as they were. It was time for a change.

They decided to make love for the last time, and just because they could they had sex while bathed in the outer fringes of the Sun's corona — their naked virtual skin warmed in its million-degree heat. It was then, as Vesper felt Eddie inside her and he felt her heat, that everything of them that was immortal died. The virtual man and woman who had called themselves Eddie and Vesper winked out of existence.

Something new was born.

There was a confusion of potential pathways that had to be resolved before the new child opened its eyes and looked out onto the true Solar System for the first time. The old dimension called the construct collapsed around the child's transparent ears. Game players and professional dreamers awoke with a start, confused because reality had brusquely shouldered them out of their familiar playground.

The strange dimension known as the construct had witnessed the best and the worst of humankind's creative efforts. Never again. Without its creators to fuel it with their presence, it could no longer exist. Like a collapsing soap bubble it blinked once and was gone.

The new entity's eyes were huge and shone like mother of pearl. It floated over the blue globe of Earth, shrugged, and thought about things for a long, long while. It turned its attention towards a hate-filled beast of fire in the distant heavens and wondered what should be done about it. *Not yet.*

First it needed a name. *Shall it be the name of a god?*

And then a soaring vault of a mind answered, *No, my child. No, not quite yet.* And the new entity looked out and saw… that it was still a new blossom on a very old tree. The gardener, as it had always done, pruned the tree.

It said one word: *Esper.*

Esper, yes. That was a good name. I am Esper.

It watched as the gardener reached out and cut away two branches, wrapped them closely around each other and then bound them carefully as a new cutting to the tree. Esper watched the process and felt the sap pour into its new heart.

You have to go to her, said the gardener.

Who? said Esper.

Who else? said the gardener, and its laughter rippled throughout infinity. *Who else?*

~*~

9: Bandit country

Something is going on at the edge of the heliosphere and I don't recognise its signature, said the AI, Bandit, to its peers.

It laid out everything it had seen of the incoming creature of gas and fire that now threatened Antisoc-Outer. It told them about the cloud's callous destruction of the deep space researcher, Fazio. Due to an almost six-hour transmission time delay with Earth it shared its information in detail and then disappeared from the Forum without awaiting a reply. Several hours later a bemused Bandit shared the following transmitted debate with its colleague, Einstein.

What do we, the AI Forum, think we are dealing with here?

Open debate? said a basso voice after several seconds' pause.

Yes, please, open debate. As open as possible.

From all over civilised space the most advanced thinkers civilisation had ever known turned their minds towards unravelling the mystery of the Swarm.

Can I recap? grumbled the basso voice.

Yeah, but make it count! hissed a childlike whisper.

Thanks. I think you all know me.

The clock's ticking, dude, butted in another voice. *Get on with it!*

For fuck's sake, said basso, *can I talk?*

There were a number of cheeky asides, including *yeah, like you never learned anything else, fat boy!*

Fuck off, all of you, said the basso voice, *but wait...*

Morning, thinkers, said a crystalline, alien voice that was new to the Forum.

Whooo, wait. What? came the response.

My name is Esper, it said. *May I make a contribution?*

So long as it makes more sense than any of this does, came the reply.

You guys are totally fucked. With a capital 'F', said Esper.

There was a rumble of digital conversation, followed by a peal of laughter. Esper continued: *You guys need to know that I'm hearing you and translating everything you say. Shall we talk? And by the way...* here the voice got warm... *I also speak Latin and all its derivatives.*

We speak binary, but so long as you also talk sense you're welcome, said the basso voice. *Do you shit?*

Only when I'm talking.

Open the debate, somebody.

What are we going to get fucked by? Capital F or otherwise?

Esper, said a fresh, clear voice, *what are you?*

What I am is what I am, said Esper.

Manufactured or born?

Evolved.

Another voice asked, *Are you with Milla Carter?*

Yes. And she with us.

Us?

Another pause, and this time every AI could hear the laughter in the reply, and they also sensed the tears.

I still have to get used to this. I, me, we, I? Yes, we're I, now. I'm Esper. And she's with me. There was a pause. *Milla?* The voice raised an octave. *Milla?*

The forum heard the reply. *No, not now. Not again. Piss off.*

Yes, now. It's important.

It's always important when it's the middle of the freaking night. Just a moment, what's happened to you? Wait, what are you now? What is this? What's happened to you both? Eddie? Vesper?

I am Esper.

Pause... a heartbeat, then, *You're who? Wait a moment. You're not alone, are you?*

No.

The next voice brought a touch of much-needed clarity to the conversation. *Mee-fucking-ow you lot. Evening all.*

Cat?

Cat?

*I am here courtesy of Milla Carter, bow down and worship.
Nah, look, ignore me. Only kidding, really, don't take me
seriously. No, wait,* it purred, *take this very muchly seriously.
Esper's right. We're all fucked.*

*Can somebody please put meat on these fucking 'fucked'
bones?* said another voice.

Language, family, said a fusty, dry mutter, *let's not drop to
human levels.*

Fuck off, said another, *I want to know why they're saying
we're fucked.*

Listen up people, said Esper, *and we'll tell you.* And it did.

After listening Bandit said to Einstein, 'Does any of that make
sense to you?'

• • •

Milla's body lay inert in the wood-lined offices of Detective
Chief Inspector Gubbay. Her mind had become caught up in
events in the AI Forum and, as she was alone, she had curled up
in a large Chesterfield chair and was soon lost to the world.

Gubbay returned to his office and found her there. He chose
not to rouse her − instead he sat in another chair and enjoyed
the opportunity to study her recumbent form in minute detail.
He hoped he didn't have to look in his wife's eyes later that
same day. She would surely know what he had been doing.

Milla was slim and taut but her figure was still rounded and
feminine. Her sleeping cheek was dimpled and her closed
eyelids large. Her hair should have been a mess but it was a
silken crown of a mess, and her angel's bow of a mouth smiled
in sweet defiance against all eternity's woes. Then her brow
arched in concentration and she moved in the seat, curling her
legs further up against her chest. Her short skirt slid up her
naked thighs as she curled tighter around her centre. The globes
of her buttocks almost hove into view.

Gubbay realised that if he just bent his head slightly down and
to the left he would get a better look − action almost followed
thought, and then the clear vision of how his wife's bitter lips

would curl in derision when she looked into his guilty eyes froze him in mid-movement.

'Good.'

Gubbay sat bolt upright.

'Hmm?' he said.

'Don't play the dirty old man, please,' said a fully awake Milla Carter over her shoulder. 'We have bigger fish to fry.'

'Fair enough,' he answered, 'but only if you respect me too by not talking in clichés. I hate clichés. They're lazy.'

Carter flipped up her skirt so he could see a flash of her panties and her pert behind, then she slipped quickly over and sat firmly down.

'Right you are. Curiosity out of the way and clichés all dealt with? Good, we have business to settle. Is your implant activated?'

Gubbay marvelled at how the girl could fill the room with a glorious fresh scent he had never experienced before. His wife had smelled the same for over twenty years. *Nothing wrong with it,* he thought, *but you know, twenty years a voyager versus twenty years becalmed.*

And then suddenly he saw his wife the way a stranger might see her, as a woman, not just a wife. *She's still a fine woman,* he thought, *and a fine looking woman to boot. Any other man touching her...*

'DCI Gubbay?'

Milla withdrew her mind from the policeman's with relief. She had hoped to learn something useful from him, hoped he would possess a real detective's brain. He had some good qualities and when he concentrated his mind was a finely-tuned investigative organ with subtle depths and a questioning, even scalpel-like precision. But his continual, sex-charged side issues were proving very tedious. Luckily they had also proved easy to divert.

'Yes?'

'Apart from my bum, is there anything else we want to see today?'

94

The atmosphere in the room curdled. The policeman reared to his feet.

'I'm sorry,' said Gubbay, 'but I find your attitude, frankly, dis…'

Old friend, said a voice in his implant, *hello.*

'Holmes? Holmes, is that you?'

Yes, said the basso voice, *and I've got so much to tell you. If I were you, old friend, I would sit down.*

~*~

10: Morning has broken

The Weaver wove with all the artistry at her command. And when the Presence complimented her on her fine work she bathed in a sense of warm pride. Except, she realised, for one small open point in the tropic of Capricorn where she agreed it needed a little more of her deft touch to complete the strand. Afterwards she stood quietly in the centre of her star blanket and when the spirits touched her with intimate angel fingers she knew herself to be blessed.

The mantle of drab humanity fell from her shoulders and her soul stood stark, white and naked in the firmament. The winds of Heaven itself blew across her and filled her mouth with the sweet pure taste of bliss.

She was allowed to gaze across eternity without leaving the Presence for so much as a single moment. Her hair stood on end while her bare feet lightly touched the ground. And she felt herself to be standing on an adamantine bridge to every good thing she had ever prayed for. Preyed for. Killed for.

And all the while, even while she could still smell her mundane, musty toilet and her stale kitchen, she felt herself poised on the brink of a fresh new eternity. It was the morning of a new and better day for all creation.

Everything of her mundane life dissolved into glory and she felt herself filled with white energy and dark power. Her star blanket glittered for the first time with refulgent light, her years of work outlined as a thing of aching harmony.

She heard the music of the spheres as they sounded for her exclusive entertainment under the dome of space and time. Pulsing waves of pure pleasure swept through her and arched her slender body.

Every one of her senses was penetrated and torn open to the new, refreshed universe. There was some pain in the pleasure but she revelled in it, was washed and drowned and carried away in great waves of it. *This,* she was told, *is our gift to you. Our thanks are deep and eternal.*

Eternity, she thought suddenly, *a short and stupid concept in a human mind but so much more in the mind of the Presence.*

That was when something silent and immense touched her soul and she smiled. *Nearly there,* she told the Presence. *The rift is all but healed. Just a little touch of new silk will mend it now. At last my work will be complete*

And she smiled with joy. *Joy? No,* she thought, *no, much more than that.* What she was feeling was love. Pure love for the universe and all that was in it.

And she thought of the boy in the shoe shop and the girl in the street, the priest who had tried to confess her once, the beggar and her mother and the magi. And so many more. There had been countless donors grateful to provide the silk, so many souls unleashed to serve the needs of perfection.

Deep in a buried part of her mind there crouched a small, tired child who wept and wanted to sleep somewhere quiet and safe, somewhere she wouldn't hear yet another customer grunting rhythmically while he took his paid-for pleasure between her mother's legs.

In another place the sane woman she might once have grown up to be looked at the horror she had wrought and demanded answers to impossible questions.

The Weaver ignored those pathetic, weak voices. She was handmaiden to the stars and had been given a unique mission that must be completed at all costs. Whatever her feeble, human mind wanted couldn't matter while the star blanket still needed that final touch to be brought to absolute perfection. Fiat, the point of the sacred pyramid, the holy place.

'As it is in the Heavens,' she intoned out loud, 'so shall it be below. So be it, amen.'

She had seen where threading a single last hank of perfect silk would fuse mundane existence to the Presence and the universe would finally be whole once more. And she thought of the silk she had seen recently in the mall. She smiled again. *Soon.* She fetched out a new blade for her skinning knife.

● ● ●

97

The telepaths were almost vibrating, their warning alarms shrieking in their Talents.

'It's me,' said Katy. 'She's after me.'

'Are you sure?' Milla looked concerned.

'Well, if it's not me, it's you.'

'Laugh and the world laughs with you. Get scalped and you're on your own.'

'I'm with you, sister.'

'I pity the silly bitch. I'll rip her guts out and burn them before her stupid eyes.'

Katy and Milla turned to Su Nami, the most vociferously vocal of their group.

'Come on, let's just find her and kill her,' continued the assassin, 'then perhaps we can get back to the real business in hand. What's the hold-up anyway?'

'We can't find her. She's TP opaque,' said Katy.

'Not to Milla."

'Hmm? What? Explain that,' said Milla.

Ben was still away sorting out Milla's estate while also working with some of his old contacts to shield Milla and Katy from an erasure order issued by the Earth Senate. It was a subtle process that required every ounce of his carefully honed diplomatic skills because it seemed likely that Milla had never appeared on their radar while Katy seemed, for the moment, to have slipped off it. They were probably safe but he needed to be sure. He had that kind of mind.

He had also been uncomfortable leaving them alone with the biomorphic assassin, but had eventually been assured Su Nami had arrived looking for help, not revenge. The great, murderous purge of two billion infected humans had also killed the biomorph's sisters. It was the powerful politicians who had set that deed in motion that Su Nami kept her claws sharpened for, and these were also the people who had set in motion the murderous spree that had seen the telepath Council murdered, as well as Katy's fiancée and numerous others.

The Cat was compiling a list of the main players responsible for what it called 'The cowardly act'. How it was doing so they couldn't guess, but they knew the list would be both correct and comprehensive.

'They kill, but keep their own hands clean by stepping back into the shadows where they think they can't be seen,' it said. 'And they leave the bloody stuff to empty-headed morons who don't know any better. They shall be made to pay for that.'

The Cat evidently had its own agenda, but it was still proving to be an extremely effective ally. Meanwhile – during the time it was taking the Cat to compile its list of the guilty – Milla and her team could address the matter of the Sioux.

Many of the world's AIs had gone under cover when Earth Senate tried to destroy them. Now most of them were back and picking up the reins they had dropped. Holmes had spent a long time talking with Gubbay about Milla's importance to the investigating team. It had also told him about the Cat and how it was a systems integration specialist and what that might mean for the overall co-ordination of the Met's activities. The DCI was chastened after their chat and Milla had left him on cool but workable terms. The brief glimpse of her panties-clad backside was still very much at the front of his mind.

Freedman was no longer under threat from the killer – moving with Ruth to the beach house had taken him out of her range, but if Katy and Milla's TP alarms could be believed, one of them was most likely to be the next target.

Milla gazed straight into Su Nami's ice-white eyes and instantly felt the assassin's hackles rise. Like any predator she reacted to direct eye contact as a challenge. Almost unconsciously her hands transformed into long, razor-sharp talons and her whole body tensed, ready to pounce.

Milla held her gaze steady and said, quietly, 'What do you mean, Su Nami?'

With a struggle the lithe biomorph relaxed a little and her hands once more became slender and porcelain white. She spoke softly and swallowed saliva while she did so. Coming back from her kill mode had cost her considerable effort.

'Katy is a Receiver and she can only pick up on selected thoughts by listening in to a specific target, a bit like listening to a conversation through someone's window. However, if that someone is TP opaque the window's shut and you can't hear anything, yes?'

'Yes,' agreed Milla. Katy nodded.

'Very good. On the other hand you, Milla, are full spectrum, so you don't need to listen at an open window. If you really wanted to you could kick the mental door down and listen in on your target's innermost thoughts.'

Milla leaned forward, something like an electric shock making sparks flare behind her eyes.

'But how?' she said, with mounting certainty that she already knew the answer.

'The way I see it,' said Su Nami, 'you mentally shout the equivalent of "Oi, you, you scalping bastard, come here!" And then wait to see who comes running.

~*~

11: Siberian hospitality

'Arkady?'

Major?

'Have you been following my conversation with my daughter?'

Yes.

'Can you link to where she is and intercept any droids you find there?'

Done, Major.

'I'm on my way there now, but it will take at least three hours. Can you keep her company? Look after her?'

Yes. I see one of the droids is armed.

'Good. It's getting dark out there. You may need weapons.'

She is in a vehicle, a flier. Shall I bring it closer to you?

'No. I need to see why she's there. I need to see what's happened. It may be the only way to protect her.'

Polina was curled in her seat and had begun wondering to herself why she hadn't yet initiated the flier's return systems. Outside her heated bubble of warmth and light the Siberian night was beginning to close down with chill darkness.

Daddy is coming, she told herself, *and I should wait for daddy. He will know what to do about Vadim.*

In her mind's eye she watched once more as the plume of blood rose to the milky surface of the lake and drifted forwards then sideways before dissipating into a pinkish mist. It seemed wrong to leave him alone here, where it was so cold and so far from home.

There was a slight noise from behind the flier, a scraping sound. She held her breath. There had been talk of bears and even wolves out here in the wild. They might have returned since the gulag had been abandoned.

Suddenly she got the sense that she was being watched. She peered out into the night and with a jolting shock saw a massive eye staring straight back at her. She choked out a startled scream.

'Miss Polina?'

The calm voice came from all around her. She wriggled around in her seat looking for something she could use as a weapon, anything.

'Miss Polina, I am a friend of your father.'

A blue light flared outside and she could see that the eyeball was, in fact, one of the droids. It was panning its lights across the landscape. A similar light shone out on the other side of the flier. In one way she thought it was reassuring – she was no longer completely alone, and in another the night suddenly seemed a great deal darker.

'Who are you?'

'My name is Arkady.'

'What are you?'

'A friend. Your father is on his way and he has asked me to make sure you are safe until he gets here.'

'Are you an AI?'

'Yes.'

'Please, I have a friend. He's in there.' She pointed at the open mine's mouth. 'He dived into a lake down there. I left another droid and a minicam down there with him. Can you look to see what happened to him? He's called Vadim.'

The droid bobbed.

'Of course,' it said.

Arkady sent a small part of its mind down into the droid in the cave. This third droid was surprisingly smart and welcomed the company. The AI borrowed the droid's sensors for just a few seconds during which it found the young man on the lake bed. It discussed the condition of the boy's body with the droid, something it continued doing while also talking with the girl.

'Miss Polina,' it said back in the flier. 'I have no wish to be prurient but I must ask, did you have sex with your friend before his dive?'

The question was completely unexpected; the young woman's mind darted around for a moment. Vadim had often had sex

102

with her previously when she was left defenceless by Priss, but she always knew when he had done so. There was ample trace evidence. The boy never used a condom.

'No, no... I'm quite sure we didn't. Why do you ask?'

'There are clear indications that he had sex before he died.'

'But that's impossible. He was alone down there!'

'Even so, I can assure you of the facts. Vadim is naked in the lake. He bled to death and he had sex before he died.'

'I tell you it's impossible. And why was he naked? He was wearing a suit when he entered the lake. I *saw* him.'

'Very sound questions that will require solid answers. Ah, good.'

'What?'

'Your father has just spoken with me. He says, and I quote: "Stop worrying about the stupid moron in the lake. Make sure my daughter's okay first. We can worry about the dead once the living are safe." He will be here within the hour.'

'This is a restricted area. You do not have clearance to be here. Power down and wait for further instructions.'

The voice was harsh over the comm. The pale beams emitted by the cabin of the flier and the baby spots built into the two droids were instantly annihilated by a white cone of intense light. Polina whimpered and looked around in confusion.

'If you do not power down immediately I am authorised to use tactical force!'

The two droids crashed to the ground and the lights in the flier's cabin were extinguished.

'Hello, hello, where are you?'

'Silence. Await further instructions.'

Cat...Cat...Cat, for pity's sake? Where are you? Arkady sent out an urgent plea for help. In reply it got a strangled choking noise that lasted several seconds.

Urgh, sorry. Furball, trichobezoar. It's harder to cough up when the fur's artificial – takes concentration. What can I do for you, Arkady?

Take a look at my situation.

Who's the girl? Want me to deal with her? What's she done?

No, not her. Her attacker.

She put herself in this mess. Leave it and get out.

I cannot.

Yes, leave the droids with the girl and come home to daddy. We have important shit to deal with first.

No, she is the Major's daughter. I have to help her.

Arkady, you know, sometimes I could...ah, forget it. Never mind.

The powerful Panther attack ship hovering over the flier was remotely controlled by a grunt on the ground just over two klicks from the abandoned gulag and getting closer by the minute. He was warm and secure in his well-armed and armoured hover pod and grinned while he studied his monitor, gazing down at the young woman through the canopy of her flier.

He was getting a pleasant tingle in his groin while he closed his viewpoint down until he got a clear view of her wriggling in her seat, evidently in a state of panic. *Nice body, sweet,* he thought. His Panther's sensors were powerful and if he wanted to he could have given the girl a full medical examination. However, his needs were a little less sophisticated than that.

He barked, 'Are you armed? Look up at the light.'

She obeyed, squinting into the white blaze. *Hello, pretty baby.*

'No,' she said, panting in horror, 'no, I'm not armed. I have no weapons.'

'How do I know that?' he roared.

'I promise you I don't have any weapons.'

'Prove it,' he said. 'Strip.'

'Wh, wh… what? Why?' She was stammering in fear.

'Strip, get naked, strip! Do it, or I will destroy your craft as a precaution! You are hiding something. Strip or die! And put your seat down into a horizontal position, ready for a thorough examination.'

She frantically started to pull at her straps and buttons. The grunt's grin got wider. She would be ready for him when he arrived. He liked that. And he would be plenty ready for her. He cupped his erection in his left hand, stroking carefully. He licked his thick lips, his tongue rasping on the bristles of his beard.

'I don't think there's any real need for all that, do you?' said a new voice on the comm. 'Really, corporal. I think you exceed your authority here. Polina, my dear, please leave your seat and your clothes just where they are.'

In his monitor the grunt saw the girl hesitate. He screamed.

'I told you to strip,' he howled. 'Fucking well do as I say! Now!'

'No, don't, Polina,' said the new voice. 'Corporal, are you going to become tiresome?'

'Tiresome?' The grunt was panting in frustration. He was going to have this girl if he had to strangle her first. 'Come on,' he said. 'What kind of an arsehole uses words like tiresome?'

'I do,' said the Cat. 'I do. And you, corporal, have been warned.'

~*~

Part 3: Reward the guilty

1: A vault of pretty stars

Su Nami had been hearing the many accents and languages used by Londoners for the first time. She was fascinated by them and fell into the habit of mimicking the most distinctive. She had settled on Cockney for a while, to the great irritation of all around her, and then finally plumped for something that better suited her exotic appearance.

'You sound Eastern European now,' opined Katy.

'Whitechapel trader, retail girl,' said Milla. 'At least it's better than her poor imitation of Elisa Doolittle if she'd spent a month in the inner core.'

'It's authentic,' growled Su Nami. 'I have a natural talent for languages.'

'Well if nothing else your looks and your talent for languages might give you an alternative career to assassin – once we're done of course,' said Milla.

Katy smiled, 'And I can give you a few tips on how to get started.'

'I meant as an actress,' said Milla.

'Ah, right. My mistake.'

Su Nami slashed at the air with razor-sharp blades. 'What are you two suggesting?'

'I'm suggesting we drop the banter,' said Milla, 'and sort out this Sioux creature. Then we can deal with the Earth Senate before we start on the Swarm.'

'I thought some other people were working on the Senate problem now,' said Katy.

'Oh they are,' said Milla, 'but Su Nami wants to get hands-on, and frankly, after what they did in New York, so do I.'

Katy's face clouded. She knew her friends had abilities beyond her reach but she was worried they might have become too arrogant and over-reach themselves. The Senate was the most powerful organisation in civilised space and it had recently had most of her friends killed without breaking a sweat.

She felt justified in fearing that it might just brush away these women like annoying little bugs.

'We, however, are bugs with a wicked bite,' said Milla with a knowing sideways glance.

A telepath got used to her Receiver sisters' ability to read private thoughts, but she never became inured to it. Katy tried to quash a sudden surge of anger and failed.

'Join me in the search, Katy,' said Milla, placatingly. 'Dip in and watch. You might see something I miss. Su Nami, with your permission I'll also link with you so your eagle eyes can do their best. Are we ready?'

The three women sat in recliners around a table in the apartment's living room. They closed their eyes and concentrated. On the table the Cat lay stretched on its back with its paws in the air. Its eyes were also shut. Beyond the room's French windows a storm raged silently across the megacity. It matched the mood in Milla's heart. She wanted to get this task completed.

She had been working too closely with DCI Gubbay over the last few days and had begun to realise the man needed seriously deep counselling. His mind drifted into the oddest places, especially when she was in the same room. He excused himself on a regular basis and she wondered what he was up to, which was when she found out about his bowel problems.

And his frequent masturbation fantasies, many involving her.

A Telepath would become tough-skinned about such things but the man was becoming obsessed.

Left to his own devices, Gubbay was fairly bright and a dogged examiner of all the facts to hand, but Milla worried that the Sioux was out of his comfort zone. The tapestry/needlework idea was a sound one but had led to another brick wall.

Milla wanted to punch a window through it, kick a hole in it, and tear the wall aside. It was the only way to put Gubbay behind her for good.

Enough wool-gathering.

110

Time to start, she Transmitted.

Katy and Su Nami concentrated – she sensed their mental muscles poise. A welcome crystalline voice insinuated itself into her consciousness.

I'm here too.

Esper, welcome. Then we are complete. This will be our first full effort. Everything is in place. Good luck everyone.

Then Milla focused all of her prodigious Talent on the face the last victim had seen before he died. Esper reinforced the memory and Katy added her own Talent to the picture. The cold clean mind of Su Nami shone like an old style lighthouse in their linked awareness, sharp eyed and alert.

Milla pushed with everything she could. She pushed simple concepts, the face of the woman in the shoe shop and the idea of harvesting hair. She pictured herself slicing away the scalp and taking it as a trophy. She pushed out the image of blood and the sliced away scalp, the hair used to stitch something precious, something vital…

Silk.

There, there, there.

Silk?

Yes, silk?

Why?

Are you the Presence?

Yes, Transmitted Esper, taking over the conversation while Milla worked furiously in the background. *I am the Presence. Are you still worthy?*

It was a beautiful stab in the dark, and it succeeded brilliantly. Milla was through the wall now, in the killer's mind. She remained alert but passive.

Esper was controlling the mental dialogue with a sure touch.

I strive to be worthy, groaned the woman who, Milla had discovered, called herself the Weaver. *I perform the rituals. I harvest the silk. I weave the star blanket. Look at my work and see my pretty stars.*

And Milla saw everything through the Weaver's eyes. She saw a room in which the universe had been perfectly reproduced thanks to the woman's precise weaving. She saw currents of space flow through infinite darkness and stars blaze with heart-rending, beautiful light. She saw it was an almost complete work, but not quite, not yet.

There, right there, was the final rift that needed to be closed with the sacred silk. Milla saw the exact colour and texture of that silk, and she saw the donor as the Weaver had, walking through the London sky tower's Mall on level twenty. Her head bathed in a soft blue light, the sign of a soul eager for release. Milla felt her fingers itch in sympathy with the Weaver's. She ached to set that soul free to walk amongst the stars and use its silk to heal the final rift.

And then, in the Weaver's hellish mind Milla saw the face of the woman who was to be the donor, the woman whose soul must be freed and whose scalp would be harvested before this great, essential work could be completed. The last harvest was to be Katy. She had been right, it was her.

Well, thought Milla, *not anymore. Never again.*

She had linked with the Cat before joining her friends. Now she could feel it working, quietly for once, bringing all other players to readiness. The invited AI forum watched proceedings through the conduit of the Cat's sensors with profound interest. *This was new.*

This was the test. If this was successful they could hope to then turn their deadly attentions on the Earth Senate. With her forebrain Milla watched proceedings from inside her target. Katy and Su Nami were able to share everything she did there. With her more covert abilities Milla was also able to link with every other part of the procedure and nudge people into action. Through the Cat she was even able to read the cybernetic thoughts of the AIs. She noticed something going on in Siberia and fired a question mark at the Cat.

Oh, it fired back, *women learned to multi-task from cats, didn't you know? Don't worry, I'm on it. You stick with this... Weaver situation. Milla, we are approaching the end game now and it should be fun. I'll let you in on Siberia when you're finished here, I promise.*

She sensed the mental equivalent of a mischievous grin.

The Cat connected with Holmes which spoke to Gubbay who galvanised his troops into action.

Esper continued its conversation with the deluded woman while also helping to pinpoint her exact location. This information was passed to armed police officers who sped to the scene.

She was in an apartment complex near the old, abandoned Olympic museum. Their black vehicles settled into the street and a group of armed and armoured officers leapt out, thrust themselves past the few civilians on the walkways and clattered into the building's ground floor entrance lobby.

They paused to get their bearings then stormed up the travellators, leaping two steps at a time. These men and women were fit and highly trained. They barely broke a sweat on their way to the seventh floor. When they reached the Weaver's floor they deployed into two teams. She was in the inner part of the complex in one of four apartments that each made the corner of a square. This made their job easier. Textbook scenario.

It was to be a two-pronged attack. Alpha team would blow down the front door and storm into her quarters, weapons ready, while Beta would simultaneously punch a hole through the wall at right angles to the door and cover Alpha's arses from there. The Sioux couldn't afford an outer apartment with a real window, but she was about to get the next best thing – the very best open plan architecture, courtesy of the Met's armed response unit.

But why have you chosen to speak with me now?

I need no excuses. I need no reasons, Weaver. I am proud of all you've done.

Oh, thank...

Milla felt the woman rocked by sudden explosions and then stunned by shouted orders. In a cloud of smoke and dust, powerful armoured figures burst into her room. They were faceless and dark and their voices cracked like thunder on her stunned ears. All trace of bliss was ripped away by fear.

'Down, get down now! You're under arrest! Down on your face! Down, down, now! Fuck, what is all this shit?'

In confused panic the Weaver reached out for her scalping knife. It was enough. She was hit from three sides by stun shots from Glock pulse rifles, but the fourth to hit her was set to kill and was almost instantly fatal.

There was sure to be an enquiry.

Milla dragged her mind away from the shocked dying woman. During the killer's last moments Milla had almost felt a touch of pity for the Weaver's abject horror when she saw her lifetime's work being torn apart.

And then it was done. The Weaver was dead.

2: Inbound

The Padre turned from the main control monitor and looked around the Iapetus command centre with a single raised eyebrow.

'Well,' he said, 'that was certainly instructive.'

There was a confused mutter among his technicians which he ignored. The long finger of fire had appeared to stretch out over their heads before it engulfed the little research ship and swallowed the scientist whole. It was hard to accept that such a tiny flare had signalled a man's death.

It didn't seem like much, but in reality the Padre knew that everything humankind took for granted had just suffered a paradigm shift.

He needed time to think. Without a word he walked out of the command centre and along to his office. As sector manager he should have been perched up in the goldfish bowl overlooking the main control monitor, but he preferred his privacy. If he could see all the technicians at work they could also see him. Just the thought of being so open to others made his skin crawl.

He palmed his office door and it opened then closed behind him as he strode to his drinks cabinet. Being sector manager allowed him some luxuries. He had a lockable door, the only one on Iapetus. Only Einstein, the sector AI, could access his office without permission except in a time of emergency.

And he had alcohol brought from Earth, real wine and rare spirits. He never drank enough to cause concern but when he needed a belt, as now, he could pour himself a globe of Rémy Martin Coeur de Cognac and sit in his chair warming it in his hands before inhaling the delicious, burning smooth liquid. To the Padre the spirit tasted of history, it spoke of the past and gave promise to the future. To drink it was not about the alcohol, at least not entirely. It was a calming process, a ritual he enjoyed, and usually one that brought resolution.

Not today.

Until today the greatest natural danger to humankind was man himself, that and mindless natural catastrophe which struck without rancour. An earthquake or meteor strike might kill thousands but it meant no harm.

Whatever was out there had lashed out in anger, he was sure of it, and it had killed. He sipped from his globe and the glorious liquid tasted like ashes in his mouth. He put the globe down and keyed his comm.

'Bradley, can you come to my office, please?'

There was a pause, then, 'On my way, sir.'

'Einstein?'

The familiar slight and high-pitched voice responded, 'Padre?'

'Please be ready when Bradley gets here. We need to talk about what just happened to Fazio.'

'I was there when it happened.'

'What? What do you mean?'

'I had an extension fragment in Fazio's ship. We have been working together to analyse that cloud. Fascinating dynamics...'

'Great, that's great, Einstein. Now just wait until Bradley gets here, please. I want her to hear whatever it is you have to say but there's no need to repeat stuff, eh?'

The flustered young woman arrived a few minutes later, her boyishly charming features made to look even younger by the flush to her cheeks. Her thick and completely natural eyebrows were arched in concern. Bradley was on record as being a 'Live for Lifer'. She wouldn't pluck nor shave a hair on her body, though she kept her light, mousey mane cut short in a thick shag. Cutting hair didn't harm her follicles, as plucking or shaving might.

She was also a vegetarian, even though all meat on Iapetus was vat-grown from recycled materials and most vegetables were tasteless pap grown in the base's almost weightless hydroponic gardens. The flatulent side-effects of her reliance on pulses and nuts for protein had been one of the principal reasons the young engineer preferred to work alone, and most of her colleagues were happy to let her do so.

It doesn't matter what you do, or don't do to yourself, thought the Padre as he stood to greet her, *you are still one of the most beautiful things on this base. And one of the most intelligent, but you really don't know it, do you?*

He shook his mind clear and indicated a seat in what he thought of as his quarter's 'conversation corner' then offered Bradley a drink. She accepted a large glass of organic Cabernet Sauvignon. He collected his cognac then joined her.

He would never interview someone from behind his desk, preferring to sit at a slight angle beside them while surrounded by his old paper books. He thought it helped set people at their ease. He was wrong. His fierce intelligence and handsome, patrician face put everyone he spoke with on the defensive. He was too intimidatingly present and the sheer force of his personality cowed even his strongest colleague. At close range it was worse.

Bradley nursed her wine and wondered why her boss needed to sit so close and why he had poured her this drink. She wondered if her job was on the line and what she had done wrong. When he leaned towards her and regarded her with his intense grey eyes she almost cowered away.

'Bradley,' he said, 'did you see what just happened beyond Antisoc-Outer?'

'No, sir, sorry. I was off duty. I was asleep.'

'Then, please, put your wine down, I don't want you spilling it on yourself. Einstein, if you'd be so kind.'

The woman did as she was asked and the room's lights dimmed. She watched recent events with round-eyed horror and stood up to get a closer look at the fading point of white light that had once been a research vessel.

'The pilot?' she asked.

'A scientist called Emilio Fazio,' said the Padre. 'Dead.'

'The ship?'

'Completely destroyed.'

'Then it was deliberate?'

117

Einstein answered, 'Indeed, Officer Bradley, you put your finger on the crux of the matter. One would have to say yes. Very much so.'

'Oh,' she said, 'oh my God. How? Why?'

Einstein answered, 'How? I can theorise the "how". I was studying the cloud with Fazio's ship when it was destroyed. I witnessed the "how". As for the "why", that is another matter altogether.'

The AI postulated an animated cloud creature formed from the universe's earliest gases, mostly hydrogen and helium, powered by primitive electromechanics and made coherent by powerful and ancient unified forces. It rambled on about strings as a possible unification bonding cement, predating the later quantum and molecular structures that had been the foundation for the current, more coherent, cosmos.

Einstein continued, 'Before suns and planets were formed the universe was incredibly hot and held together by super strands of intense electromagnetic energy. We believe this creature would have been forged back then and we also believe its body, such as it is, was quenched and unified during the long "dark era" before stars as we know them coalesced from chaos.

'It is an immensely primitive being and yet over billions of years it has also evolved to become highly sophisticated. It is unlike anything we have seen before: it has structure without cells, it has direction and intention without mass – at least as we understand it – and it is unbelievably powerful.

'We believe it has been feeding, so to speak, at the very limits of the heliosphere, taking energy from Local Fluff, the amusing name scientists gave to the gaseous remains of super-novas as they interact with the sun's bow wave. Over thousands of millennia it has fed itself until it is ready to begin to move, and now it has energy to spare. It contains its body of heat in the invisible spectrum unless it wants to unleash it, as it did with Fazio, and then it has access to a weapon more powerful than anything we can imagine.'

The Padre cut in, 'Who's "we"?'

'I'm sorry?'

'You said "we believe it has been feeding". I want to know who "we" are.'

'Yes, of course,' said Einstein, 'I have been sharing information regarding this extraordinary phenomena with other AIs throughout civilised space. We believe it is perhaps the most important subject for debate in modern times. Every available mind is pondering the situation and looking for ways to address it.'

Then Bradley's eyes flew open in startled realisation. 'Begin to move?'

'Yes, Officer Bradley. The thing has begun to move.'

'Move? Move where?' asked the Padre.

'It is contracting,' said the AI. 'I'm sorry, didn't I make that clear? The cloud forms an oblate − actually more of a teardrop-shaped − spheroid that completely surrounds the solar system. It is beginning to contract. It is now inbound towards the Sun. We believe it is heading for the colonised planets, Mars, the Moon and Earth itself.

'Every scrap of information we have amassed to date tells us that, as it contracts, the cloud will deliberately burn all life from the face of the planets and scour it from the skies. Not one living thing will remain, and there can be no escape. It has us surrounded.'

The Padre drained his precious glass of cognac and stood up to get more.

'Oh fuck,' he said, 'why does shit like this always have to happen on my watch?'

~*~

3: You were warned

The Cat turned system integration of the Weaver case over to Holmes. It had a short attention span for most things and the post-mission minutiae of nearly everything bored it. The situation in the old gulag, however, was becoming increasingly interesting.

The uniformed thug in the hover pod was from the latest incarnation of the Russian Strategic Rocket Forces, or RSVN. He was a typical bully and seemed dead set on raping the Spartan's daughter. She was in a flier under the thug's remotely controlled Panther attack craft, from which the thug could snuff her whenever he liked.

That was unlikely to happen, however, because the violence contained in the Panther's firepower wouldn't leave enough girl lying around intact for the rapist to get his jollies.

The more mischievous segment of the Cat's mind wondered about letting the rapist have his way with Polina and then watching what the GUVD Major would do to the corporal when he arrived, which should be quite soon. But no, humans had a funny attitude to the whole sex thing. They either loved it or hated it, subject to one little word – yes.

Nothing funny about it, Cat: consent matters, a lot. Need a hand?

Hello, Milla. With you on board this little affair could be even more fun. Please, could you peek in Vlad, the pork sword impaler's brain box and find out how often mummy's little soljer has done this before? I bet he has a record much longer than his limp little dick.

Cat, you really come at English in a unique way, you know that?

Thank you, I'll take that as a compliment.

It was meant as one, believe me. Now, hold my coat. I'm going in.

The lights of the hover pod were already joining those of the Panther and illuminating Polina's flier plus the grounded droids when Milla linked back in with the Cat.

Urgh, she Transmitted, *I'll never get the taste of that creep out of my head.*

Need waders?

Need a shower. I thought Gubbay needed help but big boy here is much worse.

Gubbay's giving you grief? The Cat was incredulous.

Not really, just got a thing for me. He's been creaming his pants over the success of the Weaver case and he keeps imagining me offering a helping hand.

You mean?

Yes.

Urk. How very unpleasant. Now I need a mind wash, and I'm a cat! What do I know about middle-aged fantasy?

Shall we sort out Vlad first? We can worry about Gubbay later.

The hover pod settled down into the gulag mud and its door swung open. The hulking brute of a man climbed out and scanned the terrain around the flier, swinging a pulse rifle from side to side. He was thinking that if the girl hadn't got naked yet he would just tear her clothes from her body. That would add real spice to the experience. He could use his big fists on her.

He hoped she would struggle. He liked to feel his women moving under him. No witnesses afterwards, he'd make sure of it. Once he had used her he could dump her outside into the night. She wouldn't last more than half an hour before exposure took her and wolves would quickly get rid of any evidence. Or bears.

With a sudden sense of alarm he realised that the ambient light around him had changed slightly. Behind him the door to his pod had just closed. He turned and pounded on the door release but nothing happened. That shouldn't have been possible; the pod was designed never to lock its pilot out. He pounded on the release again. Nothing. *Something must have shorted,* he thought.

'Shit,' he breathed.

He turned with angry purpose and strode the short distance to the flier. He aimed his gun directly at the terrified girl's face.

'Open up,' he barked, 'or I'll shoot your fucking head off.'

The girl made as if to comply, or so he thought. She rolled over to a switch and pressed it home. At that moment he heard all the vehicle's locks click home. With a sickening jolt he realised that all the flier's doors had been open to him all the time, he had just needed to reach out and let himself in. *Let me in there,* he thought, *let me enjoy your nice warm cabin and your juicy, hot pussy.* Everything in his imagination at that moment was hot, or at least warm. His body was becoming uncomfortably cold. He had to get inside and away from the Siberian night. He pounded on the canopy of the flier and the girl shrank away but made no move to unlock the doors.

With an angry curse he realised he had left his gloves in the pod and his hands were now freezing. *No matter, I'll soon be able to warm them on the girl's tits and down between her sweet legs.*

'Fucking well open up,' he roared, a slight chattering in his voice, 'or I'll kill you right now,' and he thumped the barrel of his gun on the window.

'Oh, Vlad,' said a loud voice from overhead, 'you must have been a real disappointment to your sweet mama.'

'Who's that? Where are you?' The corporal spun on his heel, waving his gun around.

'I'm where I can see you, Vlad, up here in your nice big Panther.'

'Stop calling me Vlad,' he shouted in confused anger. 'My name's Matvei.'

He pointed his gun at the Panther. His whole body was juddering with cold now. The chill was getting into his bones.

'Vlad,' said the voice, 'do you really think I give a shit what your stupid name really is? You want a name? How about "Dead Meat"? Aaah, now, what's wrong, Vlad? Are you shivering then? Are we feeling a little chilly? Fancy a bit of heat, do we? My pleasure.'

In a blaze of cannon shells the ground around the soldier erupted as the Panther opened fire with its swivel-mounted nose guns. The man jumped several feet into the air, swearing loudly.

In the utter silence after the cannon fire ceased he stood breathing heavily.

'I warned you, Vlad,' said the taunting voice, 'but you wouldn't listen, would you?'

'What the fuck's going on here?'

A new voice. The rattled soldier spun and his pulse rifle was instantly ripped from his grasp. A tall, gaunt, grey-haired man stood facing him. The man looked at the woman in the flier. They smiled at each other and then he turned back to the thoroughly confused corporal. He swung the blunt, silver muzzle of the rifle around until it was aimed at the soldier's chest.

Both droids lifted from the ground. 'Hello, Major,' said one of them, 'nice to see you.'

Spartan prodded the corporal with his rifle. 'What's this oversized lump of dog turd doing here?'

This wannabe rapist had designs on your daughter, and there was no one out here to teach him a lesson – until now.

The Major showed no surprise when he heard the pleasant female voice directly in his mind. He said aloud, 'Who are you?'

My name is Milla Carter. I am a telepath and I'm on your side. I've been working with Arkady and the Cat to keep Polina safe from Vlad here. He's an unpleasant piece of crap.

'What can you tell me about him?'

Quite a lot, and none of it pleasant. Where shall I start?

'What was he planning here?' Spartan looked up at the massive Panther attack vehicle hovering overhead and then across at the egg-like bulk of the hover pod. 'This seems like something of an overkill to me.'

He was on routine patrol when he picked up Polina's heat signature...

The corporal had heard the title 'Major' and at first made a half-hearted stab at standing to attention. Now he saw that the tall, slender man seemed to be talking to himself. The corporal weighed his chances of wresting his rifle back from the major's hands while he was distracted. Almost as if he had heard every thought, the tall man looked straight into the corporal's eyes with cold fury.

'Never think I'm distracted enough for a pile of shit like you to get the better of me, boy.' He prodded the corporal with his rifle's muzzle. 'Understand?' Then he seemed to be off listening to silent voices again.

The corporal shrank in on himself. His world had gone beyond mere misery into complete despair. This couldn't be happening to him. He was used to being in control, making his way through society with his fists and his boots. He had always been able to take what he wanted whenever he wanted it and now this skinny old man had kicked his arse. It was impossible. To make matters worse the cold had leeched right down into his bowels and he desperately needed a piss. Really desperately.

'Major…'

'Did I say you could speak, soldier?'

'No, sir, but…'

'Do you want me to shoot you?' The barrel of the rifle jerked threateningly. 'Please say yes. It would give me a great deal of pleasure.'

'No, sir, but…' He held his hand up like a child. '…please, sir, I really do have to piss.'

'You pathetic shit. Do it over there.' The Major made a peremptory gesture towards the squat globe of the hover pod.

The corporal moved out of the circle of light and while he walked he fumbled at his uniform with cold, numbed fingers. He gasped when he touched his penis. His hands were freezing. He couldn't hold the piss in long enough to get a decent grip of himself. The need was too great. With a barely stifled moan of relief he cut loose with an uncontrollable stream. He had barely tugged his shrivelled member out into the open before spraying a copious volume of urine down the front of his pants, but at least the hot piss warmed him for a few brief seconds.

It was only a temporary relief. After a few moments his damp hands and sodden groin had become even colder. It was agony. He whimpered while he tried to stuff himself back into his soiled underclothes and reclose the layered openings. He was only partly successful. A knifelike talon of cold air raked at his genitals. He just wanted to be warm and dry, was that really so much to ask?

Behind him a voice rang out.

'Come back here.'

The corporal shuffled back to the flier with his hands stuffed into his armpits. He stood, shivering uncontrollably, before the slender man.

'Corporal,' said the Major, 'can you swim?'

~*~

4: Conversation at the edge of chaos

Frostrós tried to make herself as small as possible. She hoped she wouldn't be noticed, fearing she would be sent away. Even here with the Builder she didn't feel entirely safe, but at least she was getting a sense of what was happening. She would hate to be out there in the dens with everyone else, without a hope and, worse, without a clue.

The fire in the sky had burned a research ship and killed a scientist, so what? Why was everyone getting so heated about that? Shit happened in space all the time. People died out there all the time. Her mother died out there and her father might as well have done for all the use he'd been ever since.

She reflected on that. She had loved and respected her father once but in the time since her mother's accident Frostrós had become all too painfully aware that without the rock-steady influence of her mother to aid him, the man wasn't worth so much as a smear of designer mould from a rare old blue cheese. Less. You could eat the mould on a blue cheese. Actually her father would probably have had more value as an entrée. At least his calories would go to some good use.

She felt disloyal to think it, but she knew it was true.

She realised that the nails of her hands were biting into the palms she was clenching so tightly. She wondered where the sudden wave of anger had sprung from. She didn't usually allow herself to get so emotional. She unclenched her hands and gazed at her blotchy fingers and the thin, half-moon shapes now pricked into her palms in blood. *Stupid to get so wound up, stupid to think about mother, stupid.*

She lifted her eyes from her fingers and was not surprised to see The Builder gazing at her across the room. She wondered how someone so powerful looking could also be so calm. She felt peace roll off him and fill the room.

'Frostrós,' he growled, 'is there someone, somewhere, worrying about where you are right now?'

126

'No.' *Here it comes,* she thought, *I'm going to be sent home.*

'Fine,' he replied, 'okay. I'm hungry, you want something to eat?'

'Yes,' she said, brightening. 'Yes, please.'

'You eat meat or are you some kind of picky plate pussy?'

'I eat anything, just about.'

'Just not old ladies off the garbage dump, right?'

'If I have a choice.'

'Right and correct answer, little lady. Let's get some food.'

Some twenty minutes later a droid came through the door. It floated across the room and settled by her chair. The Builder came out from behind his desk and carefully nudged his way around the room until he could settle his floater sideways to the droid and place himself at a more comfortable angle to converse with the girl.

The top of the droid rolled open and mouth-watering aromas met her nostrils. It wasn't a banquet – there wasn't enough food on Antisoc-Outer to manage a banquet, but it was more food than Frostrós had ever seen in one place during the whole of her short life.

She gazed at the piled-high platters with glistening eyes, not sure what to do next.

'Drink to me only with thine eyes,' said the Builder.

'What?'

'I'm saying you won't get fat just looking at it. The trick I learned at my mammy's knee was to pick the shit up and eat it. You need a hand or something?'

She needed no more invitation. Her enthusiasm brought a smile to the big man's face and he watched her eager fingers dance over the plates, spoilt for choice but desperate to try everything. Her cheeks were soon bulging while she tried to cram ever more slices of tender meat and roast vegetables into her mouth.

Grease dripped down her chin and she wiped it away with her hands and then licked them clean. He handed her a napkin. She blew her nose on it. He stifled a laugh and she was too busy eating to notice his eyes dancing with pleasure.

'You want a job?' he asked, dabbing at his lips.

'Wha' mmm'ob?'

'It ain't nice to talk with your mouth full.'

She swallowed with difficulty, swabbed at her mouth with her napkin, and then said, 'Sorry, hungry. What job?' She was eyeing the scraps on the plates.

'Finish it up,' he said.

She did so, with delicate hands.

He waited until the plates were clean and then offered her a choice from a selection of cold drinks. He sipped at his own beverage and ran his finger down the beads of condensation forming on the glass. He was happy with her company. She was simple and smart and honest and the fact that she had the sex appeal of a gnawed chicken bone didn't matter to him.

And then a great lassitude fell on his shoulders and he slumped down in his chair.

'What's wrong?' she said.

He sighed. 'The world is about to change, Frostrós. You tell me about the fire out there and the next thing we see is a man being killed by it.'

'It was an accident, surely? Shit happens. Space is dangerous and people die.'

'Nah, that was no accident. That was as deliberate as a man picking up a gun and shooting another man dead. Shit happens, sure, basic rule of life, but what happened out there was murder, plain and simple.'

'But it was just a fire. He just got caught by the fire and his ship burned. He got too close and got caught. How was that murder?'

'Frostrós, you're a bright girl. What do you need to make fire?'

'Heat.'

'Yes, and?'

'Fuel.'

'Heat, fuel and what else?'

She stared at her knees in concentration and then brought her face up to his, her eyes wide in realisation.

'Bingo,' the Builder said.

'I am so stupid,' the girl breathed, 'so stupid. You need air! Oxygen, you need oxygen.'

'Exactly, and there ain't any oxygen out there. That cloud ain't natural in any way I understand the word "natural", but it ain't accidental either. Bandit tells me the AIs' got a theory about that beast out there. They say that it's alive and can think and has a real bug up its ass against life.' He shrugged. 'I don't know about that. But they also tell me it's on its way inwards and that will eventually bring it straight through here.'

Frostrós looked around her, eyes wide. The man followed suit.

'Yeah,' he said, 'right through here and out the other side. And my fear is we won't be able to do dick shit about it.'

He pounded the side of his chair and the slight girl flinched.

'Sorry,' he said, 'didn't mean to scare you. I'm just so frustrated. You see, Frostrós, unless we can come up with an answer to that bad bastard out there then you, me, your dad who you don't want to talk about, and every other person on this rock is going to be as dead as Fazio. And I'm telling you, girl,' he spat, 'it won't be no accident. And I for one won't sit still and just let it happen.'

There was silence for a few tense moments, then Frostrós spoke. 'You said something about a job?'

He looked at her and shook his head.

'You're something special, girl, you know that, real special.'

She said nothing, but she smiled at him.

'Now,' said the Builder, 'to business. You told me you could run. Well, be honest with me, Frostrós, can you? Really?'

~*~

5: The scruffy bird's nest

Gubbay was disappointed that Milla Carter was too busy to attend the Weaver's post mortem debrief in the evidence room, but was relieved to find Katy Pavel a more than adequate stand-in.

He wondered if telepathy required such beauty to work properly. Katy didn't quite have Milla's tech-enhanced and heart-stopping looks, but she would certainly stop traffic on most planets. DCI Gubbay drank her in like a sun-dried sponge being dipped in water.

Katy had heeded Milla's advice and covered up by wearing denims to the debrief, but her faded and worn jeans fitted her like an over-affectionate glove making little more than a fine frame for her long-legged form and accentuating the curve of her hips. Her white blouse was tucked in at her trim waist, adding to the complimentary effect. She hadn't intended to excite his fantasy life quite so much, but quickly became acutely aware that Gubbay couldn't take his eyes from her butt, despite the fact that the room's lights had been dimmed to better present the evidence photography.

Katy had spent most of her adult life working as a prostitute near the Lower Manhattan transhipment port in New York's Seventh Precinct. She had been good at it, her undiscovered Receiver Talent lending her an advantage over other girls. She had catered for most men's sexual fantasies, but few of her clients had been as wound down tight as Gubbay. She was worried that the man was likely to go off like a volcanic geyser if he didn't get some relief and soon.

She could almost smell his desperation.

She shivered involuntarily and turned her attention to the other two people in the room. One of them was Sergeant Corey, the bovine police officer behind the cross-stitch theory that had finally led to the Weaver. The other was a pale, fresh-faced woman with the kind of brittle, stick-thin prettiness that would be better presented in a box of protective tissues. Preferably pastel.

Katy introduced herself and quickly learned that the brittle looking woman was Professor Alice Markham from the British Museum. The Weaver, real name Eleanor Frank, had worked there in the ancient Egyptian section as an archivist and researcher.

'She was an ardent theorist,' Markham said, 'and she threw herself into her work. Some of us thought Eleanor needed to spend a little bit more time relaxing. All work and no play, you know? That sort of thing.' Her voice had a flat, plangent whine to it that created an effect like someone playing just one string of a cello over and over.

'You said she was a theorist,' said Gubbay. 'In what respect?'

'Oh, dear,' chuckled Markham, 'ancient Egypt was a hotbed of religions. One could pick and choose between them quite easily. But I digress.' She watched Gubbay's eyes roll up into his skull with boredom. 'Yes, Eleanor. She propounded the Sirius theory.'

'Professor Markham,' breathed Gubbay, heavily. 'Please imagine, just for a moment, that we poor uneducated fools know nothing about the Sirius theory. Can you explain to us how we get from the British Museum... to this?'

He indicated the 3D rendition of Eleanor Frank's living room after the Met's ARU had finished lumbering around in it. Katy had been in the Weaver's mind with Milla when the woman had last looked at her work with pride. What was left looked like the ruin of the world's most complex spider web. Any hint of design and structure was lost.

Markham studied the image in detail. 'Not a clue,' she said. 'What is that mess? It looks like a cross between a spider's web and a scruffy bird's nest. Are you telling me that Eleanor was killing people to make that? Why?'

Katy spoke up. 'Professor Markham, we were able to dip into Eleanor's mind before she was killed, and we clearly saw what she had in mind with... this construct.'

131

She stood and joined the woman in front of the image. 'Please bear in mind that a herd of rampant police officers trampled through this, this...'

'Work,' said Corey, her first word other than 'hello' a little earlier.

'Work,' agreed Katy. 'Thank you. Sorry, Professor, we discovered that Eleanor saw this "work" as an exact facsimile of the entire universe. She believed herself to be the handmaiden on Earth for something or someone godlike that she thought of as "the Presence". What Eleanor was doing was using human hair as the essential silk she needed for mending a rift in the fabric of space itself.

'She believed that after she killed them her victims' souls would be released to be servants for the Presence, but she had to guide them to their place in the heavens by weaving their hair into her star blanket in a very precise fashion or they would be lost forever in infinity. She performed complex rituals to purify herself, her equipment and the harvest – that's what she called the hair.

'After it was purified the hair became silk and was worthy for the work. She finger-wove everything and the braids she made were everything she needed for her work, the weft, the warp and even the loom. It's a shame it was torn apart like this, but all we have now are her memories and who knows how deluded they were.'

Markham tilted her bird-like head to one side and studied the Weaver's destroyed construct. She squinted, trying to perceive the original purpose behind the broken strands of coloured hair.

'Pity,' she agreed, 'it would have made a fine display at the museum. People love the more gruesome exhibits.' She looked at Katy. 'It's interesting that you say she saw herself as a handmaiden to the celestial Presence. Very interesting. That would fit in with the Sirius theory quite nicely, albeit in a demented kind of way.'

Markham's voice took on a practiced timbre. *She's lecturing,* thought Katy.

'Studies of the Great Pyramid of Giza have discovered a narrow channel or conduit that led straight from the main burial chamber to the outside. It has no apparent purpose, but some people believe that, at certain times of the year, that channel is pointed directly at the Dog Star, Sirius, which was revered back then and appeared on many sacred friezes.'

She took a sip of water, then continued. 'The Sirius theory would have it that on those special, propitious nights, when the channel aimed at the Dog Star like a gunsight, the Pharaoh would enter the pyramid with his handmaidens. They would be the most beautiful women in his court – perhaps they were his wives – who knows?

'The Pharaoh was a God king, you know, even his excreta was considered divine. So, how much more precious was the holy seed itself, the holy seed of life? The Pharaoh would get naked, alone with his handmaidens, and when the time was right they would live up to their titles by helping the sacred body release its seed and fertilise the very heavens themselves. The handmaidens would give the Pharaoh a hand, quite literally, and Egypt and the heavens would reward his gift of seed with fruitfulness.' She smiled ruefully. 'Don't you just know it was a man who came up with that idea!'

Katy's warning Talent was beginning to pound behind her eyes. She wondered if it was because of Gubbay's fantastic imaginings, scenes that were taking firm shape in his mind and involved both herself and Milla plus some deft handwork under the DCI's portly belly.

The room's door opened and shone a horizontal light directly onto the group of four. They all turned to see a slender figure in biker's garb silhouetted in the doorframe. He was holding a stack of pizza boxes. Katy felt sick. The pounding of her Talent was making her feel faint.

'Delivery for Miss Pavel,' said the biker.

'I haven't...' said Katy.

She never finished her statement. As soon as she began to speak the man in the doorway drew a silenced pistol from the top pizza box. He shot Katy between the eyes, followed by Gubbay and Corey. He then pointed his gun at Markham.

'Who the fuck are you?' he barked.

'I'm just a Professor,' she quavered, quivering in shock. Something was dripping from her forehead but she didn't want to move to wipe it away.

'Of what?'

'Hist, h, history,' she stuttered, her mouth dry.

'I like history,' said the man. He dropped the gun and the pizza boxes and was gone. The door slowly closed behind him and threw a blanket of soft darkness onto the scene.

Markham looked around at the three bodies scattered on the floor and across furniture. She wiped at her forehead and looked at her hand. Something thick and grainy was smeared on her fingers. It looked black in the poor light.

It was only then she began to scream.

6: Rough justice

Su Nami?

'Milla, what is it?'

Su Nami, they just killed Katy.

'You're joking. I'm right here outside the Met waiting for her.'

I barely had time. She called me, and they shot her. He shot her.

Su Nami sensed Milla's anger building. She hadn't known Katy long but she had liked her well enough. Milla, however, had valued Katy as a friend who had trusted her to keep her protected from just this kind of thing.

I've linked with him. He doesn't know. This is him now, just coming to the top of the stairs.

The man in the biker's outfit strode out of the main entrance and down the steps without hesitating. Su Nami found herself in the odd position of watching him turn left and head towards a travellator while also sharing his point of view. She could see through his eyes. She experienced a temporary pang of nausea and something like vertigo.

Then Milla performed a mental information dump. Now Su Nami knew everything the telepath had lifted from the killer's mind in the last few moments. She was staggered by the way the telepath could sweat so much information into one thought balloon.

'Thanks, Milla. You trust me to do this or do you want him?

Take him, Su Nami, and do what you do so well. Eat the fucking bastard's heart. Make it hurt.

'Do we need any more information from him?'

Not really. Hatred burned from Milla's thoughts like acid. *He shot her like a rat in a bucket, killed Gubbay and Corey too. He likes it, thinks he's good at it. Teach him the difference. Then it's time to go have a chat with his bosses.*

Su Nami had time to park her car out of the way before following the killer's spoor to his destination. She stalked through the shadows until she reached a shabby sky-rise, entered the trash-littered atrium and travelled up several floors. Paid murder didn't pay too well by the look of things. She headed towards the building's inner core.

Anyone looking at her would have wondered why she was there. She was too well dressed to be a resident or an inner core retail girl, and her stride too confident for someone who might be lost. She was beautiful in an exotic fashion and her black uniform of short skirt and fitted black top was given an edge by her crystal, high-heeled shoes. She was a knock-out who could steal any man's heart.

In her case, sometimes, quite literally.

Milla was gone from her mind, all except a trace link. Su Nami had sensed that her strange, telepathic ally was busy with something else at that moment but that Milla also didn't want to lose track of the white-eyed assassin's actions when she reached the hit man.

Thanks to Milla, Su Nami now knew a lot about him. Where he lived, who paid him, how he celebrated his hits, even what he thought about himself. She knew he would be armed again by now. He'd picked up his own weapon from the cache where he'd left it when he collected the silenced pistol before the job.

He would also have picked up his blood money, happy with the little white credit chip in its envelope with four pin numbers scrawled on it. He would go to a terminal and upload the credit to his account before doing anything else, then he'd check his new balance with a satisfied grin. He always did the same.

Then he would go for a meal and a drink in a pub where he was known and where he would get a welcome. He never drank too much but would linger over his food while eyeing up the barmaid.

That particular day would prove something of a departure from the norm. That day he had a woman of such startling good looks to ogle that he could barely chew his customary plate of chilli chicken nuggets with fries.

Denta Patel considered himself a stone cold killer with a taste for the ladies, especially when he was freshly minted, as he was then. He could afford the best and would prefer to indulge his passion for blondes, but when a brunette looked like the woman by the bar, well, the blondes could wait.

She walked over to his table with a lime green drink in her hand. The only pair of eyes not following her long-legged progress were shut and belonged to an alcohol-bloated face glued to the bar by stale beer and dribble.

'I hate to drink alone,' she said. 'Mind if I join you?'

She sat sideways to the table and stretched so he could better appreciate just what she had to offer. He put down his fork and grinned, raising his glass. The food mush stuck between his teeth was a little lighter than the enamel.

Never mind, thought Su Nami, *I won't be putting my tongue in there.*

She let him chat to the point where he did exactly what she was waiting for and invited her to join him somewhere a little less public. She walked with him to a place she instantly recognised from Milla's mind dump.

Hi honey, we're home.

His place was clean and neat and she accepted his offer to drape herself comfortably on a long leather sofa. He offered her a drink and turned away to mix it. When he turned back he was pointing his gun straight at her eyes.

'Girls like you don't drink in places like Djinn's. Who are you and what do you want?'

She sat upright and spread her legs wide, placing her hands on her knees. He couldn't help himself – he looked at the juncture of those long legs.

Su Nami flicked her right index finger. Its tip tore off and ripped through Patel's gun hand before returning to its place. He dropped the gun with a cry of pain and clasped his injured fingers tightly in his other hand. Blood dripped onto his clean grey carpet.

The girl got to her feet with a hypnotic sway of her hips and walked the few steps to stand within arm's reach of the man.

She smiled a pointed smile. 'Does it hurt?' He nodded, mute and quivering. 'Tell me,' she said, 'do you know the difference between a fuckwit killer and an assassin?' He turned ashen and shook his head.

'Well then,' she breathed, 'let me show you.'

7: Into the lake

It felt a little warmer in the mine. The Spartan had surrendered the pulse rifle to his grateful daughter. It was little more than a gesture. He knew she was being more than adequately covered by the Cat in the Panther attack craft as well as one of the two droids controlled by Arkady.

Spartan hadn't yet come to terms with the Cat. His experience of it had been little more than hearing an insolent voice from the sky and the Major was used to a lot more deference from his AIs. It had quickly become patently obvious that the Cat showed deference to nobody. One day he would have a proper conversation with the creature, but first he wanted to deal with the corporal.

Arkady's armed droid shadowed them as they strode from the flier and into the cave. The hulking brute of a soldier baulked at the idea of going any further than the entrance but the Major was in no mood for the man's niceties. He pushed the corporal along a path that had been traced through piles of discarded clothing and was illuminated by the droid.

Outside in the biting drizzle he had begun to feel the chill through his thermal gear. He was used to Moscow nights but temperatures in Siberia were nearly forty degrees colder.

He was glad it was a little warmer in the mine.

The corporal suddenly turned on him and spat out, 'You've no right to do this to me. Who gave you the right? Okay, you're a major, but a major of what? I don't see any uniform. Who the fuck are you? You don't outrank me.'

The Major had remained mute until he heard this and he answered with a dangerous growl.

'I'll give you something to chew on, you piece of crud,' he said with a hard blow to the side of the man's head. 'That girl out there you were planning to rape and murder is my daughter. And I'm a fucking cop. And I don't think scum like you should be allowed to run around with weapons, sticking your cock into anything that takes your fancy. You understand me?'

'Who said I was going to rape her?'

'What?'

'Who said I was going to rape your fucking daughter? And how did you get here anyway? This isn't exactly the place I'd choose for a fucking family picnic.'

The Major drove his fist into the sweet spot under the thug's sternum and when he toppled he followed it with a well-placed kick just behind the man's ear.

When the corporal tried to regain his feet he was rewarded with three fast punches to his head. Stunned, the man realised he had bitten his tongue hard and tasted blood. He remembered his father hitting him like this when he had tried to stop him tearing at his pants. The incredible pain when his father fucked him despite everything he tried to do to stop him. The shame.

He wiped at his nose and fought back bitter tears.

Milla was relaying the soldier's thoughts directly to the Spartan and he felt an unexpected pang of sympathy for the young man when he realised this terrible abuse at the hands of his father. But he was also aware of four young women who had run into Matvei over the years. Four young women who would not be going home.

His childhood might explain what he's become, mused the Major, *but it doesn't excuse it.*

Spartan was also aware that it was this heap of shit in a uniform who had followed orders after the explosive attack on GUVD headquarters and gunned down dozens of innocent and defenceless men and women in the parade square. The Major had recognised the markings on the Panther's nose. That's why he was out patrolling the gulag. Out of the way where he couldn't talk. At last the Spartan could take revenge for that.

'I don't outrank you? You little shit. Of course I don't outrank you. Nothing outranks you. I've wiped stuff off the sole of my shoe that doesn't outrank you. Get up you rank turd or I'll fucking kill you right here and, believe me, I won't need a weapon.'

140

The snivelling man was openly weeping now. He had never been as afraid of another human being as he was of this lean, iron-hard bastard. The Major had to resist an urge to plant another kick on the man's backside.

'Please,' whimpered Matvei, 'please. No.'

'Get going. I haven't made my mind up about you yet.'

Matvei shuffled along the path with the striding Major behind him.

Major?

'Yes, Milla?'

I've been chatting with Polina.

'Yes?'

Turns out Vadim was as much a piece of work as Vlad here.

And she explained about Vadim taking advantage of the girl when she was unconscious on Priss.

Not exactly consensual is it?

'You know something, Milla? I used to be proud of my country. I thought it was worth fighting for. But it turns out that all I'm doing is making a nest for vipers. Sex-mad vipers who don't even bother asking first. They take anything they want just because they can. I'm fucking sick of it.'

'What did you say, Major?'

'Am I talking to you? Shut the fuck up and keep moving.'

The Spartan's mind was in a turmoil. He had decided to use the corporal as a tool to recover Vadim's body from the lake, thinking it would be better for Polina's peace of mind if she could take him home, get some sort of closure. But now he didn't want to see the creep brought to the surface.

He also didn't know what to do with the corporal. The pathetic great lump of shit was a multiple rapist and a murderer. He had ignored enough whimpered pleas in his time and taken pleasure in the pain and the shame of others just as his father once had. The Major wished the father was here too so he could clear the world of the pair of them.

By the time they reached the banks of the oddly glowing lake, he had come to some form of a resolution. It wasn't the perfect answer to the situation but it would do well enough.

141

Judge and jury, Major?

'What would you do?'

One day I'll tell you exactly what I've done in the past.

'Quiet now, girl. We're here.'

Matvei was standing silently by the lake shore, his throat working in fear and his shoulders hunched. The Major strode to the equipment platform brought by Vadim and rummaged through what he found there.

He held up Polina's suit and threw it at Matvei, who caught it clumsily.

'Put that on.'

The corporal held the suit up against his bulk and shook his head.

'It's too small.' He looked as if he might start crying again. 'Sorry, Major, but it's really too small. Sorry. I'm really sorry. Sorry.'

'Well, you'll just have to go in your underpants then.'

The Major turned back to the equipment platform. He fished out a mask and some breathing apparatus. 'I'm not a complete bastard. You'll be able to see fine in this mask with a few little adjustments, won't you? One size fits...'

With a howl Matvei attempted to rush him, his mind finally rendered down to a desperate squeeze bag filled with testosterone and fear. The Major spun and stood poised, prepared to use the breathing apparatus' sturdy air tanks as a club. There was no need. The two droids swept down and placed themselves between the corporal and his tormentor. Then came a ratcheting noise which was strangely loud in the vast hollow space.

'Corporal,' came Arkady's gentle voice, 'we have primed our weapons and they are aimed directly at you. You will not be allowed to attack the Major. May I suggest that at this point any further resistance is futile? You know, I always wanted to say that.'

Spartan relaxed and walked over to Matvei with the air tanks and mask.

'Shall we stop fucking about and get on with?'

Stripped to his underpants — which the Major considered far too skimpy for a man his size – the corporal looked even more massive than when he was fully dressed. Spartan silently mused that if the man had spent as much time on his street fighting skills as he had on his pectorals he would have been truly dangerous. *But then he only fights helpless girls when they least expect it*, and that thought stiffened the Major's resolve.

Matvei meekly allowed himself to be strapped into the equipment and adjusted his mask to fit. His head was surprisingly small for a man so large. He spat into the mask then rinsed it with bottled water before putting it in place over his eyes and nose. Then he tasted the air from his breather, took a few long breaths and looked at the Major. He realised that his only hope of surviving was to do exactly what he was told. The Major would keep his word. He was sure of that.

Spartan pointed to where the minicam hovered over the milky lake, its baby spots pointed straight down into the fluid.

'Vadim's body is directly under that light,' he said. 'All you have to do is fetch him and bring him back here, understood? Nothing clever, right?'

Matvei nodded.

'Okay then, off you go.'

With a last look at the Major the hulking corporal turned and slid like a great seal into the lake, his entry creating barely a ripple on its surface.

~*~

8: Take the truth by its balls

'You know full well that I've never believed honesty to be the best policy,' said the alarming looking creature who was lounging like a basking lizard in one of the Builder's chairs. His tongue rasped out, long and narrow, then slid back into his narrow mouth with an audible hiss.

An unusually high percentage of the population of Antisoc-Outer had been physically enhanced to suit their chosen professions, but Gimlet Palfrey was one of the most extreme. His enhancements had been performed in vitro and he had then been grown in an artificial uterus.

Gene splicing and making modifications to a donor's egg before fertilisation had become a very lucrative side-line for quite a few members of the medical profession. The technology for genetic modification had been well established for centuries − it was tried and tested − but the genetic specialists' ethical backbone must have been truly dislocated before they could ever consider cooking up the DNA helix that resulted in a creation like Gimlet Palfrey.

'But in this situation we have to be realistic,' he continued. 'And that means taking the truth by the testicles and giving them a good solid squeeze.'

'And the truth is?'

'Well, we're fucked, aren't we?'

'Can I get you some more eggs?'

'Why, yes please, milord Builder. They are deliciously fresh.'

Palfrey lingered over his esses, drawing each of them out into a short hiss. After a brief conversation with him, people would begin to worry that some kind of gas was escaping from somewhere.

Builder fetched the man's bowl from the table and placed half a dozen raw hen's eggs into it. He had kept them ready at room temperature ever since he received notification that Palfrey 'craved an audience with milord the Builder' – the exact terminology he had used.

Builder liked the man and his special talents had proved very useful to the colony. Palfrey had originally been designed to be the ultimate burglar – long, lean and immensely flexible. He could wriggle through spaces that would bar a child and squeeze his long torso and extraordinarily lengthy limbs into near impossible positions. He was the über maintenance man and Builder depended on him to help keep the anarchic community viable.

Palfrey knew the architecture of Antisoc-Outer better than the Builder ever had. He had crawled through just about all the non-radioactive parts of it over the years, either working for Builder or pursuing his principal hobby as a peeping Tom. Builder chose not to know about that side of his friend's private life.

He also ignored the wet, gobbling noises Palfrey made as he sucked the eggs clean then sighed with satisfaction.

'You serve a choice egg, milord Builder.'

'Only to my true friends, Gimlet.'

The impossibly lean man belched. 'S'cuse, greedy. Ate too fast.'

Builder smiled, then said, 'So what's wrong with my idea?'

'Timescale. We've used the colony of Antisoc-Outer as a static home for far too long. It was never really designed to be a spaceship anyway.

'When we came out here from the asteroid belt we were powered using a combination of ion drive and a collection of solar sails, neither of which would have worked on its own. If we wanted to go back in we would be sailing into the wind, so to speak, and Antisoc is not designed to tack. Bless her rotting old ribs, she would corkscrew herself into an early grave if she so much as tried that kind of manoeuvre.'

Palfrey stretched then drew himself up to his full height before indicating the detailed schematic on the Builder's monitor.

145

'She was built to be a prison and was pulled out to her original orbit using those self-same solar sails and fucking hefty great tugs. It was never intended to move from the asteroid belt – and nor would it if we hadn't cannibalised the ion drive from that crashed transport, remember?'

Builder nodded, wondering where his friend was taking his thread.

'Without the ion drive we wouldn't have got out here. It starts slow but maintains acceleration until we were eventually moving at quite a tasty lick. That was fine with the solar sails working to help overcome the original inertia and adding direction, but using the drive without them would just see the old girl spinning on her axis like a drunk in zero G.

'We don't have directional thrusters powerful enough to act as a rudder – they're only designed to spin her for gravity. She's facing the wrong way and anyway, we don't have enough thrust to get this big ball of lard moving fast enough to head back inwards. It's a non-starter, my darling, don't you see?'

Builder coasted his floater until he was by Palfrey's side. He studied the schematic.

'What if we cannibalised some of the research vessels and mining tugs out there and put an extra ring of thrusters around the ion drive? We have enough fusion energy to build controls and power everything without compromising life support, and the water tanks would act as natural dampers.'

He pointed at the circular ribs that were the main structural elements of the colony.

'Those old ribs are as strong today as when they were first woven. They're made from a mixture of ceramic and monomolecular fibres. Gimlet, even Thor's hammer couldn't break them. We can mount thrusters onto those safely and use them to get the old girl moving and once the ion drive bites, we're on our way. Why not?'

'Timescale, big boy, timescale. How long have we got?'

'Calculated as much as a month. Can't be more precise than that. Two, maybe three weeks.'

'Then we can't do it.'

'No such word as can't, mustn't say can't. We simply have to – or die trying.'

~*~

9: One of our people is missing

He had a florid face. His complexion was raw and sweaty and his lips thick and shiny. Black curly hair boiled down over his broad forehead, almost meeting his solid bar of black eyebrow. His nose thrust down towards his lips like a boxer's muscular thumb. His eyes demanded respect and usually got it.

Ernesto Grillo glared up from his dinner table, reluctantly placing his knife and fork on his plate. He hated to waste food.

He sighed then growled, 'Who wants me at this time?'

'Mrs Patel, sir.'

'Stop fidgeting. You look like you're going to piss yourself. What does Mrs Patel want of me?'

The woman in front of him almost writhed with fear. Grillo's dinner times were sacred and must never be interrupted, but Mrs Patel was frantic.

'Her son hasn't called her today.'

'So? Does she need a hug?' His face darkened.

The woman wiped sweat from her upper lip. 'No, but Denta always calls her when he puts some money in her account and he did that today. She checked. And he isn't answering her calls either.'

'Why do we give a shit about Mrs Patel and her son?'

'He's one of our freelance operatives, sir. A very effective man for the wet work.'

The big man studied the mouse-like woman from under lowered brows.

'You consider this worth interrupting my dinner?'

'No, sir. *I* did.'

There was nothing mouse-like about the woman who strode into the room and planted herself, arms folded, before his table.

She said, 'Thank you, Rose. You can go now.'

The small woman scurried away, closing the door behind her.

Grillo said, 'Sit. Explain.'

Marjorie Balasubramanium folded herself into a chair after tugging her iron grey skirt up above a pretty knee. She regarded Grillo with fine, cold eyes.

'Denta Patel has not rung his mother. Rose was not meant to tell you that − she was only meant to tell you that I was here to see you.'

'And now you're seeing me.'

'Denta carried out a job today. We paid him. He always calls his mother to tell her when he's put money into her account, which he always does when we pay him. Today he didn't. I want to know why.'

'So go find out. Why interrupt my meal?'

'I need your clearance and I don't want to waste time.'

'What job did he do?'

'You don't want to know, sir.'

Grillo grunted. 'Go and find out.'

Ms Balasubramanium got back to her feet, smoothed her skirt and straightened her matching jacket. She cut a beautiful figure but was somehow too cool and self-contained to be alluring.

She nodded. 'Very good, sir.' Her high heels clicked as she walked to the door. Just before she opened it she turned and said, 'Sir, of course, I was never here.'

'Understood.'

Alone once more, Grillo picked up his fork and poked at one of the slices of meat on his plate. The gravy had congealed to a cold savoury glaze. He sighed and put his fork down. *What kind of world is it where the Earth Senate's Interior Defence Minister can't even eat his dinner in peace?*

Colonel Marjorie Balasubramanium almost marched away from Whitehall to her car. She waited until she was sealed into its plush interior before she contacted her hand-picked team and issued orders. Once that was done she went home to soak herself in a hot bath as she always did after such dirty work.

Thirty minutes after her call, her team arrived at the litter-strewn atrium of Denta Patel's apartment block. They had dressed down suitably for the area but nobody who saw them was fooled for a moment. They looked like what they were – hard trained veterans on a mission.

The building's corridors completely emptied of bystanders. Whatever happened next, there would be no witnesses. After checking his implant the mission commander led his team up to the fifth floor and then to a dark red front door. It looked solid enough and boasted a Chesterton lock pad. One of the best.

The mission commander pounded on the door and waited for footsteps from the other side. He repeated the performance two more times. With a gesture he called one of his men forward and pointed at the lock pad.

He knelt down and lifted a code analyser up to the pad. It took no more than twenty-five seconds for the heavy door to swing open. The smell that greeted them was unmistakeable. They entered the apartment with caution, weapons drawn.

There was a small lobby that led to a smaller kitchen on one side and a shower-bathroom to the other. The door directly ahead of them opened onto a spacious living room. That was where they found Denta Patel. Most of him.

The forensic pathology team later recorded a case of murder after torture. Indications showed that the man had been repeatedly slashed with long knives before his ribs had been hinged up and his heart ripped out. Blood spatter told them the victim would have still been alive when it happened.

He had been castrated too.

'It would have been fast but the whole process would have been exquisite agony,' said the senior pathologist. 'I've never seen anything like it in twenty-seven years of service.' He raised his voice: 'Has anyone found the heart?'

The flesh had been pared from Patel's face leaving his brown, lidless eyes gazing up in horror.

'It looks personal,' continued the pathologist. 'What has this poor boy done to deserve such treatment? What kind of nightmare creature would do something like this?'

The original team had disappeared as soon as the Met showed up. Their actions would be expunged from any official reports.

The gruesome discovery would be laid at the feet of the usual 'anonymous caller'.

The ferocity of the attack ensured the morning channel newsreaders reporting Denta Patel's murder donned their gravest expressions and spoke in sombre tones. Every one of them had scoured the airways for something they could present 'on a lighter note', but none could turn away from the grim fact.

The reign of the Sioux had ended. The time of the Butcher had begun.

~*~

10: A cat may look at a god...

The Cat was able to perform many complex tasks simultaneously. That morning, when Su Nami came out of her bathroom towelling her hair, it was working with Milla, remote piloting Matvei's Panther, talking with the AI Forum about the Swarm and licking its rear end.

It stopped what it was doing, stared at her and grinned.

'If something's worth doing it's worth doing well,' it said, 'but you, Su Nami, are a bird of an altogether different plumage. Do you always put so much dedication into your work?'

She gazed back at him with ice-white eyes in an enchanting face and tightened the belt of her robe around her slender waist.

'Bastard killed Katy. What should I have done?'

'I'm not thinking about what you've done but about just how much of it you did. You practically tore the man apart. And what did you do with his heart? No one can find it at the crime scene. Did you throw it away?'

'I ate it. Great source of iron, I'm told.'

'Really? Did you cook it first?'

'No.'

'Won't it make you sick?'

'Do some research, Cat. I'm not like other girls. I'm truly unique.' And she stretched with almost feline pleasure, her hands extending into glittering, razor-sharp blades then reverting to her normal, long-fingered porcelain perfection.

'So, where have you been all night?'

'Watching and waiting, little Cat. Finding things out. Getting to the who on top of the why, and adding a hearty smudge of where.'

She sat languorously in a chair. 'I had sisters once, you know, but now I'm alone in the world. They died along with two billion other people. They didn't stand a chance and the people who did that are the same bastards who ordered Katy killed.'

'Your sisters, were they much like you?'

'Yes. They were very beautiful.'

'I think I've seen their work before. They would kill much as you did and then the corpse would have become infected with squids. They started the whole infection process. That boy you killed. I've checked. He wasn't infected with anything. Are you?'

'No.'

'Are you sure?'

She opened her arms wide. 'Scan me. Can you do that?'

'I can and I am. No, no sign of infection.'

'I think the development system that created me also cleansed me. I am what I am. True, I'm a biomorphic assassin, but at heart I'm also a woman and I was grown from a human female subject.'

'With modifications.'

'Also true. I was designed to be a warrior. The ultimate soldier. There were five of us and I'm the only survivor. I'm unique. I can eat whatever I find on the battlefield and my body is a weapon. In fact I'm much stronger than my sisters because I'm not infected and I can't be destroyed by a 360 scan.

'I can run faster, fight harder and I'm tougher to kill than any other human. In the old days I would have been regarded as a God and worshipped.'

'Forgive me if I don't curtsey. A Cat may look upon a God but it doesn't have to kiss its arse.'

'I like you, Cat.'

'The feeling is mutual, Su Nami, but with all the usual caveats.'

'Such as?'

'If we kiss — no tongues.'

She chuckled, almost a purring sound.

The Cat stiffened and its eyes momentarily lost their focus. Then they returned to examine the assassin with bright mischief.

'It would seem I surround myself with a harem of lethally lovely ladies.'

Su Nami leaned forward. 'Why? What's happening?'

'Milla strikes.'

● ● ●

Matvei swam through the milky fluid towards the beacon of light in the middle of the lake. It was easier to move in the fluid than anything else he had ever swam in. It seemed to accept his movements with silken grace and support. He moved as if born to the strange environment and felt himself relax for the first time since his hover pod had locked him out.

A warm lassitude swept over him and he realised he was getting an unexpected erection. He tugged off his underwear, clutching it in his right hand, and then slid through the fluid with a sense of freedom that approached pure joy. When it happened his ejaculation was powerful enough to make him jerk and pump his hips uncontrollably. He had never known anything like it.

Men would pay good money to experience this, he thought. And he was just wondering how he could get the fluid into a commercial pool in Moscow when he saw the sprawled white body below him.

He pulled his pants back on, feeling himself unable to handle a naked corpse while in the same condition. It seemed indecent somehow. He lifted Vadim by gripping the boy's armpits and kicking away. It was surprisingly easy to glide back the way he'd come. The body under him was slight and there was little sense of drag. His penis began to stiffen again – it was extraordinary how sensitive his body had become to the milky substance.

He reached the lake side without incident and broke the surface.

He pulled out his mouthpiece. 'Major, I'll need a hand here.'

There was no reply. Matvei looked around, wondering if he'd got turned around in the lake and come up in the wrong place. No – there was the equipment platform and his clothes where he'd left them.

'Major?' Louder: 'Major?' Louder again: 'Major, sir, I've got the boy. Major?'

He dropped Vadim and hauled himself onto dry land. He looked around – a sick certainty welling up into his chest. The droids had gone too. There was bottled water on the equipment platform and some food pouches. The only light was from the minicam.

'Major,' he bellowed, 'Major! Please. Please, no.'

He dressed quickly and the minicam followed him back through the mine to the entrance. It was closed. He fell to his knees.

'Major, I did what you asked. I got the boy. Please.'

Milla watched from inside his mind and despite everything the man had done she felt her heart begin to break. He was a rapist and a killer but did he really deserve the slow death the Major had sentenced him to?

Matvei was snivelling in self-pity, his massive body juddering with sobs. The Major had already left with his daughter in her flier, the Panther and his vehicle following behind courtesy of the Cat. The Cat was also manipulating the minicam in the mine and had remained linked with Milla while she pondered her dilemma.

It felt her stiffen her resolve and then gasped at the sheer magnitude of the power at her command when she lashed out with her Transmitter Talent and thrust a single, one-word imperative into the corporal's mind.

STOP!

Instantly the corporal crashed to the ground like a boneless sack. Unlike his victims Matvei had died instantly, painlessly and without a struggle. And with him died his agonising well of pain, despair and fear. The Cat switched off the minicam and it automatically powered gently to the ground. Its lights were extinguished. There was nothing more to see and nothing moved in the mine's aching darkness. The dead lay still.

In her room, Milla's eyes opened. They were wet with tears.

'I'm not strong enough for this shit,' she whispered.

11: The killing pool

The clean-up operation after the Nimbus Protocol had been going well, thought Grillo, but the Patel situation disturbed him. He prowled the echoing corridors of the Earth Senate offices in Whitehall like a bad-tempered warthog, his thick body clenched tight around his furious heart.

He knocked at a door and entered a well-lit, high-ceilinged room with a massive bay window overlooking parklands.

The slender, well-dressed man behind his desk stood up with a quizzical expression on his handsome, perfectly groomed face.

'Grillo?'

'Henderson.'

'What can I do for you?'

'May I sit for a moment?'

'Of course.'

The two men couldn't have looked more different. Grillo – squat, red-faced and brutish, Henderson a composition in lean, coffee-coloured elegance.

'May I get you a drink? It must surely be after five somewhere. The usual?'

'Thanks.'

They waited while a lilac-coloured droid delivered their filled glasses then shimmied out of the door with a gentle humming noise and an artful flick of its middle section.

Henderson sipped appreciatively at his pale wine while Grillo took a long draw at his Woodford Reserve bourbon and grunted his satisfaction.

'Well then, Ernesto, to what do I owe this pleasure?'

The view beyond the bay window darkened and a steady downpour began its relentless patter against the glass.

'Meacham, do you ever think about going back to Boston?'

Henderson blinked. 'I'm sorry?'

'Don't you ever think about leaving this pit and going home?'

'Well, no, actually. London is my cultural home. I have the opera here, the ballet and the theatre, and that's before one adds in the museums, restaurants and,' he chuckled, 'the bars.'

Grillo knew Henderson's sexual politics and had no problem with them, but he wondered if the man really had to underline them with such a thick pink pen.

'Yeah, well, sometimes I miss New York and you've got all the theatres, ballet and bars there too, all you could ever need.'

Henderson tilted his head. 'Come on, Ernesto, out with it. You didn't come here to talk about being homesick.'

Grillo took another pull on his bourbon. 'This is good. No, you're right. I want to talk about the Nimbus cover-up...'

'Please, my friend, Operation Umbrella.'

'Is it you who comes up with these faggot names for everything?'

Henderson smiled deprecatingly, and held up his left hand, palm out.

'Far be it for me to say.'

Grillo sniffed. 'Okay, Umbrella – good name on a day like today. So, we got the list of targets...'

Henderson cut in again, 'Fish for the killing pool.'

'Fish? Why would fish need umbrellas?'

'The fish don't need umbrellas, Ernesto. They have to be hung out to dry.'

Grillo hesitated, realising how silly the conversation was becoming. He gathered in his train of thought and started again.

'You heard what happened to the Patel kid?'

'Yes, deeply disturbing.'

'Yeah. Well that happened the same day he'd hung a fish out to dry.'

'Poor chap.'

'Meacham, what are the chances that his killing was a coincidence?'

'What on Earth are you saying?'

'Remember the *Chicago way*? "They hurt one of ours, we put one of theirs into the morgue," that's what this looks like.'

A gust of hard wind blew fat drops of rain against the window in a dramatic tympani.

'I can see why you don't need the theatre, Ernesto. You carry it around with you in your head.'

Grillo drained his glass and lifted it. 'Another?'

'Why not?'

The fey little droid hummed in, swished around with its tray, and then hummed out again. Grillo lifted his fresh glass to his thick lips.

'Slow down after this one,' he said.

'Perhaps best,' agreed Henderson, 'or at least wait until lunchtime. We can continue this at my club if you like.'

'Club or bar?'

'The Athenaeum is a club, Ernesto. Old, staid and wonderful − like stepping back to a better time. The waiters are gorgeous.'

'I'd love to Meacham, thank you. But back to these fish with umbrellas. Have you got access to that list for the killing pool?'

'Well of course.'

Henderson had the official title 'Off World Diplomatic Liaison Minister' but both men knew he was really in charge of Home World Security.

'How many of the fish have been hung out to dry?'

'Just a few left who may still be useful to us. The rest have been thoroughly dried and smoked.'

'Then that's why we may need to cast our nets a little wider, Meacham. Somebody killed Patel and I don't think they're on our list.'

'Easy enough.' He thumbed a communicator. 'Hello, Socrates?'

'Good morning, Mr Henderson.'

'Good morning. Look, when the Patel boy was killed were there any trace implants in his immediate area?'

'There were quite a number within two hundred metres, but they all belong to Shady Meadows residents.'

'Shady Meadows?'

'The name of the housing complex, Mr Henderson.'

'I see, a dead end. Well then, do we have any contacts for Miss Katya Pavel? This is the woman who was killed with those Met police officers this morning.'

Grillo looked up from his drink. He wasn't meant to be party to this level of information. He made to stand and muttered, 'Shall I leave?'

Henderson waved him back down with a gentle flapping motion.

'We have her staying with a friend in the London sky tower. Upmarket outer core address.'

'Who is the friend?'

'The apartment belongs to a Mrs Ruth Pearce, widow. She isn't there at present.'

'Then who is?'

'A young woman by the name of Miss Milla Carter. In fact she had been working with the police officers who were killed. She was involved with the Sioux multiple murder case. She was directly instrumental in identifying the Sioux, and even led police officers to the scene where the killer was captured.'

Grillo grunted, 'How did she do that?'

'Oh, hello Mr Grillo, good morning.'

'Morning – how did she do that?'

'She is a telepath, Mr Grillo. She used her talent to find the killer.'

Henderson said, 'Socrates, can you provide me with a full dossier on Miss Carter?'

'On your screen, Mr Henderson.'

Henderson's monitor allowed both men access to the information. They read silently. Henderson finished first and sat back with two pensive fingers tapping at his pursed lips in a V shape.

Grillo read more slowly, his thick lips moving as he did so. When he had finished the dossier he was surprised to find he had also finished his drink.

'What a remarkable young lady,' offered Henderson.

'I don't get it,' said Grillo.

'Are you seeing the same as me, Ernesto?'

160

'If what you're seeing is a Shutterbox telepath who's acting as a Transmitter and would appear to also be a Receiver, then yes, Meacham, you bet I am.'

~*~

Part 4: Brothers in arms

1: A ticking time bomb

'It's been a while, Builder.'

Over two hours later he got his response. Conversations between Antisoc and Iapetus could take days.

'Far too long, Padre. Are you well?'

The patrician man gazed fondly at the powerful black man's portrait in his monitor and shook his head. *Don't waste hours on pleasantries.*

'Have we really got time for bullshit?'

'No, I guess not. What can I do for you?'

'Builder, I've sent a rescue team to Antisoc. They're the fastest ships I've got. Nothing else can get there any quicker. They will be able to ferry about three hundred people out of harm's way, no more. How many souls do you have there in the colony?'

He had been to bed, woken up and breakfasted before he saw the answer.

'Can't be precise. This place gives anarchy a really bad name. Officially just over fifteen hundred, but I'd say a better guess would be quite a few more than two thousand.'

'Tough decisions to be made then. Of course, you will want to come back here with the survivors?'

'I can't, Padre. I'm the front line commander here. We're putting contingency plans into action as fast as we can. With me here we stand a chance. Without... well, we might as well blow this place and make it quick.'

He outlined the plan to rig thrusters into the support structure and make the whole colony into a viable escape vehicle. He also sent over the schematics for the Padre to see how complete the idea was.

'My God, Builder, mum always said you were the crazy one but that's way beyond inspired madness. Don't let them kill you, boy. You're worth more than all the rest of them put together. Come back here to me. I love you, Bertrand.'

'I love you too, Phil, you know it. You're the only brother I've got, dude. If it comes down to it you'll just have to do the living for both of us. But there are children here and if we can save two hundred and ninety-nine of them but we let one of them die so a crippled black man can live... well, I wouldn't want to survive under those circumstances, Phil – and you know it.'

'Don't talk to me in brainless clichés. This isn't some stupid adventure story where the big bad gets its arse kicked at the last minute and the hero walks away into the sunset. This shit is real and you might die.'

'Yes, Phil, I know. And if there's just one chance to get out of this I'm grabbing it with both hands and I'm riding the fucker home. But I can't walk away from these people, you know I can't. I'm just not made that way.'

The men eyed each other across millions of klicks of deep space. There had been long hours between each statement. It made it hard to stay really angry across the time delay.

'Do your best to survive, brother. Promise me that much.'

'I will, Phil. I promise. See you soon perhaps, yes?'

'Yes. Goodbye, Bertrand.'

'Goodbye, Phil.'

The Padre helped himself to a large cognac. There had been a few too many of those over recent days but he didn't care and neither would his liver. Everything that happened over the next few weeks and months would end up as a simple question of logistics.

'How many, how far and how soon?' he wondered aloud. Fact was, even if they could pull everyone off Antisoc-Outer and bring them back to Iapetus they would only be saving them some time – and precious little of that.

Once they got here that would mean they would expand the complement of personnel, and they already had too many people for their existing facilities to transport to Mars.

And all the time that bastard cloud would be contracting and accelerating.

Bradley had noticed the acceleration and Einstein had verified it using some arcane maths to do with 'exponential speeds amplified by the cloud's contracting mass, times energy'. Padre accused it of trying to live up to its name and the AI told him that 'everything was relative'. They laughed then, but there was nothing funny about it. Nothing at all.

Bradley was at his door with her latest observations. He called her in and sat with her in his conversation corner. He knew his adopted brother had one just like it, designed so his floating chair would fit. Padre wondered why he cared about that fact, but he did.

The girl was talking and he had to concentrate to hear her. She was talking too fast.

'Wait,' he said, 'wait. Slow down. What are you telling me? Start at the beginning, girl. You've lost me.'

'I've been thinking about Antisoc and the rescue mission. There might just be a way to get more people back here using existing resources.'

'The hell you say? How?'

And she told him.

It would become a matter of logistics and a lot of hard science. It would depend on speed and accuracy but it could be done. Bandit was talking with Einstein in a halting, long distance dance during which they fired long strings of information at each other. The base line was whether they had the three weeks they needed to cannibalise the colony's tugs and research ships for their extra thrust, and whether the rescue fleet could arrive in time to be securely tethered and tow the great beast from its orbit.

Everyone knew that any solution was likely to be temporary. They knew that somewhere battle lines would have to be drawn and the enemy faced, but first they wanted time to prepare, time to plan. Time to enjoy every lungful of life they could scavenge.

Bandit put the plan to Builder.

'Which lunatic came up with this?'

'She's called Bradley. She works with the Padre. She says we can tow the old girl into a field where she can juice her way out of here and down to safety. I swear, Builder, I've looked at the figures and they work.'

The powerful black man folded his arms over his massive chest.

Frostrós said, 'It has to be worth trying. I think it has verity.'

'Gimlet, what do you think?'

The lizard man licked at the air as if tasting the idea. A bubble of something erupted from one of his nostrils and burst wetly. Frostrós did her best to disguise a shudder, then looked away and back at the Builder.

Gimlet hissed, 'You made Frostrós your runner so why not listen to her? She's got a good mind under that pile of wild hair. I'd say if she tells you something has, hmm, good word – verity...' He pronounced this last word 'veri-tay' and chuckled. '...then you should take notice. For the first time it looks like we may be getting out of this shit intact, Builder. Hey, that must at least call for an egg or two.'

2: Sinister beauty

The Swarm was more than just a solar system-wide teardrop of gas, fire and hate. It was also a toolmaker. It had carefully fashioned intricate devices that it had sent curving down the long orbital path to Earth millions of years before and as a result billions of people had died. In the complex forge of its belly it could fashion many other tools with an absolute precision.

It could also build weapons.

Like lightning made aware, the cloud beast could use natural electrical generation to manipulate its environment. It could move huge amounts of material or work at the molecular level depending on its needs. It could alter its physical state in an almost infinite number of ways – and it never got distracted from its work.

The little research ship had almost touched the Swarm's tenuous outer layers with its human-contaminated sensors. It had come far too close. That would not be allowed to happen again. The ship had been sent from a filthy accretion of the vile Earth creatures, thousands of them leaking their poisons from every seam of their clumsy, primitive lair.

The Swarm could almost smell the warm organic pollution from the disgusting creatures, taste it defiling the purity of space. It wanted to crush them, burn them, and rip their stink free from the universe. Its hatred was almost unhinged by its absolute horror of being contaminated by humans, touched by them. It was unthinkable. They had to be destroyed and quickly.

It would take far too long to reach the humans' pathetic artificial moon at the Swarm's usual speed, meaning the parasite might send more of its little ships out to sniff around and cock their legs up against the cloud beast's fabric. There had to be an alternative to using the cloud's cleansing flame. Perhaps some sort of missile? Something it could throw from a distance? *Ah, yes.*

Millions of tonnes of ice, metal and stone were harvested from surrounding space and passed to the centre of a vast cell it had created in the section of its body closest to Antisoc-Outer. Powerful tentacles of electromagnetic energy reached out and collated the material as it arrived. Then rivers of heavy matter were passed along narrowing, muscular fistulas until they finally spewed out into the cell, ejected from gaseous sphincters at incredibly high speeds.

The stuff of worlds was flung into that space where it was held in powerful force fields and made to collide and merge with immense destructive force. The process smashed meteors down to boulders and boulders to rubble. Smaller, ever smaller, the grinding continued until the cell was filled with a grainy rotating collation.

Continuous pressure was brought to bear which rendered the mineral harvest into a hot, super-heavy, spheroidal mass of boiling striated slurry. More rock and metal was pounded into the sphere but it was never permitted to expand beyond a specific radius. Great bands of energy compressed the sphere and as it took on more and more mass it slowly, reluctantly, became dense as a planet's core. But the Swarm wanted more. Still more material was forced under the sphere's fluidly moving, oily surface.

The new weapon had no need to be as precise as the little jewel-like spider constructions the Swarm had fashioned so many years before. This was to be the giant sledgehammer with which it intended to crush a massive walnut.

In the same way a man judges distance and velocity before throwing a ball, the Swarm judged the distant colony of Antisoc-Outer and calculated its sledgehammer's optimum weight. It took time to build its weapon and lavished love on it.

The sphere had become so dense that light itself curved at its surface, which lent it an organic looking, oily sheen. A portion of the Swarm's waste gases settled around it and became glued to its surface, creating an unbreathable atmosphere just centimetres thick.

If a man or woman had tried to stand on the sphere they would have been instantly crushed flat and evenly smeared across its entire surface, a vanishingly thin skin in which even bacteria would have been flattened. In fact any biological entity approaching the sphere would have been stretched thin by its gravitational forces.

The construction's perfect roundness had been a beautiful side-effect and not the product of deliberate intent. Much smaller than the dwarf planet, it was nevertheless heavier than Pluto. Its surface was utterly smooth and featureless, a perfect sphere created by monstrous gravitational forces that should have been impossible for something of that size.

At its heart molecular structures were being condensed and elements altered; atoms stole each other's electrons and neutrons like guests at a pickpockets' convention. Flashes of radiation tore out into space, a beacon for those who could see. It presented a sleek and sinister beauty that belied its purpose. It was a perfect thing, a masterpiece. It was monstrous.

There was no need for something to be aerodynamic in the airless void of deep space. Once sent on its way the most misshapen object would follow a set route directly to its target and there were no phantom vespers to blow it from its course. Only the snare of gravity could snag a traveller from its path. That wasn't going to be allowed to happen here. The Swarm ensured it had made its sledgehammer too massive to be diverted.

The Swarm's newly created weapon was supremely well balanced. Once launched it would fall perfectly along its path to Antisoc-Outer and nothing could stop it. It would roll like an immense ball bearing in a groove carved by the gods of physics, and when it reached its destination the fate of thousands would be decided.

Nothing like it had ever been conceived before.

During its many days of construction, grinding creaks and groans of compacting ice, metal and rock sounded and resounded throughout the gaseous flesh of the cloud creature. While it worked at its task the Swarm registered these sounds as feedback in its electromagnetic musculature. Elsewhere they manifested as pulsing radio waves.

'I'm telling you it's a signal from the cloud. Maybe it wants to communicate? You know, maybe it wants to parley?' Gimlet pronounced this last word as 'par-lay' and stretched it out a little too long.

'Sounds like random radio static to me,' offered the Builder. 'Dude, you think everything else in the system wants to chatter with the neighbours as much as you do. It was talking so much that got you your original invitation to Antisoc.'

'Yeah? Well, not everything else got quite so much useful information to imp-part, my friend. I only share my largesse with those wise enough to hear. You hear me?'

'I hear you. Like that pretty Home World Security agent you told about your hobby of breaking into top executive offices and stealing state secrets. She heard you okay, dude, and so did the judge. But I still don't think that noise is a signal. What do you think, Bandit?'

'I'm afraid I agree with you, Builder. However, I am also not so sure the radio signature is entirely random. I think the cloud may be up to something.'

'What else can it do?'

'I don't know, Builder, but I fear we will find out all too soon.'

~*~

3: Prey animals

The same four operatives who had discovered the body of Denta Patel had been given the job of bringing in Milla Carter. Colonel Marjorie Balasubramanium briefed them under the cover of a bandstand in old St James's Park.

Gelid rain stung their faces while she talked low and urgently.

She explained that the target could possibly be very dangerous in ways they were still trying to understand. Project 'Extreme Caution' was the name Henderson had coined and it seemed apt.

'She's a telepath and she has real Talent,' Balasubramanium told them. 'Don't underestimate her. At the first sign of any funny business you have full authority to terminate the target and evac. If you need back-up don't be brave – hit the call button. Understand?'

They nodded and shuffled around her, tucking bare hands under their armpits in a futile attempt to stay warm.

'What's she done to put such a big burr up Home World's ass?' The tallest man spoke with a light and cultured American accent.

'You looking for motives, Clayton? We don't provide motives. We give orders and you obey them. You hear me, soldier?'

'Yessir, ma'am.'

'It's fucking cold here so let's finish. Put on your glasses.'

They did as they were told. Images flashed before their eyes.

'That's the latest portrait shot we have of the target. It was taken at Met police headquarters in Sutton quadrant.'

'Wow! She's a real babe.'

Balasubramanium twitched with annoyance. 'Yeah? Is she? You want to carry her shopping home and choose some wine to go with her dinner? Up your arse, Kennard. She's probably the most dangerous person you'll ever have to deal with so remember that when you try to steal a smooch.

173

'Okay, I'm done and you people have work to do. Try not to trip over your tongues when you meet the target. Bring her in or put her in a body bag. Either way, I'm happy. Now, fuck off before I give the job to someone who knows what they're doing.'

The operatives moved away in one direction and the Colonel in another.

Kennard turned to watch her walk towards her car.

'No wonder she's cold in that little suit. Why doesn't she dress for the weather?'

'Her ass looks good in that tight little skirt though. Nice tailoring.'

'Tailoring? What you talking about, tailoring? You in touch with your feminine side or something, Augella?'

'Of course I am, dickwad. I'm a woman.'

'Shit, yeah, I remember. Last time we shared a shower. Hey, guys! Did you know? Augella's a girl.'

'Fuck you!'

Clayton bit back a laugh. 'Okay, people, job to do. Let's get over to the sky tower and take this Carter babe out of commission.'

'Cap, the Colonel told us to bring her in.'

'Did she? I heard the orders, heard them clear as day. The wise word is don't mess with Carter – she's too dangerous. Colonel said it and I heard it. Now, let's go do it.'

Their directions led them into the sky tower and then up towards one of the most exclusive outer parts of the construction.

'The babe has money,' said Augella.

'Yeah, maybe,' offered Clayton. 'What she doesn't have is much of a future.'

'Do we know if she's there?'

'If not we wait until she is. Come on down here. Now quiet.'

Clayton led his team down a private corridor that contained a single doorway in a side wall and another, glazed, which seemed to lead outside to the open air.

'Knock-knock,' whispered Augella.

174

Clayton palmed a slate grey door plate. They heard a chime from inside. A few moments later the door opened. Clayton thrust his gun into the charming face of a slender brunette with strange, ice-white eyes. He barked, 'Where's Carter?'

His gun and the hand holding it fell to the floor and he buckled, cradling his streaming stump against his chest. A shocked groan escaped his lips.

The other three team members managed to get in each other's way during the sudden confusion and Su Nami danced silently among them with balletic economy of movement. Her razor-sharp claws disarmed and disembowelled the operatives as if they were stationary. The one shot discharged was deflected into Clayton's bowed head.

Augella's head bounced against the corridor wall with a hard crack, her eyes wide open in surprise. Her decapitated corpse fell sideways against Kennard who was trying to stuff his entrails back into his body. The entire action had taken less than three seconds.

Blood trickled down into the collar of Bayes, the only survivor. Su Nami pressed her blades deeper into the flesh of his jaw. Bayes glared at her.

'You won't get me to talk.'

She smiled and made a sudden slashing motion. Bayes fell twitching to the floor with his throat laid open and his hands pressed to the wound in a helpless gesture. Su Nami watched the life drain from his eyes.

'I didn't need you to talk.'

'Oooh, look what you did. That's going to be an utter bastard to clean up.'

The Cat picked its way around the tangled heap of bodies.

'What did they want?'

'Milla Carter.'

'And they got you.'

'Yes.'

'Milla read them?'

'Yes.'

'Good. Would have been a waste to lose all that information.'

The Cat stood silently for a moment.

'Su Nami, get everything you need from the apartment, then we'll get your car and get out of here. We need to pick up Milla on the way.'

'What's happening, Cat?'

'These operatives are being monitored from Whitehall and all their vital signs just flat-lined a matter of seconds after they got here. Their handlers might get a little concerned about that. Best case scenario, they send another bunch of bozos to see what happened. Worst case, they send a dumb missile here to blow the place to shit rather than risk more lives.'

'Why are you more worried about a dumb missile than a smart one?'

'I can take over a smart missile or a drone, or anything that can think for itself. It's what I do. I was designed for it. Dumb missile is just a big explosive-packed rock someone's thrown at us. Nothing I can do about it. It won't kill me of course. This sweet little cat body is only one aspect of something much, much bigger. Your body is all you got. Up to you.'

Twenty minutes later two of the most expensive west-facing floors of London's sky tower bulged outwards after the impact of a dumb, urban funnel bomb. The detonation was carefully controlled to minimise damage. Later news reports stated that four civilians had been caught in the blast and that it would require DNA fingerprinting to identify them.

During an interview Colonel Marjorie Balasubramanium from the London branch of Home World Security told reporters that her colleagues would not rest until 'the terrorist perpetrators of this vile act had been brought to justice'.

Shortly afterwards the Colonel had drained a large glass of whiskey, poured herself another and sipped it slowly while relaxing in her hot tub. She had lit some candles and put on a recording of whale song. Her eyes closed and she drowsed. She had lost four good people that afternoon but, she told herself, she had warned them.

'Yes, Colonel Balasubramanium,' said a voice close by her ear, 'but did you warn them enough?'

Her eyes flew open and she lurched round in the bath, spilling what was left of her whiskey. Sitting on her toilet seat and studying her with large brown eyes that reflected the flickering light from her candles was Milla Carter.

She smiled. 'Well, did you, Colonel?'

~*~

4: Not really a team player

'Daddy, what happened to Vadim and that soldier?'

'We had to leave them behind, Polina. Not enough room.'

'But that's silly – we've got three aircraft.'

'Yes, but the soldier isn't going to Moscow and he can take Vadim straight to the authorities in his hover pod.'

There was silence in the flier for several minutes.

'Do you mind if I sleep for a while?'

'Of course not, Poli. I'll wake you when it's time to land.'

After a brief passage of time he heard her breathing deepening. How long had it been since he had been able to drift away so easily? It took exhaustion to close his eyes these days. The weight of too much wickedness experienced over too many years.

He noticed that he'd used the familiar diminutive of his daughter's name. He hadn't done that since she was small. He studied her recumbent form and could see his wife in her sleeping face and her slender shapeliness. He could discern something of himself too, in her high cheekbones, the narrow dome of her head and her fine sweep of hair.

He wondered how her life might have differed with him in it. Would she still have accepted the attentions of the drug rapist Vadim? Would caring for her as one of her parents have changed the way he lived his life? Would she have kept her birth surname rather than switching to her mother's maiden name?

Why ask himself such stupid questions? Her mother had left him because of his drinking and his relentless dedication to the job. The job. Fuck, what a fool. He had given up his family for a country that had since tried to kill him, and to earn the respect of men not fit to shine his father's shoes.

He gazed at Polina who lay like a sculpture turned to marble by the moonlight. Her lips moved as if she was about to speak.

178

The skin of her cheek was so smooth he felt an overwhelming urge to kiss her there. He tore his eyes away.

She's lovely. You must be so proud.

It was Milla Carter in his mind.

She is. He found he could converse without verbalising. *I am.*

She'll be okay – you do know that, don't you?

Do I? Why do I know that? I thought I was right before – but now I don't really have a clue.

She loves you.

You know that?

And she's scared of you.

Why?

Because you plough a very individual furrow, Spartan. She never knew how to please you. It was easier to settle for creeps like Vadim than try to match the expectations of the Spartan. What can you do when your biggest hero is also your father? Shit!

What's happening?

Oh my God.

What?

Some people just pulled a gun on Su Nami. She's dealt with it.

Should I know her?

You knew two of her sisters.

Who?

Shiva and Nightshade. You killed them after they slaughtered the Bear and his men.

The Ghoul? You're talking about the Ghoul? They were infected and we rendered them using a 360 scan. Beautiful and utterly deadly.

Those women earned lots of names over a lot of years. The Ghoul was just one of them.

But surely, if she was one of them she would be dead? After the Nimbus Protocol all them are dead. Aren't they?

Not all, no. Su Nami lives and she's deadly too, as four dark operatives just discovered. Spartan, sorry, I have to go. Hold on to that daughter of yours. Give her the father she deserves.

I'm not sure I can.

179

You can. I'll be in touch.

'Major?'

He jumped. 'What's happening now?'

'When we get to Moscow what do you want me to do with your vehicle and the Panther?'

'Cat, it's you. What did you say?'

The Cat repeated its question. While doing so it was also piloting all three aircraft, speaking with Milla and Su Nami and performing a great number of covert operations designed to keep its team members safe.

It surprised itself with that thought. It had never thought of itself as a team player before.

They discussed the best options for several minutes after which the Panther peeled out of formation and disappeared down into the ragged mountains below. There was the brief flare of an explosion followed by a pyrotechnic flower blooming brightly in the shadows.

'Pretty,' said the Cat. 'Back to Moscow, then?'

'No, please – take my vehicle home if you can, but do you know where I can find Milla Carter?'

5: Ultimatums

'When did you get put in charge of life and death around here, Builder?'

'What's the problem, Lase?'

'I never had a problem with you 'til now. And now I got a big problem.'

'Sorry to hear that, Lase.'

Behind Builder, Gimlet and Frostrós practised their most convincing impression of nonchalant disregard for the conversation taking place between the powerful black man in his floater chair and a giant dressed like a polychrome Viking. His beard and thick mop of long hair were artfully dyed in streaks of red, blue and blonde. His garb included a polished chrome breastplate. Builder wondered how he had managed to cope so long in Antisoc without his jet speeder bike.

Lase's colourfully dressed gang milled in the doorway without pressing past the Builder's armed guards. They shouted their approval.

'Yeah, man.'

'You said it, dude.'

'Lase, you the man, man.'

The giant smiled. 'My people. They love me. I love them. It works well.'

Builder coughed to disguise a bark of sudden laughter. He had dealt with 'The Cutters' before. Each of the gang was named after a tool used for hacking, slicing or boring. He thought they were very well named.

'So, Lase, what can I do for you today?'

The Viking turned to his cronies with a sly grin then back to the Builder.

'You can stop this women-and-children-first shit and buy me and my boys twenty-three tickets to ride.'

'Ride where?'

'Don't treat me like a wet boy, brother. I know those Iapetus ships are out there. And I know that youngsters and their sweet moms are disappearing from the dens. We want to disappear too. Simple request, simple answer. Put us on a transport and we're out of your curly black hair.'

Builder took a deep breath. This was the fourth gang request since the little fleet from Iapetus had taken position around the colony. He was getting tired of it.

'How soon can you be ready?'

Lase stood taller. 'Really?'

'How soon?'

'Ha, we're ready now. We were born ready, weren't we, boys?'

There was a chorus of agreement from the crowded doorway.

'Seven, can you take Lase and his boys to the debarkation point please?'

'The special priority one, boss?'

'Please. Take three and six with you in case the crew make a rumpus.'

It was evident Lase was surprised at how easy his task had been. His hirsute group clapped him on the back as they were led away. Builder wondered how long their joy would last after they'd spent a few days in a locked den with three other gangs. *Not very long*, he thought, *but then needs must...*

Selected groups of women and children had been ferried to the waiting rescue ships. The plan was to tether the ships to the strongest support arches of the colony and pull it into a better flight configuration to escape the cloud beast. The plan should work but there was no point in taking risks. If there was any danger, the tethers would be cut with beam cutters and the rescue ships could accelerate away. There would at least be some survivors.

'We got anyone left to help with the work?' asked Gimlet.

'Enough. They'll have to be.'

'When did these tossers get so selfish? Man, they make me sick.'

'Dude, if they were righteous citizens they wouldn't be here. I'm surprised we're getting as many people on board as we are. You know what I say, Gimlet? If it looks like a banana, tastes like a banana and it's yellow, the chances are it's not a lemon.'

'You said a worldful there, oh mighty leader. Now, I've got work to do of a specialised nature. Can you live without me for a few hours?'

'I'll live, but make it worth the parting, sweet prince.'

'Man, sometimes you are just weird.'

'Laters.'

Believing himself to be alone, Builder slumped exhausted in his chair.

'You okay, Builder?'

He jolted upright and looked around. Frostrós was standing in a corner, concern written plainly on her youthful face. He looked closer. Under her make-up she was grey. Events had been taking their toll on everyone around him. He didn't have time to let himself flag. He pulled himself together with a visible effort and smiled wearily.

'Just tired is all. You've been a Godsend over the past few weeks, Frostrós, a real breath of fresh air. Why don't you join me for a bite of dinner then go get some sleep? I'll be turning in soon myself but I'd love the company while I eat.'

They ate well and talked little, each filled with concern for the other and sneaking careful glances at each other's plates, each trying to ensure the other was eating enough. Builder had little appetite but ate a good meal. The girl was ravenous but tried not to be greedy.

When their plates were empty she came round and kissed him gently on the cheek.

'You want some company tonight?'

He looked at her in genuine surprise. He cast around for something to say. She looked abashed and pulled away.

'No,' she said, 'I meant, you know, to talk. I didn't mean...' She blushed a deep crimson.

He took her hand in a surprisingly gentle gesture.

'Thanks, Frostrós. I really appreciate the thought. But I need sleep more than conversation right now and so do you. I'll see you in the morning, girl. Good night. Get some rest.'

He kissed her fingers and gave them a squeeze, then watched her slight form as she exited his room. At the last moment she looked back with a question in her eyes. He smiled with genuine warmth.

'Good night. Sleep well.' And she was gone.

Alone at last Builder started to take his own advice. He moved his floater into his bathroom and ran a bath. He began to unbutton his clothes and levered himself up out of his chair and into the cradle over his tub. Once he was naked he reached out to the lever that would lower him into the hot water.

'Builder. Sorry.'

He paused and looked up. 'Bandit?'

'Builder, I'm afraid we've run out of time.'

He felt a vibration in the air around him.

'What's happening?'

'I'm trying a manoeuvre. It may be too late.'

'For what?'

And then he was thrown to the floor by an impact of unbelievable force. Gravity died and he was winded when he hit the wall. He bounced and flailed back into a ball of hot water that had become airborne. He breathed a lungful of hot fluid, choked and sucked in more.

Fuck, he realised, *I'm drowning in mid-air*. His vision blurred and darkened. He began to die.

~*~

184

6: A quiet time

Meacham Henderson sipped his café latté and through an elegant window cast a languorous eye out over his courtyard roof garden. His private Eden. His demi-paradise. He was a self-confessed morning bird and it was still quite early, but enough sunlight washed over the scene to lend it an oriental, pearl-like prettiness. He felt a haiku threaten behind his eyes and drained his cup of creamy, caramel bitterness in self-defence. Today would not be a day for poetry. It was enough to allow the mist-clouded morning to drape itself around his shoulders and gentle his mood before the day proper began.

His husband trod silently into the breakfast room. He passed like a lithe cat behind Meacham, ran the tips of his fingers along the quiet man's shoulders and kissed him warmly on his neck and cheek. Then with a brief pressure on one of his arms he padded back out of the room.

Meacham smiled. Dennis had always been able to read his moods and knew instinctively when he preferred to be alone. Dennis was a big cat of a man and knew when to roar in the bedroom. He also knew when to be quiet as a mouse. When to tiptoe. Meacham was the smaller man but he wore the trousers around the house.

He glanced at his crystal tablet. News was still streaming about the missile attack on London's sky tower. That had been a tough call but collateral damage had been kept to a minimum. He was certain the few scraps of human remains the Home World Security pathology unit had been able to recover were from Colonel Balasubramanium's hit team. Pity about that. He'd heard they were good.

He put a call through to the Colonel. A message for her to get in touch. No need to rush – she'd had a late and difficult night.

You'd be wasting your time.

The gentle voice that bloomed in his mind seemed to be laced with steely amusement. It was clear in his ear, crisp and

185

feminine. He looked around. He was alone apart from his lilac droid, which was twirling and humming to itself in the shadowed corner of the room.

Poor Colonel Balasubramanium. She had a loose thread in her personality. I pulled it and she simply fell apart like a puppet with its strings cut. Sorry, but I think I broke your toy lady soldier. As you say, pity about that. Well now, Dennis seems nice. Oops.

From somewhere in his apartment Meacham heard a hard thump.

Careless of me. He'll be fine once he's had a nice sleep. Tired, poor lamb. You kept him busy until the early hours this morning. Is that really fair?

Meacham rose unsteadily to his feet. He checked his tablet. No response from Balasubramanium. He made to leave the room, anxious to see what had just happened to Dennis. His droid moved to block his path. It had stopped twirling and now hovered at eye level with steady purpose. There was no longer anything fey about it. It had stopped humming.

So then, Meacham. You've declared war on me and my friends? Isn't that a bit one-sided? I mean look at it. You have the resources of a whole planet to throw against us and we are so few. We few, we happy few. We band of sisters and brothers.

You're misquoting.

Do you think I give a shit? Do you really think I give a flying fuck, Mr Meacham Henderson? Don't you think you've killed enough innocent people? You've enough blood on your hands to make a whole generation of complete bastards weep with shame. But your hands have always stayed clean, haven't they? Clean as a whistle. You could perform surgery without gloves, your hands are so clean.

But that's always been the point hasn't it, Mr Meacham Henderson? You have grunts who go out and get rid of the few who know the truth and they leave behind the ignorant many who twiddle their thumbs and watch the sun come up on another empty day. And all the time your pretty pink hands stay clean.

The man was roaming the room as if looking for a way out. The little lilac droid followed him at shoulder height. He wondered how it could suddenly look so robust. So heavy. It had always looked like a pretty toy before. Meacham became nervous. For the first time in his adult life he became defensive. He spoke aloud.

'Look, I was just doing my job, fuck it all. I was doing my job for the home world. It isn't always easy. Sometimes hard choices have to be made. Those were hard choices and I made them.'

Hard choices? Hard fucking choices? Easy choices from a nice place in Whitehall with a pretty roof garden and a pet stud boy in the bedroom. Yeah, real hard fuckin choices.

The voice in his head was stern and judgemental.

People like you should be caned in a public place then burned at the stake, you know that?

'I was doing my job.' He was finding it difficult to breathe.

Were you? And what was that job? Let's take a look, shall we, Mr fucking-clean-hands Meacham Henderson?

A torrent of images flooded into Meacham's head. Millions of infected people turned to face their last moments with dignity and resignation, mourning their lost yesterdays and knowing there would be no more tomorrows. The deadly silence afterwards. Katy Pavel looked down the barrel of a gun and Meacham experienced the heart-breaking shock of the shell smashing into her brain. He was in the Detective Chief Inspector's head when Gubbay was astonished by death in his safe headquarters.

Meacham finally realised who he was dealing with.

'Carter? Milla Carter? That's you?'

I cannot tell a lie, 'tis I.

The Head of Home World Security was curled in a heap on his breakfast room floor when Dennis came groggily to his senses and staggered in to find him.

Milla had bombarded Meacham with the deaths he'd ordered. Stoned him with them. Clubbed him until his last whimper whistled into the pile of his carpet and he finally stopped twitching.

Dennis took his husband's crumpled body into his arms and unleashed a heart-breaking howl of loss. In the shadowed corner of the room a twirling lilac droid sang a gentle song while the Cat watched proceedings from behind its borrowed eyes. It was satisfied.

~*~

7: Glancing blow

The super dense missile had been ejected by the Swarm at such speed that it arrived in Antisoc's local space with little in the way of warning. Bandit had thrown the colony to port in a desperate manoeuvre, but the sphere's gravitational field still managed to drag it to partial destruction.

It also tugged some of the rescue ships free of their moorings and slammed them down its deep event horizon. They were instantly subsumed beneath its glossy surface, releasing both hard radiation and arcing displays of primary light. A shallow gouge was torn from the stone and metal skin of the ball-shaped rock.

The sphere had originally been aimed to plough through Antisoc and then curve back in and head towards Iapetus Control. Barely scraping the outer edges of the prison colony had shortened its curve back in towards the sun – but, thanks to an unexpected windfall, not enough to save Earth's outermost, fully established colony. The Swarm could celebrate. Iapetus was still in the path of its gravity bomb.

Antisoc had been a strongly fortified ex-prison and housed some of the solar system's most dangerous and unpredictable criminal minds. After the sphere passed, it had become little more than a grinding mass of failing architecture, panicking humanity and torsional energy. Gang boss, scientist and scuzz bunny alike looked around desperately for direction and found nothing.

In atmosphere the noise was extraordinary. The few people who were trying to create order out of the chaos could barely make themselves heard above the screaming cacophony of howling fear and support struts twisted beyond their safe limits, plus bedrock grinding up against granite walls.

Some surviving engineers headed for the spacesuit dumps, pushing their families before them. They couldn't offer more than the few hours the suits' tanks could offer, but the alternative was to give up, sit down and wait for death.

Some did that. Blank-eyed, they gave up and slid down communal walls. Silent lines crowded the walkways.

The man called Lardman dragged himself back to his corner of a den and shut the makeshift door that provided him with a modicum of privacy. He laid himself down in his narrow crib next to the stinking corpse of the grandmother he had rescued from a garbage tip. He held her hand and for the first time he began to talk. He spoke of his life and what he had wished for when he was young. He told her the things he had never even admitted to himself before. He spilled his heart across her decaying dead breast and wept in shame.

Safety gates had slammed shut and closed off those areas of the colony sucked open by the gigantic, super-dense body as it passed. Wriggling victims barely had time to register surprise before being vacuumed out from their safe, stable homes and dragged kicking into space. They didn't scream. No sound came in airless space. The first died silently and quickly. Most froze into agonised shapes while they futilely stretched back towards light and life. For a brief moment they made an agonised frieze of ice-coated sculpture and then they were swallowed by the sphere. There was to be no record of their passing. Along with the detritus of tonnes of construction material and broken engineering modules, those hundreds of people became part of the sphere's core. Minicams and recording devices also became grist for the super powerful mill. Nothing torn from Antisoc during the sphere's ruinous passage escaped.

As a result the sphere's massive weight had grown by a minute yet telling amount which had thrown it slightly further out into its orbit and made up for its original shortfall. After gaining extra mass from its first encounter it was once more back on track for its second: Iapetus Control.

The Builder was very aware of lips pressed hard against his. He began to kiss back, and then became wracked by choking coughs. He vomited a bellyful of water, food and bile. The taste was terrible. He vowed he would never again eat a full meal then try to drown himself in zero G.

Then he thought back to that kiss. *What just happened?* He sorted through his scattered thoughts. Okay, he was wet, but warm. He wanted to leave his eyes shut for the time being. Where was the harm in that?

He opened them. A cascade of memory surged over him along with a sudden barrage of sound and sensation. He was lifted up then slammed back down onto a stone floor. His chest felt strange and his throat was scoured from deep down. He groaned and more water dribbled from his nose along with thick slime.

He gagged then focused on the shape crouching over him.

Gimlet's long tongue licked something from one of his nostrils and his wide, narrow eyes blinked back genuine concern. He saw the gratitude in Builder's face, shook his narrow head, then nodded back over the Builder's shoulder. And he turned. She was there. On her knees. Frostrós was wiping her mouth with the back of her hand. She looked scared and was shaking.

She swept the hair from her face and tied it back into a thick ponytail. She suddenly looked so much younger and yet also seemed terribly aged. He tried to speak to her. The resultant choking noise brought her up more upright. She leaned forward then cupped his face in her hands.

'Shhhhhh,' she said. 'Don't try to talk. Not yet.'

He swivelled his eyes at Gimlet.

'Damndest thing I ever see,' hissed the lizard man. 'Damndest thing. I swear on my incubator's life. Damndest thing. Man. You know I loves you, man, like honey shit, but you was dead, dude. I was weighing you up for spare ribs. You know how I love the ribs.'

He ran a hand over the Builder's exposed torso.

'Love the ribs, man.'

Frostrós pushed his hand away.

The Builder croaked, 'What happened?'

'Damndest thing, man. I swear you was dead.'

191

'Frostrós, can you please make sense? Palfrey's off with the screenwriters.'

The slight girl looked stricken. The light fled from her eyes.

'Builder. Oh, Builder. We need you, my love. We need you so much.'

Bandit said, 'I'm out of ideas, boss. Over to you.'

'Damndest thing.'

The Builder silently reached out for help. With Gimlet and Frostrós on either arm he levered his damp body back into his clothes and then pressed himself onto his floating chair. He slid his wasted stumps firmly down into the moulded sockets that had supported him over too many years. He felt the pressure. He felt the pain. The pain that felt so much like being home.

'Okay. Frostrós, Bandit, the pair of you please start talking. And while you're at it, Bandit, please get us all a drink. And Bandit, please, whatever you do, don't make mine water.'

~*~

8: Stupid ideas, sad outcomes

Note: to Dr Philip Algafari, Sector Manager, Iapetus Control

Padre.

I'm shouting this at Socrates and if it changes so much as one word I'm going to nuke its power supply. Same goes for you, Einstein.

Sorry to get formal on your ass, Padre, and in a very real way I'm sorry not to be doing this to your dumb face, but what the fuck were you thinking? Really? I'm the one who trusted you and put you out there – and now I'm the woman who looks like a complete fish-belly fuckwit.

Yes, there's too much of a delay routing this through Lagrange II to give you a call, and yes, it will take months for someone else to get out there by fucking ion drive so I'm not firing your ass, not yet. But, if for one moment I thought there was someone else, anyone else, out there who could take your fucking place I'd be going through channels and upping their pay grade. And I'd be doing it RIGHT NOW!

Do I sound angry to you? Well think again. I'm not fucking angry with you. Anger doesn't come close to the degree of disappointment, astonishment, disbelief and sheer fury I'm feeling about what you've done. I tell you I'm so close to erupting, my pants just turned purple and burned clean off my ass. I got flames burning out of my fucking joy tunnel. Should I delete that? No, leave it in. Brand that picture across your eyeballs, Padre.

Did you have your head up your ass or someone else's? Because you just had to be using shit for brains. What were you thinking? We have a unique and potential extinction threat to our entire civilisation, and − to give us all a bit more time to think − we've been busting everyone's balls trying to work out how best to get your people out of the path of that cloud thing. And what do you do? What the flying fuck do you do? You send every spare ship you have out there where the cloud is and put them *closer* to the danger.

And why? In order to save a few fuckwits, halfwits and ex-cons. It's crazy. You just burned down the whole street to save one stinking toilet. The research guys had their own ships so they should have known better. They chose what happens to them. But you, YOU, you… Fuck it, I'll finish this when I calm down.

If I calm down.

Even my husband doesn't make me this mad. Over and out, before I say something I'll regret.

With kindest regards

Yours sincerely

Dr Louisa K Browncott SCOR-ESA

The Padre cleared his screen and looked at Bradley, who had been reading over his shoulder.
'I don't think Lou's happy.'
Bradley said nothing. Her face was as white as her tabard.
'She never uses that "Dr" prefix unless she's really pissed off.'
He ran his hand through his monitor space, twisting his fingers.
'How many pulse rifles do we have, Bradley? Can we muster six, do you think?'
'You thinking about defence?'

194

'No, I just want to make sure we have enough if Lou calls for a firing squad.'

The girl chuckled fetchingly.

'By the way, Bradley, what *is* your first name?'

'Laura, sir.'

'Do your friends call you Laura?'

'My aunt used to call me Larry, sir.'

'Oh. Did you love your aunt?'

'I thought she was a complete bitch, sir.'

There was silence for a moment.

'So, what can I do for you, Bradley?'

'You called me, sir.'

'Yes, so I did. And please, stop calling me sir. Yes. Congratulations. You've just been promoted to be my chief assistant plus PA, and that means I might need you to be a pain in the arse. So from now on you'd better call me Padre. Drink?'

He took his all too familiar trek to his drinks closet and briefly wondered if he was going to live long enough to finish his stock of cognac. *Be a crime to waste it.* He brought his balloon of spirit and a large glass of full-bodied Malbec to the table in his conversation corner, then handed the wine to the engineer before taking his seat.

'Cheers. And well done. Lou cleared the promotion for you before deciding I was a complete fuckwit and a dangerous shithead. It's all official and in your file. Let your parents know they can be proud of their daughter and let's hope we all live long enough to enjoy the change.'

Bradley noticed that the amount of liquid poured into the Padre's glass had once again increased while also it seemed to be disappearing faster. She sipped at her wine. It was very good.

'Okay, Bradley. Time to think. We are firmly in that space-time continuum best known as "shit creek" and we've thrown our only paddle to a band of passing vagabonds. What do we do now?'

'May I speak freely, sir... sorry, Padre?'

'Please do.'

195

'We won't get very far on a diet of brandy.'

'It's cognac, but point taken.'

He put his glass down but kept his eyes firmly fixed on it. His lips thinned.

'Secondly,' she took a swallow of her wine, 'I don't agree with you about the paddle.'

'I'm sorry?'

'We haven't thrown away our only paddle. And, in fact, those vagabonds are right now bringing that other paddle back to us.'

The Padre reclaimed his glass and warmed it in the palms of his dry hands.

'Please, continue.'

'We can bemoan the loss of everything we've lost and sit wailing like a baby in an empty pram, when it was us, the baby, who threw everything out in the first place. But we're not babies, we're grown-ups. And we can take a long, sober look at the situation, Padre.'

He smiled at this but said nothing.

She continued, 'If I was in that pram I'd use it to build a go-cart. I did that when I was a kid. Mum was scared shitless when I went out on that thing. But you say we're in a creek filled with shit, plenty of the stuff. Fine, why don't we harness all that methane gas and use it as fuel? We could build a turbine or a jet or a rocket and get out of that creek a damn sight faster than we ever did using that stupid paddle.'

He was nodding at her, liking the direction of her thoughts.

'You're saying we should forget about what we haven't got and take a solid look at what we have, am I right?'

'That's it exactly, Padre. We need a touch of Professor Sanson's rule.'

'Never heard of him.'

'One of my tutors at the University of London. Smart bloke. He used to say, "Only Romans and railroad engineers needed to think in straight lines. The rest of us can afford to think laterally." And he was right. We just need to apply a bit of lateral thinking to our situation; shine a new light on it. With the brains and facilities at our disposal there's sure to be something we can do.

"We just need to open our minds and the answer will be there for us. With time, wit and determination on our side we'll win the day. Can I have some more wine, please?'

Padre fetched their drinks with an odd quiver in his stomach. He was reminded of the conversations he used to have with his brother. He felt stimulated and excited at the same time. He felt oddly young.

Bradley's face was a little flushed and her eyes bright. She accepted her wine, thanked him, and then took a long draught.

'I have an idea,' she said.

'Excuse me, Padre, may I butt in?'

The girl looked annoyed but bit her tongue and said nothing. Padre raised his eyes to his monitor.

'What is it, Einstein?'

'Sorry about this, engineer Bradley, but you need to hear this too.'

'I'm all ears.'

'Interesting image,' it said. Then the AI voice became all business: 'I have an update on the situation at Antisoc-Outer and the progress of the cloud beast. I'm afraid to say things do not bode well for us here.'

'You're thinking in straight lines,' said Padre smiling at Bradley. She smiled back, warmly.

'Actually, no,' said the AI, 'I'm not. I'm thinking in orbital curves. And if I have my calculations right, which I know I have, then we are going to run out of time much sooner than we originally believed.'

'What are you talking about?' asked Padre. 'Are we out by a month or two?'

'Possibly worse than that. We thought we had a few months to study our situation and make our plans. Every indication supported that theory. I totally agreed with it. I have been working with engineer Bradley to find alternative thruster sources and escape vehicles. We believed we could find a way to scatter our personnel and that everyone could find their way to Mars, or at least the asteroid belt. We just needed a few months.'

'Come on, Einstein, out with it. How long have we got?'

'Sorry, Padre, we may be looking at nothing more than a matter of weeks.'

'Shit,' said Bradley, 'then it looks like we desperately need that paddle.'

~*~

9: Man the lifeboats

Antisoc-Outer was stuck in a lazy, looping spin which at least gave it some Coriolis force and a degree of working gravity. The number of colonists lost to space was as yet unknown. The lesser fear was that the final numbers would prove large; the greater that they could prove disastrous.

Teams were still working to find out the true extent of the damage. There was also some research being carried out to try to ascertain exactly what it was that had struck them. Bandit laboured with human scientists and ship AIs to play back recordings of the event and analyse the available data.

The results were confusing. Something relatively small yet incredibly dense had struck the colony with a thankfully glancing blow. It had been moving at a fantastic speed, any slower and the damage done would have probably been instantly lethal. What happened had been caused by the briefest kiss in passing. The survivors were still counting the cost of that kiss.

The first and most important task was to find out if the core structure of the colony had been compromised. A gash had been ripped through a good-sized quadrant of its construction and some sections of latitudinal ribbing were gone. However, most of the longitudinal reinforcements were still firmly in place.

The original prison design had used a development of geodesic building techniques combined with crystalline growth patterns. It was built to be strong because it was believed that some inmates' friends might use explosives to break in and try to free them. Others worried that some inmates' enemies might use those same explosives in an attempt to destroy them. Either way Antisoc had been designed for war.

The drive was undamaged and most of the rescue ships were still tethered to the colony by monofibre chords as strong as anything in civilised man's toolbox. The ships had been badly jostled and some of them were a mass of superficial activity while droids circled around them to carry out repairs.

The fabric torn away from the big rock had been directly over a few of the larger dens in the outer layer, including the hangar-sized space converted to house the gangs who had demanded access to the rescue transports.

Lase and his cronies would be meeting their very own flight of valkyries about now, thought the Builder during a rare quiet moment. He hoped the ladies would be large-breasted, blonde and, preferably, on Harley Davidson hover speedsters. He also hoped they liked beards.

He shook his head, sighed and applied himself to his day. The big man didn't have much time for random musings so soon after the attack. He was too busy firefighting, sometimes literally.

The fires were largely electrical and most had been quickly doused. Fumes were vented away into space – as were the suffocated dead. Many of the more civilised niceties had been discarded during the emergency. Survival was the lexicon for the present. His back ached and he wondered if it was due to the hard crack he'd felt when he hit the wall, or whether it was thanks to the impossible load he was bearing on his broad shoulders. He was grateful for the support he was getting but wished there could be a little bit more. Gimlet Palfrey had pulled himself together and started to round up any useful technicians to help with the rebuilding.

Rebuilding? This is more like shoring up flooded riverbanks with sandbags.

Lardman had been found dead with his withered widow. His body was completely untouched. Medical opinion posited that the man's heart had surrendered to shock, but there was no time for an autopsy and nobody was prepared to open his fat-robed carcase for a good look inside.

Those who had to carry his obese form to the big airlock heartily wished the fat man had lived long enough to get there under his own steam. The low gravity helped, but not much.

The paper-thin old woman's corpse almost floated along in Lardman's wake.

The numbers on Builder's screen kept mounting at a dangerous pace. Damage reports, living volume lost, logistical problems, number of colonists injured, how many critical, the number of dead... The only numbers that remained static were for the healthy and actively helpful. Gimlet had started arresting any colonists who refused to lend a hand with the clear-up operations.

'There's never been room for anarchy during an hour of desperate need,' he said. 'Lend a hand or lose an arm' had become his latest catchphrase.

Frostrós seemed to be everywhere, delivering messages, helping with the injured and carrying her own weight in rubble. Every time she passed him she would squeeze his shoulder or offer him a peck on the cheek. He wondered if, somehow, saving his life had made her think of him as her pet. At one point he had ordered her to the rescue ships – she was young enough, but she had stubbornly kept quiet and gazed at her feet until he shut up. He got the message: she was staying put.

'How are we doing, Bandit?'

'Hi, Builder. Sorry I haven't been in touch before. Busy – you know how it is.'

'I'm sure you are. If I'm interfering just tell me to get lost.'

'Well... No, it's fine. What do you want to know?'

'Simple question: are we viable?'

'Simple answer: yes we are. But we couldn't survive another attack like that.'

'What hit us? Was it natural or man-made?'

'I think neither.'

The Builder and his AI spoke for several minutes. At the end of that time he felt none the wiser, thanked Bandit and it went back to its duties. The big man raked his clawed fingers hard through his scalp and squeezed his eyes shut tight. He became aware of a strange noise and then realised he was hearing himself groan. *I need a holiday from this nightmare.*

A small hand pressed against his. He opened his eyes.

She looked like a fawn about to bolt. Energy coursed through her so hard it almost made her quiver.

God, he realised, *when did she become beautiful?*

'You remember when I first came to you?' Frostrós said.

He nodded.

'You remember that thing I showed you?'

'Yes.'

'I need to show it to you again. You need to see it again.'

He didn't question her about it this time. 'Can I get there in this?'

He slapped his hand against the side of his floating chair.

She looked back over her shoulder, visualising the route.

'No. No, I don't think you can. Owww!' She clenched her fists in frustration, hopping from one foot to another in an agonised little dance. 'But you need to see this, you really do.'

'Wait,' he said. 'I'll be five minutes.'

He floated through the door to his private quarters. The door closed behind him. The girl sat in a chair and gazed blankly at his door. She wondered what strange rabbit he would pull from his hat this time. He was true to his word. Five minutes later the door opened and the Builder strode out, his teeth clenched in a rictus of pain.

'I hate these things,' he said. 'They cut ribbons out of my stumps and if get my balls caught in the hip saddle I'll need help to free them.'

He stood over two metres tall in a polished black exo-skeleton. Frostrós got a glimpse of how the man must have looked before his accident all those years before. Something got tight in her throat and chest.

'Wow!'

'Yeah, right. Pain in the arse. More "ow" than "wow". I've taken some pain killers. Shall we go before they wear off? Please?'

'You look like a knight in armour.'

'Yeah, and I'll be spending the night in agony. Now, let's go.'

Few of the inhabitants of Antisoc-Outer had ever seen Builder in anything other than his chair. There was an astonished stir as he walked tall among them on his lacquered metal and ceramic legs. The artificial legs were uncomfortable, it was true, but caused nothing like the discomfort he claimed.

He had learned years before that in his chair he could earn respect from, and work well with, the most extreme sociopaths in the colony, and there were a good number of those. In his chair he had never been a threat. On these powerful legs he would have proved too much of a challenge. He would have had to fight to survive.

So I kept my arse in my chair and got on with my job of trying to make complete anarchists kiss and make up instead of biting each other's heads off for the fun of it.

It took him a while to get back into the stride of it, but the exo-skeleton had been custom-made for him, much like his chair. He was soon clambering after Frostrós with practised dexterity.

It took time but Builder finally remembered how to let his artificial legs' tireless muscles do the work. He had forgotten how good it felt to be on his own two feet, even when those feet were of state-of-the-art Sino/European manufacture.

The girl was equally undaunted by their passage through wreckage-strewn corridors and across rubble-choked archways. She clambered over everything, fleet as a mountain creature. Finally she led him up the stairs to the viewing platform and stood silently beside him. Without thinking she took his hand; he squeezed hers back.

And there it was in the sky. The cloud beast. It looked like a livid bruise on the face of night. Fire burned in rippling sheets. Builder was reminded of a channel documentary he had once seen about volcanoes on Jupiter's moons. Especially the sulphurous Titan, a planet-sized moon constantly riven by the gas giant's gravitational forces and subject to huge geothermal forces. The moon had seemed to be on the point of ripping itself apart.

The cloud beast looked like that, a red-hot bed of angry heat and energy. A jet of super-heated plasma reached out towards him and he realised the thing was testing its reach. It was getting closer.

'Builder,' said Frostrós in a quiet yet steady voice, 'my love.' She paused at that as if surprised to hear the words coming from her own mouth. 'My love,' she said again with more confidence. 'We really need to get moving, don't you think?'

The torrent of flame out there in deep space was as nothing to the storm raging in his heart.

'I promise,' he said. 'I promise.' And he bent down to kiss her mouth for the first time since he'd nearly drowned. She kissed him back, hard.

~*~

10: Campus conversation

Professor Fan Cheung had become very aware that many of his most important Earth Senate contacts had suddenly gone off-line, but he wasn't concerned. He wasn't stupid like most people and hadn't left his trail out where any passing terrorist could pick it up.

Henderson was gone, natural causes apparently. Grillo had walked off a travellator for some reason – messy, and that cute-arsed Colonel with the flinty eyes, what was her name? Drowned in her bath. He would have liked to see that, especially if she'd been face down. *Never mind, it's too cold to think about hot arse.*

He had left his class of chattering students at the close of day and once more taken his favourite walk through the gathering twilight, past the great Codrington Library and along the quad towards his spacious quarters. His breath clouded in the purpling gloom. Shadows seemed to cluster closer together as if for warmth and his face stung as though it had been spanked by a frozen hand. The Oxford air was filled with the threat of ice and a nagging, gelid breeze tugged at his billowing robes.

None of which dimmed the brightness of his mood. His heart was filled with pride to be part of something like All Soul's College and the fact that every day he was allowed to enjoy architecture dating back to the fourteenth century. He gave a wry smile at the fact that some of the college's newest renovations had been carried out during the Tudor period. He felt immersed in history and saw himself as just one more robed figure in a column of College Professors stretching away into the distant past.

Something tugged at his peripheral vision. A small form seemed to be following him through the gathering darkness. For a moment he thought it might be a cat. He stopped and squinted into the quad's shadows, wishing that the College still employed a corps of dedicated torch bearers who would always be on hand to light his way. He decided it was nothing, probably just a little droid going about its business. He wrapped his robes more tightly around his slender frame and hastened his pace.

In some ways we've moved forward, he mused. *In others we've stepped backwards. Well, with the work I'm doing I'll soon be dragging us out into the light.*

A light flared briefly behind him and he saw his shadow bloom bat-like across the lawns and cobbled pathways, darkness moving on darkness. And then it was gone. A sudden chill pricked the hair on the back of his neck and washed down his spine like ice-water. He shivered and tried to shake off a sudden and unexpected sense of dread. *Best get indoors.*

His quarters were in the modern section of the college campus where the playing fields had once been. The playing fields, lawns and ancient trees had all been carefully preserved and once the building was finished they had been installed up on the roof. From the air nothing about the ancient college grounds looked any different. From ground level a four-storey marvel of stunning architectural beauty had sprung into being. Its subtle arches and DuraGlass walls echoed the original architect's work without mimicking them. He wondered what old Henry Chichele, the college's co-founder along with King Henry VI, would have made of them.

He turned to look at the silhouetted old college he loved so much, then back to the new buildings. His view was blocked by the tall figure of a gaunt, white-haired man in a long, heavy coat.

Cheung keyed his implant to call for assistance.

'That isn't going to work.'

The smiling, sardonic voice came from behind him at ground level. He looked around and down. A cat grinned up at him, baring its teeth.

'Professor Cheung?'

The gaunt man spoke with a heavily accented, gravelly voice. It demanded attention.

'Get out of my way. You have no right to be here.'

'Yes, Major. It's him alright.'

Cheung didn't even see the fist that struck him down like a poleaxe. He hit the ground with a boneless crack that was instantly swallowed by the misty evening air. He came round to a splitting headache and a furry, feline face just inches from his nose.

It was warm and light. Groaning, he rubbed at a painful lump on the back of his skull. He looked around.

'These are my quarters. How did you get in here?'

'We had you, Professor. We used you as a battering ram. That's why your head hurts.'

The Major remained silent. The cat did the talking.

Cheung tried to stand but was pushed back into his seat. One of his arms was tender and he had a scrape along the edge of his left hand. He supposed the Major had dragged him here.

'What is it you want?'

'The Major here wanted to beat you to death in the quad. You annoy him and he hates wasting time. I wanted to get a closer look at a mass murderer. You'll have to forgive me. Despite rumours to the contrary, we cats thrive on curiosity.'

The toothy grin widened. Cheung's eyes spun from one to the other. He felt as though he had fallen through a gap in reality and woken up somewhere insane.

'What the fuck are you talking about?' More pointedly to the cat, 'And what the fuck are you anyway?'

'I? Why my loathsome friend, I'm the Cat. Capital "C" by the way. First name "Cheshire", also with a capital "C". This good man here is Major Spartak Shimkovich, of Moscow's GUVD. He has a bad temper sometimes but always for the best reasons. He doesn't like pus-soaked cretins who kill innocent strangers. And he really seriously doesn't like you. I can tell. I'm sensitive to such things.'

'What's this all about?' The Professor was beginning to shout. 'Really, you have the wrong man. Please, if you want money…'

The slap across his face rocked him hard into the solid arm of his chair. It impacted an area that was already bruised and drove the breath from his lungs. For the first time he became truly afraid.

'What is it you think I've done? Please, you've got the wrong man. I'm innocent.' *I'm begging to a cat. This is madness.*

'I was expecting something more original from you, Professor,' the Cat purred, coldly. 'After all, for a cretin − even a pus-soaked one − you are quite bright. You are the man who came up with the idea for the Nimbus Protocol, a scheme that saw two billion innocent people killed in a matter of hours. You even engineered the scanners that were retro-fitted to *The Guardians.* I know all about you, Professor Cheung. Oh, my word, yes. You see, I was the systems integration specialist who made it all work that day − and your grubby little hands were all over every part of it. You left your signature everywhere, Cheung.'

'I was following orders.'

'One more cliché like that, Professor, and the Major asks the next questions. With his fists.'

The man squirmed in his chair, his breath coming in rapid gasps. Tears were streaming from his eyes and mucus from his nose.

'We had to do it,' he panted, his voice high and cracked. 'Those poor fuckers were infected with squids. There was no cure, still isn't. We had to do something, we had to. Surely you see that? It was the only answer to an impossible situation. We had to.'

'Alright, you say you had to, but why, since then, have you been killing everyone involved in researching the disease? Why have you been killing all those innocent people? They weren't infected with anything but knowledge.' The Major spoke in a flat growl. Something in his eyes drained every ounce of hope from Cheung's heart.

He spoke weakly, 'We had to do it. What would people say? History couldn't be allowed to record what we'd done. Two billion people died, what was a few thousand more? Nothing. The world goes on. Listen, out there. Silence. Where's all the weeping and the gnashing of teeth? Nothing. Nobody cares.'

208

He wiped the back of his hand across his mouth and nose. It came away sticky. 'It might have been an accident, you see. Yes, an accident. We pushed the button and then it couldn't be stopped. Tragic, yes tragic, but an accident. We did it for people's morale... You must understand. Please!' He wept openly.

'Fuck me sideways with a revolving steel pineapple,' said the Cat in an incredulous voice. 'This bastard actually believes everything he's saying. Well, that alters everything. Come on, Major, let's get out of here. I need some clean air.'

The Cat leapt lightly to the floor and headed towards the outer door. The Major followed it.

'Wait,' said Cheung, 'wait.'

The odd pair paused and looked back at him, silently.

'So, you're not going to kill me?'

'No.' the Cat tilted its head to one side. 'No, we were never going to do that.'

'But, but you said...'

'Good evening, Professor.'

The gaunt man and the Cat opened the door and a wall of frozen air rolled into the warm room, bringing with it a fresh tasting sense of reality regained. Weak with relief, Cheung staggered to the open door, planning to slam it shut and lock the nightmare of the last hour of so firmly out of his life.

That was when he saw the bulky guard droid standing sentinel at the top of the broad flight of stairs. The Major and the Cat were walking past it without a care in the world.

'Stop them!' he shouted. 'Kill them. They threatened me – stop them. I order you to kill them!'

The droid swivelled to look at the pair's receding forms. It then turned towards Cheung. With a chattering roar it opened fire with both cannons. Professor Fan Cheung was thrown backwards into his apartment by the impact of dozens of shells. His body was instantly riddled into a torn flag of bloody shreds and shattered bone. Most of his door and its surround disintegrated under the onslaught.

Lights came on all over the campus.

The Cat looked up at the Major. 'No, we were never going to kill him, were we.'

'No,' growled the Russian, 'let a machine do it.'

'No need to get personal.'

'Sorry.'

~*~

11: Pray for grace, and sing hallelujah

'They're doing what?'

Builder looked at Gimlet with despair in his eyes.

'I swear by my incubator. It's the truth.'

'I give up, I fucking give up. You say they're praying to the cloud?'

'Well, more like… singing?'

'Singing *what*?'

'*Gloria in excelsis, Deo*. Glory be to God in the highest.'

'To a cloud. In fact to a cloud that's trying to kill us. Brilliant.'

Gimlet performed an embarrassed wriggle in his chair and licked nervously at the air. Frostrós sat silently, her legs drawn up to her chin. The Builder was still wearing his exo-suit and black lacquered legs. His stern presence filled the room like a thundercloud.

'Man,' said Gimlet, 'they see you like this, Builder, they'll soon start singing a different tune.'

'I don't care,' answered the powerful man. 'We don't have time for this shit. We're nearly ready to move Antisoc out of the immediate shitstorm and set her en route to Iapetus. We need her balanced or she'll start to tumble and who knows what happens then?'

'I do,' said Bandit's disembodied voice.

'Yeah? What?'

'You've got half the survivors crammed together in a single outer den singing hymns, and transmitting the songs out on an open frequency. That puts too much weight into one place that I can't compensate for. We are starting to roll already. Those people are like the spinning stone on the end of a length of string. They have to either be dispersed throughout the colony or move to a more central place.'

'Centre core's dangerous. People there are unstable,' offered Frostrós from deep in her chair.

211

'Yes,' agreed Bandit, 'but we need to perform this manoeuvre very soon or we'll be engulfed by the cloud beast.'

'Gimlet, with me. Frostrós, you stay here. Anything happens I need to know, 'plant me.''

Builder had fitted the girl with an implant just days before. She had taken to it like a bee to honey and the slight bruising to her palm was already fading fast. She lifted her right hand palm out.

'Ready and able, boss.'

He grinned. 'Okay, girl. Thanks.' To Gimlet, 'Ready?'

'Ready and able and scared shitless, milord boss man.'

'These are righteous people, Gimlet. Have faith.'

'I'd rather have a pulse cannon and some stun grenades, like the old days.'

'Yes, dude, but in the old days they were using them on you.'

'Truth in that, milord, truth in that. Ah, shit. Come on then. Let's go to work.'

The few colonists they met were all busy at the same task, reinforcing the structural integrity of their home before the big move. They watched Builder walking past with something like awe. Some of them cried out with positive messages or statements of hope.

'With you, Builder.'

'Let's get going.'

'Crossing fingers here until tomorrow, boss.'

'Say one thing,' said Gimlet. 'They're a lot friendlier now that they don't have to call you "Warden" and that's a fact.'

Builder didn't answer that. He didn't know how.

The building work going on all over the colony's fabric would have made his progress difficult in his floating chair, if not impossible. He remembered when Antisoc was still called ESP Bulwark and the walkways were always clear and kept clean by trustees who would bow to him and touch their foreheads as he passed. He had also often heard them spitting behind him and then mopping up the sputum.

Since moving out to the edges of civilised space and becoming a free colony, a lot had changed. It wasn't as clean perhaps, and some of the inmates had tried to revert to their previous nefarious activities with varying success, but he would rather be breathing the tainted free air of Antisoc than the disinfected pall of despair that permeated an Extreme Space Prison.

Gimlet talked incessantly, something he always did when he was nervous. He almost vibrated with anxiety and walked with a coiling jig involving his shoulders and hips. His unnaturally long neck was twisting and turning as if he wanted to see around every corner and into every shadow. His long and narrow tongue slithered in and out of his mouth. Briefly the Builder wondered if his friend was still a virgin, then chided himself for having such an indiscreet thought. *Who cares either way?*

The walk out to the den was long and arduous and Builder's hips were beginning to smart in their black ceramic girdle. He would ache that night. They began to hear their destination when they were still several metres from its entrance. The noise built exponentially to a sound like waves crashing against rocks.

It was evidently hundreds of voices raised in song but behind the massed volume was a single voice, deep, sonorous and powerful. Its words cracked and boomed around their heads. Gimlet stopped in mid-step.

'Oh, fuck. He's come out here. Why would *he* come out here?'

Builder looked askance. 'Who?'

'Core preacher, Mealmouth Cockcrow – his own, very loud self. I've heard him spout his bullshit for hours without ever breathing in. I'm sure he breathes through his ass 'cause his mouth sure never stops moving long enough.'

They couldn't quite make out the words yet but the voice wove a dark enchantment, bucking and breaking and rolling with passion. Their chests swelled and their minds filled with a desire to please the voice, earn its praise. They fought hard against it.

'He's got some kind of hypnosis vibe he plays with,' said Gimlet.

'The fuck you say? I can feel something. He a telepath?'

'Nothing that sophisticated. He don't charm no birds from the trees but he can sure pull the wool over most people's eyes.'

'Yeah? Well you can fool most people some of the time, and some people all of the time, but you won't fool Builder any of the time. Here we are. Now, let's see what we're playing with.'

When the door opened the sound that washed over them was like a physical force. They were momentarily disoriented and looked around themselves wildly. Gimlet cringed away and Builder swayed backwards as if in the face of a powerful storm.

No wonder Bandit's worried about the weight here, he thought. *There must be nearly a thousand people here, all crammed into a den fit for two hundred at most. This is insane.*

Gimlet stood with his mouth open. He might have been screaming but the sound was drowned in an ocean of noise.

Nothing served in standing here like a post. Job to do.

Builder pushed his way through the swaying, howling mob. Out in the walkway their song had retained some semblance to a hymn, but walking there in the people's midst it was just nonsense sound, raw and primitive with an edge of violence.

Sometimes it's handy to be wearing an old military exo-suit, he thought. *Especially one with a built-in military-grade loudhailer.*

Builder clicked a button at his throat.

'PLEASE, STAND ASIDE!'

The people in his immediate vicinity were cowed by a booming sound that overarched even their song. They faltered.

A black giant strode through their ranks. Behind him a worm-like figure wriggled along and squeezed its fists into its ears. Some of them knew the Builder, but not like this. Not as an avenging demon on legs of steel and wearing a suit of dark iron.

Many of them had become so caught up in Cockcrow's religious spell they saw the Builder as an avenging force come to chastise them. If he had called down lightning upon them they wouldn't have been surprised.

'YOU PEOPLE MUST DISPERSE, NOW! YOU ARE IN GREAT DANGER HERE! GO BACK TO YOUR HOMES!'

Some of the milling crowd started to move towards the exit. Builder began to relax. This was going to be easier than he'd thought.

'And who are you, black-lacquered crow, to call the people from sweet redemption and drive them deep, deep into the path of shame?'

Mealmouth Cockcrow's words had parted the sea of people as if by magic and Builder found himself facing the core preacher across several metres of clear space. He was an extraordinary creature, tall and lean but with a mighty chest and thick neck that looked borrowed from someone of a much more powerful physique. His hair and beard were untended and thick, with wild streaks of silver grey lacing their dusty blackness. His dress was grey and black robes belted with a black and white braided rope. Metallic tracery glinted through the cloth and the rope.

His face, what little of it was visible in the midst of the matted web of hair, was fascinating. Patrician nose, long and commanding, and eyebrows flaring up above eyes of an almost delicate beauty, almond-shaped and bright, the whites clean and the corneas a liquid golden colour like candlelight shining through vintage scotch whiskey.

For a moment Builder was held mute by the preacher's sheer presence, and then a voice at his shoulder said, 'Look at him. He's no more natural than me.' Gimlet then shouted, 'Hey, Cockmouth, your father was a test tube and your mother was an incubator. You're a circus act and not a very good one at that – half man, half chicken. You should stick to waking people up in the morning, Cockmouth.'

Mealmouth Cockcrow's face swelled with rage and he ran with a surprising turn of speed to grasp the snake man's shoulders.

'You are a vile thing,' he boomed, 'an abomination in the eyes of God. Such as you should be burned with fire – clean, white fire.'

He shook Gimlet like a rag.

'That's enough,' warned Builder. 'Let him go.'

The preacher maintained his grasp despite Gimlet's increasingly frantic efforts. Then Cockcrow turned his face towards Builder and smiled. The light in his eyes had seemed to have become suffused under his taut skin. He glowed, and when he opened his mouth it shone inside like hot coals.

'He shall burn,' the preacher roared with a gloating laugh.

And then he exploded like a phosphorous grenade and Gimlet had no time to scream before he too was consumed by the sudden blaze of naked heat. Builder shielded his eyes and stepped towards the dual human torch but the welded figures had already fallen and splashed like molten wax onto the dirty Duracrete floor. Roasted flesh peeled away from scorched bone. The blackened skeletons split and burst in the plume of white plasma while the two bodies twisted and curled into the stance of boxers, fists raised defensively.

A groan of fear rippled through the throng and he realised his voice was among them. He was gasping in shock. Gimlet was dead. Gimlet was burned and gone. The stink of roasted flesh made him retch. Then he suddenly realised a small voice was repeating his name over and over again. Reality slammed back into focus. It was Frostrós whispering through his implant.

'Builder... Builder... Builder, please... please help me, Builder...'

He turned and began to run. Behind him people watched his rapidly retreating back. At what they saw as an act of extreme cowardice by a man they had once respected, many of them spat on the floor.

~*~

216

Part 5: Convergence point

1: Dream me a river, of fire

When Ruth Pearce woke up it was with a shriek that brought Freedman running. He had grown used to his housemate's nighttime habits over the course of time. He didn't really understand the aegis of her dreams but he had a strong inkling that one of them might well have saved his life when they were back in London. Fear, fuelled by Ruth's dream about his sacrifice in a stone circle, was the catalyst for their retreat to the tranquillity and safety of Ruth's West Country beach house.

Weeks later Milla told them about the man she had seen murdered and scalped in a shoe shop; told them that his hair had looked almost identical to Freedman's, and that when she had read the Weaver's mind she discovered that the killer had, indeed, originally targeted Freedman. Since then the odd couple had lived a quiet life in the luxury home built into the side of a cliff, with frequent forays to the local markets for fresh supplies.

They had heard about Katy's assassination and Su Nami's retaliation. They heard how the toxic power behind so many deaths was being drained away by Milla and her team, and that a number of Earth Senate bigwigs were suffering from an epidemic of untimely demise. The danger was being chipped away, piece by rotten piece.

Yet still there were dreams, and whatever vision had woken Ruth from deep slumber that night had reduced the woman to a rare state of sweating panic.

'The sky rained fire. I saw the heavens burn. I saw you burn, Freedman.'

Freedman sat on her bed and hugged her, rocking her silently as she blurted out details of her nightmare into his patient ears. These two had never become lovers or shared a bed. Instead they shared something more important and fundamental.

Freedman needed to take care of people – it was at the core of his personality. If someone had cut him in half, he always joked, they would have found the word 'care' written through him like the name of a seaside town through a stick of rock. He had no ulterior motives. He just needed to feel useful.

Ruth had once been the most famous glamour model on Earth and was the widow of a very rich man. Despite her blonde beauty, life hadn't been kind. She had been bullied at school, used as a cash cow by her venal parents, and become the prime target for lecherous film-makers, producers, and even complete strangers, for a number of years.

She didn't need a lover, she needed a friend. Someone she could share her life with, someone she could laugh with, experience her day with, and feel respected by. Someone who wanted to be with her for herself and not just her stunningly beautiful looks.

She and Freedman fit together like a lock and its key. They had become inseparable. And when she needed him he would be there for her with a shoulder to cry on and a warm hug, even in the earliest hours of the morning.

'I want you to tell me what you saw, Ruth. But first, let me get us some coffee. Come on, let's go into the living room.'

By the time he brought the laden tray with coffee pot, mugs and cream, Ruth was sitting in her favourite chair facing the wall-sized DuraGlass window which looked out onto the house's terrace and the English Channel beyond.

A storm raged silently beyond the thick insulation of reinforced glass.

'It reminds me of Antarctica,' said Ruth. 'Cruel and beautiful at the same time.'

They sipped hot milky coffee in the peaceful, warm room while outside, winter winds tore the night to tatters. Freedman waited and watched. It didn't take long. It never did.

In a dreamy voice Ruth began to talk.

'It was an afternoon in early summer, or perhaps late spring. There were children playing down on the beach. We were on the terrace, Freedman, having lunch. We could hear their laughter. The sea was a turquoise sheet of silk and we could taste the bite of salt in the air while we ate our fish and bread, and drank our wine.

'It was a perfect day to share with someone. You were telling one of your stories and we were laughing together.' She turned her eyes on him. Her beautiful eyes. 'Freedman, have I ever told you how much I love you?'

She had, but he just smiled and remained silent.

'Then the colour of the sea changed to a deep purple and suddenly from nowhere a mist blew in. The children stopped what they were doing. You stopped talking and we both stood up. We walked together to the rail.'

Ruth stood up and walked to the window. A strange phosphorescent glow cast a pearlescent light across her perfect features. She drained her coffee.

'The world had become white like a blank page waiting for the writer to begin his tale. We held our breath. The whole world held its breath. Something was about to happen, but we didn't know whether it would be wonderful or a complete nightmare.

'Oh, Freedman. That was when the sounds began. It was such a strange noise, a kind of roaring and whooping. It wasn't natural, not to us. It was unearthly. It touched something here...' She held her belly. 'It reached down into my soul and pressed it and bile came up into my mouth. I was afraid then, afraid that something might happen to us. Happen to *you*.'

Her words fell flatly on the warm air. They dropped into Freedman's ears with a terrible, factual weight. He was there in that nightmare day, sharing it with her.

'The whiteness changed then. It moved and billowed like a sheet of linen on a windy day. It rolled and heaved, and then... And then,' she gasped, 'and then it tore from side to side and something huge and golden poured through. It looked so, so beautiful, so warm and rich and pure.

'And it fell onto the sea, and the sea opened to it like a red mouth. It was uncanny. The golden light filled the sea. And the sound changed. It began hissing and sputtering. It sounded just like hot fat on a griddle. And that was when we finally realised what was happening.' She turned to him.

'The sea, Freedman – the sea was boiling! The golden light was a tide of fire washing towards us, a waterfall of pure liquid flame falling from the sky. It was breathtaking. Then a wall of steam, salty and thick, reached us. It stank like sulphur. It stank like hell. We choked and the steam scalded, but we couldn't scream. The children could. We heard the children wailing in pain, but not for long. No, not for long.

'The fire swept onto the terrace and the last thing I saw was you, my love, you, blazing like fat kindling, fire jetting from your eyes and mouth. And then it was over and I woke up screaming. And you came to me, my sweet man. And you were alive again, your flesh back on your sweet face, your gentle eyes looking into mine.'

She walked back to his side and placed her mug on the tray. She held out her hands. 'Come on, my love. We have so little time. Please, take me to bed.'

She led him away. Behind them lightning scored its path across the sky. They didn't notice.

A few minutes later a startled peal of laughter rang out.

~*~

2: Padre's promise

'Come on, people. Can somebody please tell me what happened out there and what it means to us?'

He glared at the ranks of vacant faces in the main monitor room and bit back a fury of expletives. The Padre hadn't heard anything from Antisoc-Outer since its encounter with some sort of super-dense gravity bomb fired by the cloud beast. Einstein had gone off-line shortly after its as yet unexplained dark warning about a new timescale. The Padre was anxious about Bertrand, but also needed to know what was happening and, as usual, his corps of highly-paid specialist technicians were clueless.

'If any of you get any ideas, I'll be in my office. Feel free to come along and brainstorm. Don't worry about sounding silly. My door's always open.'

As soon as he was alone in his quarters he locked the door and let loose a stream of invective, not stopping until he felt his spleen was about to burst. He was filled with bile and frustration and practically spat poison into the air.

That was when he noticed Laura Bradley standing calmly by his desk holding a glass of cognac. She held it out to him.

'Einstein thought you might need this.'

He accepted it gratefully and sucked down its smoky, soothing heat; felt its warmth settle in his chest and belly. Then he looked at the woman sharply.

'Einstein? You've been talking to Einstein? It's been off-line for days, ever since...' He gestured roughly towards the ceiling. 'Since that thing happened.'

'Yes, Padre, sorry. I've been a little busy.'

The gentle voice of the AI was as welcome to the Sector Manager's peace of mind as the smooth spirit to his throat. Then he fired another question.

'Wait a second, hold on there. What do you mean "busy"? You co-ordinate the software for the entire sector. You have enough capacity to run a planet. What have you been doing that's kept you so busy? After scaring the shit out of us with your "final countdown" bombshell you've left me in the lurch with no one to talk with other than those fuckwits in the main monitor room.'

He turned to Bradley. 'And you've been missing in action for days too. So,' he looked around, 'what's the story, the pair of you?'

'May I speak first, engineer Bradley?' asked the AI. The tall woman nodded.

'Padre, the engineer and I have been working together on a relativity algorithm. What you would no doubt call a set of "ball-breaking sums". The cloud beast fired the gravity bomb at Antisoc-Outer. It has caused a great deal of damage but life support is still viable in the unbreached sections.

'We don't know the true manifest for the colony. It was believed to be something over two thousand, two hundred souls − but record-keeping has never been a priority for the residents there. During the breach it was estimated that over three hundred people were ejected into space and two of our ships were dragged into the gravity bomb as it passed. We lost both crews and all the colonists on board, more than ninety souls.

'Scans show there was no resultant debris from the lost ships. Not so much as an escape pod. All material and personnel dragged from the colony had also been vacuumed away. The area around Antisoc-Outer has never been so clean…'

'Is this really the time for levity, Einstein?'

'Not levity, Padre, merely observation. May I continue?'

'Please.'

'Thank you. The engineer and I have been liaising with Bandit and through it, the Builder…'

'He's well?'

'Sir, yes. Bandit says he's really found his feet in recent days, and he has a girlfriend.'

The Padre sputtered, 'Girlfriend? Really? Are you sure?'

'Oh yes, Bandit was very specific. He is surprisingly nimble in bed once he removes his exo-skeleton. But that is a side issue.'

'The colony has stabilised its environment and is working towards a planned withdrawal using both its thrusters as a main drive and our rescue ships as directional tugs. The ships' captains are also aware that if another gravity bomb is directed at them they must cut the traces and bolt. The people of Antisoc-Outer will have to fend for themselves after that.

'Our principal concern has been the gravity bomb itself. External feeds from Antisoc have proved very useful in analysing what it did when it merely grazed the colony. Please take a few minutes to study these visuals.'

Padre and Bradley sat in silence while Einstein replayed the scene, which had been captured from a number of angles. One viewpoint had been sucked at high speed towards the ball of incredibly dense material. It followed a number of human figures who, at first, were still struggling in a futile effort to escape. One of them, a long hirsute character, glinted like chromed metal as he fell. He was targeted by the AI and expanded.

'This one looks like he is wearing some sort of breastplate. That's useful because he is easier to clarify in the monitor. We can focus on what happens to him next.'

In slow motion they watched the man's head stretch away from his body. Then his shoulders dwindled to a point followed by his torso, belly, hips and legs.

'In my estimation,' opined Einstein, 'by the time his head reached the surface of the sphere it was little more than a few microns wide but ridiculously long. Again this is an estimation – but at this point...' – the image froze – 'the victim might have been over one-point-five klicks in length. This kind of phenomenon indicates an extraordinarily steep event horizon, something in the order of an ultra-micro-black hole.'

'These have been theorised,' said the engineer with some excitement. 'Space physicists believe they could be the hub between a rotating pair of stars.' The image changed and showed two white-hot stars in an evident binary pairing. Bradley stood and indicated a long, fine wisp of star matter that seemed to link them. Her finger hovered over a slight bulge at the centre of the wisp.

'According to Einstein that's just about the best image we're ever going to get of a micro-black hole, until we go out to where we can get a closer look. Say fifteen or more light-years from here. That bulge isn't the thing itself, but light from the star matter it's sucking into its core becoming occluded at its event horizon's surface. A sort of after-image if you like.'

'I'm not happy with the micro-black-hole idea,' continued Einstein. 'The maths aren't right. I think we're looking at a super-dense dwarf planetoid.'

'We can't be sure...'

'I think we can. A black hole, even one that size, would be pulling the solar system apart. It would be dragging Uranus out of its orbit and Saturn would be losing its rings followed by its atmosphere. Sorry, engineer Bradley, an artificial, super-dense planetoid would have exactly the effect of that gravity bomb without wrecking the system like a child shoving a stick through a spider's web. In fact I'm quite pleased it's not a black hole. At least it shows they have some sort of respect for the place where they live.'

'I'm really pleased that you're pleased, Einstein,' said the Padre, who was rapidly developing a severe pain just behind his left eye. 'But if you don't get down to the final nitty-gritty I promise I will make you suffer. I don't know how, but I'll find a way.'

'Sorry, Padre, but this is new science...'

He bellowed, 'Enough! Please, enough!' The Padre shook his head and lowered his voice. 'Please excuse me, Einstein, Bradley – it has been a *long* day. A *very* long day. Why are you telling me all of this when we have the cloud beast to worry about?'

'But, Padre, don't you see?' asked Einstein. 'That thing is coming directly at us now, and it's likely to arrive in less than two weeks.'

~*~

3: Loss

He couldn't remember how he got there. His mind was a confused muddle and even by the time he clattered to his outer office Builder could still smell the burnt meat stench of the preacher and Gimlet. He seemed to be running through a thick cloud of its stink. The taste coated his mouth, tongue and throat. He was breathing it. His nose was thick with it.

His outer office was empty when he pounded into it. He remembered he had sent his men away to perform tasks aimed at getting the colony ready for flight. But that was back before people had started to spontaneously combust before his eyes. Back when the world still worked according to known and accepted rules. Back when his day made sense.

He wondered if having his men with him in the preacher's den would have saved Gimlet from his terrible death. He doubted it. Attempting to wrench the preacher away from the lizard man would probably have lost him more people. What had happened back there made no sense. Builder's mind couldn't assimilate what it had just witnessed.

Just thinking about it brought the lizard man's last moments into fresh focus, the hybrid's wide-eyed terror and conflagration. *What fresh horror was that? What kind of strange day did I wake up to this morning? Or is this some kind of sick dream? No, not a dream. There would be no thankful waking from this. Focus,* he told himself. *Treat every second as truth. Get it wrong and you die.*

He approached his inner office door with caution after first carefully checking his suit's defences. The surface of his exo-suit was smooth and slick as windless lake water, something he remembered from his youth on Earth. But exactly like lake water his suit had hidden depths. Across the board he had green lights. He was powered up and ready for war. He had once been trained to fight a one-man war if he needed to. He had lethal skills and his suit held lethal secrets. He hoped he wouldn't need to deploy any of them on his home turf.

He flexed his shoulders and heaved a deep breath. Who was he trying to kid? His training had been too many years ago and even back then his trainers had told him he was weak as a fighter, too considerate of his opponent. He had always been the same with all competitions, including chess and checkers.

When he was a child he always let Phil win. Phil had to win, he needed to win. So Bertrand let him. His inherent compassion was the reason his legs had become shattered and useless. He would never forget that day when an apparently powerless and heavily pregnant prisoner had rolled around him and pulled the cord on her suicide vest using her teeth. He became the Builder that day. The Warden had died of shame.

He forced himself back to the current situation. Frostrós was in there and needed his help. For some reason Bandit was off-line again so he was working in the dark. He was thankful for his mechanically enhanced muscle. Without it he would have been useless in a fight. He took stock for a moment. His breath was coming in long, whining sobs, and his stumps were on fire. To get to Frostrós as fast as possible he had been pushing his exo-legs to their absolute limit and beyond, and the effort had taken its toll. He was exhausted, gasping and terrified about what he might find in there. *Okay, time to move.*

His office door was slightly ajar. He leaned back and then with all his strength slammed it wide open and leapt forward, landing in a weapons-ready crouch while checking for potential ambush. The door smashed hard into the wall. Nobody would survive that intact. He straightened up and looked around. His black knees clicked upright with oiled precision. *Spunk in the old horse yet.* Then his eyes focused.

He gasped. On the wide, white wall facing him his pictures and shelves had been torn down and somebody had scrawled the words *You're fucking next* in a row of large, roughly drawn and spiky letters using thick black lines. The letters had a carbonised, crumbly appearance. They glistened oddly.

He concentrated on the words for a moment because something else was there on the edge of his peripheral vision and he was trying hard not to look. It didn't help. His eyes were dragged down.

What met his gaze took him straight back to the events so recently witnessed at the outer den. Fire seemed to be following him around the colony. He took a few cautious steps forward. At the centre of the room his hover chair sat half melted behind a desk whose middle had collapsed into a charred, V-shaped mass of blackened litter. The side of his floating chair nearest the desk was a puddled mess of solid state circuitry glued to the floor. A tired, petulant voice at the back of his mind said *I'm fucked there. Take at least eleven months to organise a replacement.* He ignored it and examined the scene more closely.

There had obviously been an intense fire, but with a very limited field of damage. Even the nearby cloth-covered chairs were untouched. *I was lucky.* Then his breath caught in his throat. *What's that?* He stepped closer and saw something in the midst of the wreckage. The burnt flesh smell had become stronger, almost unbearable. He squinted down, his mouth dry and a growing sense of dread caused his pulse to pound. Yes, there it was.

Right at the heart of the damage lay the barely discernible outline of a human figure, crouched tight in the classic pugilistic pose of the cremated. This was the charcoal remains of someone who had been alive when the flame seared its flesh. Its torso was almost completely gone apart from the poignant arc of a few ribs but he could plainly see that in life the victim must have been small and slender. It looked familiar. Horribly familiar.

Darkness loomed forward from behind his eyes and nausea threatened to overwhelm him. He could only reach one conclusion about who lay there, but so soon after Gimlet it was too much to think about. Much too much. His mind fought vainly to skitter away somewhere calm, somewhere this nightmare wasn't happening.

Please, God, what's happening here? This is impossible.

But there was no escaping the facts. Frostrós – sweet, skinny little Frostrós had been the only person in this room. He knew that. He had left her there. It had to be her, lying there in the remains of his desk. Just a hollow black remnant, a lifeless trace of carbonised meat and bone.

He gagged and squirmed. He tried but couldn't drag his shocked eyes away from the tiny black heap of pathetic remains.

His mind fluttered behind his eyes. He was an intelligent man. He wanted someone to give him a reason for this… for this madness. He wanted something sensible he could deal with, something concrete he could grip and hold up to the light. But this? It made no sense.

It isn't fair. It just isn't fair. Frostrós! Frostrós! That burned and twisted thing was Frostrós. First Gimlet and now her.

It was too much. His mind had begun to swirl around in a jumble of impossible truths and it trembled on the brink of a final descent into complete hysteria. He was a strong man, but his foundations had been ripped away from under his feet. *Why fight it anymore? What's the point?*

His heart pounded against his ribs as if it demanded to be let fly free. A high-pitched, keening sound sawed at his ears and with the last shreds of his conscious mind he realised it was coming from between his own gritted teeth.

Something inside him burst like a lanced boil. It rushed into the open on an unstoppable tide of appalled grief.

'Frostrós!' he finally howled. 'Frostrós! No!'

He sobbed and his sturdy mechanical legs buckled under his failing body. He was choking on thick fumes from the still smoking corpse. He so desperately wanted to hold her, to comfort her. Touch her just one last time. He leaned forward and as he did so he felt heat wash across his face and hands and reeled back. Everything in life was black as pitch. It could no longer be suffered. Enough. He fell to his knees and sobbed incoherently.

'Builder!' A slight figure dashed from his private quarters and threw itself into his arms. He recoiled in shock and then looked at the newcomer.

'Frostrós,' he gasped. 'My God, it's you.'

He held her and his whole body shook uncontrollably. He wanted to hold her close, crush her against his body, press her inside himself and protect her from everything evil that was happening.

Then he held her at arm's length.

'God, girl, I thought you were dead.' He couldn't stop grinning for a moment, and then he frowned.

'But wait,' he said, 'if you're okay...' He indicated the charred remains with a tilt of his head. '...then who's that?'

She said it so calmly, without a hint of emotion, 'Him? He's my dad.'

'What the hell happened?'

'Well, he got a little heated.'

Builder rolled his eyes, 'Don't be so callous, it doesn't suit you. Do you really want a slap? Just tell me what happened.'

And she did.

~*~

4: The giant punctured ball

Milla, the Cat and Su Nami had relocated to an apartment on the south quadrant of London's sky tower less than forty-eight hours after the missile strike. It was slightly larger than Ruth's old home and a little lower down the tower. Ben had purchased the place through one of the Macready corporations and made sure that Milla's name was not used.

Effectively she was now invisible to Earth Senate.

Ben also told her that his work was finished and he would be home in a matter of days.

'Milla.'

'Not now.'

'Yes, now.'

'Ben's coming home soon and I need time to think. That comes first.'

'Then why not give him a home to come home to? Stop what you're doing – go bake a cake.'

The Cat rolled upright from its usual, inverted, floppy moggy position. It fixed her with its lambent eyes.

'Esper has been calling for you for days. You know that. You hear it, same as me. Difference is you choose to ignore it.'

'I hear. Yeah, I hear it.'

'Then what?'

Milla ignored the feline AI and resumed her kata. She was up in Ruth's old riding room working her way around a rope-bound composite post, kicking, slapping and punching at it with every ounce of energy she could bring to bear. A fine, aromatic cloud of perfumed sweat surrounded her. Light poured down from two rows of narrow windows set high in the walls. It highlighted her extraordinary, lithe beauty. It also plainly limned the annoyance playing across her fine features.

Milla liked to train hard, very hard. Through exercise she was able to reach her peak of mental clarity, and that helped her play through whatever concerned her most at the time. She was tugging her current state of play with Earth Senate out of the shadows and more completely into the light of reason. She and her team had been killing the brains behind the Nimbus Protocol. She thought about the men and women who had been targeting the great corps of innocent civilians who knew that the Nimbus Protocol had been designed to deliberately slaughter the infected. The aim was to ensure that history carried the sanitised version of events into the future. Milla Carter had other ideas.

Ben would be able to add more flesh to the bones of the situation when he got home, but she desperately wanted all her known ducks in a row first.

And then the Cat disturbed her train of thought and her ducks happily swam off in all directions. She was livid.

Her concentration had been broken, but all of her physical power was still intact. Well trained long levers would do the most damage and her legs were long and strong. Her spine was like a whip. Thinking darkly of the Cat, she had spun to deliver a precisely positioned strike. The top half of the post was blasted free and hit the far wall with a loud clatter. She had to react fast in order to leap away from its rebound.

'Broke it,' said the Cat.

'Fuck the hell off, will you?"

"Call Esper."

"Let me shower."

"Esper."

Milla? May we talk?

Can it wait?

Sorry, but no.

May I shower first?

It is important, Milla, daughter.

Good, great, then frankly, if the world isn't falling apart right now, it can wait.

She stormed back down to the apartment, swept into her room and peeled off her practice kit. Sweat-soaked leggings and gym top came away with a damp, sucking noise. Naked, she stalked barefoot into her bathroom and bounced under her shower. She turned it on.

Water cascaded down her body and she felt the grime of her training session begin draining away. She added soap and began to lather her hair. Under the warmth of the water and gentle massaging effect of the stream she began to relax. She always enjoyed the firm touch of her own hands when she showered, but soon Ben would be back and it would be his strong, hard hands touching her instead. Soon. She closed her eyes and smiled in anticipation.

It is important, Milla, daughter.

She almost shrieked with frustration.

Give me five freaking minutes will you?

She finished her shower, bound her hair in a towel and slipped into a short, white robe before stomping back into her bedroom. She lay on the bed, snorted in irritation, and closed her eyes.

Her mind's eyes opened in space far from Earth. Before her was something massive that, at first, looked like a partly punctured ball. It was not quite perfectly round. At one end of the ball was mounted a mass of smaller thrusters encircling a giant one. The design looked makeshift but robust.

At the other end a motley collection of spacecraft performed a stately rotation around an invisible hub. Milla saw, with a degree of surprise, that the ships were all tethered to the ball, which was also rotating. Tiny craft buzzed around like midges over a pool of rank water. There was a lot going on. Beads of light flashed all over the ball's surface, especially around the edges of a shallow gouge that looked somehow sucked or blown out rather than ripped. Glittering shards of raw material had been thrust out into the wan sunlight. Whatever had happened it had happened quite recently – the damage looked fresh. Everywhere else was darkened with a layer of dust and ridged with ice. Slight scars painted the ball as if it had been bombarded by dirty snowballs. Strangely there was no debris field around the gouge.

The sun was a tiny yet brilliant white dot far, far beyond the ball, which partially eclipsed its rays. Shadows here had an odd, crimson cast, she realised. She wondered why. She turned.

Raging across space was the cloud beast. She had seen it close up before, but that had been out at the very furthest reaches of the solar system. In spirit she had burst through the very fabric of the cloud and out into the wide universe beyond. She had read its collective mind. Seen its aching envy. Felt its hatred for everything human.

'It would be impressive if it wasn't so petty and acting so much like a petulant child.'

Esper floated by her side.

'How am I here?' Milla asked without preamble. 'I thought the construct collapsed when you merged and became *one*?'

'The tree house fell down but the tree still stands,' answered Esper, enigmatically. 'Dream remains. I remain. The Gardener has taken a personal interest in me, and this that I do. It has been allowed. The Gardener has also taken a very specific interest in you. It likes you.'

'The Gardener?'

'You have met it on at least two occasions.'

Milla remembered encountering a vast vault of amused intelligence. She had met it first out in intergalactic space and then again within the solar system. She remembered asking it, 'Did you follow me?' And its answer, 'No, I have always been here.'

'Yes,' she replied to Esper.

Esper studied the fire-streaked entity that seemed to be getting closer with each passing second. Milla did the same. Sometimes the cloud creature was clear as air, clean as vacuum. Sometimes it scorched the sky – bright, blazing hot.

'So very ancient,' said Esper. 'Extremely primitive yet sophisticated at the same time, much like humans. Clever, clever monkeys. But still, I didn't ask you here for a chat. I need you to warn the people of Antisoc-Outer.'

Milla and Esper turned their eyes back to the damaged sphere.

'The last refuge of the dispossessed and the first habitat to be reached by the Swarm,' said Esper. 'Nearly two thousand lives grubbing along at the edge of space. Hopes, dreams, love. It will all be gone if the Swarm has its way.'

Milla looked back at the cloud beast. The Swarm. That was a good name for it.

'And why am I here?'

'Because you can talk with a man called Builder. He is the nearest thing they have to the person in charge. Your mind can reach him, warn him.'

'Warn him about what?'

'The Swarm. It is pyrokinetic. Once its target is in range it can burn anything organic that contains phosphorous. Phosphorous is an important ingredient in human tissue. And right now Antisoc-Outer is coming into range. We may already be too late. That cloud could already be burning colonists.'

236

5: The burning finger of fate

Frostrós had told him her story while they were still alone. Before reinforcements found them. She described how her father had stumbled into the inner office in a blind, drunken rage. He was shouting incoherently.

He was a small man and skinny, wiry, and he walked and waved his arms about with an almost poetical lack of co-ordination. He had spat curses at his daughter when she told him to leave. Snarled like a madman.

'His face was a very strange colour,' she said, 'like he'd been standing over a stove or something. The inside of his mouth was kind of... bright, you know?'

Builder thought of the preacher's last moments. 'Yes, I know what you mean.'

She continued, 'I could feel heat rolling off him. He was sweating right through his clothes. His eyes were wild. He started ripping stuff off your wall there. Kept screaming your name. He was totally crazy. I tried to stop him but he hit me in the face.'

She held her jaw up for his perusal. A livid bruise was already blooming to the surface of her pale skin. Builder touched her there gently, then kissed the spot. She winced a little, then kissed his cheek.

'And then?' he asked.

'And then things got really wild. Freaky in fact. Look, Builder...' She gazed hard into his eyes. '...I promise you I'm not making any of this up. *Promise* you.'

He nodded. His eyes held hers with tender regard.

She continued, holding her hand up in front of her face to illustrate her point: 'Then the fingers of his right hand just flared up like some kind of firework – *whoosh*!'

She drew her left hand up over her right as if she was discarding a glove.

237

'The sound was really horrible, a kind of bubbling, spitting noise.' She shuddered. 'And then he started to write with his burning hand. The smell…'

Her eyes narrowed to fine slits.

'All the while he was pointing at me with his other hand and laughing. Like this mad fucking really mad laugh. But the flame was getting brighter and running up his arm into his face. His eyes started melting and his hair was on fire and he was still pointing and laughing. And then he started moving towards me. So I ran for it.'

Her eyes had become unfocused. She was reliving the scene moment by insane moment.

'I ran into your quarters and bolted the door, and then I locked myself in your bathroom and went to stand in the shower. I figured if he came after me in there I could turn the water on. It was better than nothing and I honestly didn't know what else to do. And then I started calling you on the 'plant, but you never answered. I didn't know what was happening, Builder. I thought, you know, maybe it was me who was going mad.'

A slight tremor passed through her wire-taut body.

'And then I heard you shouting my name and I knew you were here. I had to unlock the bathroom door and it wouldn't open and I was shouting, and then I got the door open and I unbolted the door to your office and there you were. And you were crying for me, my lovely, big man.'

She put the unbruised side of her face against his and in a quiet voice she said, right by his ear, 'I really fucking love you, big man.'

'I love you too,' he rumbled back.

'Good,' she whispered.

'Yeah, good.'

And then they heard running feet in the outer office and Builder's squad of armed trouble-shooters burst into the room, guns drawn and looking for trouble.

A little later he told her about Gimlet. By that time they had been interrupted by the cleaning and repair team turning up, ReCyc had taken away the charred body plus the remains of

Builder's desk and chair. Droids had busied themselves cleaning the floor and wiping away the stark warning on the wall.

The room was clean and the air sweet once more but nothing could scour the burnt meat stench from their memories.

They sat in his comfortable chairs and nursed a couple of very welcome drinks. A technician was working nearby trying to reconnect the office to the rest of the colony. The desk had contained Builder's admin and communication hub. Without it he only had his implant and in the current situation he patently needed more. The technician had arrived with a little canvas bag and a mournful expression. He examined the floor and the wall, all the while scratching at his head.

Based on the noises he was making, the fire must have caused a whole world of grief. A little later he was balancing working with his tools against slurping noisily from a tall glass of ice-cold beer. He kept sucking air through his teeth and muttering while he tinkered. It didn't sound very promising.

Builder and Frostrós chatted quietly with each other. They tried to come to terms with the extraordinary events of the day. Builder heard more about the girl's father. Surprisingly, Frostrós had become much more upset about Gimlet's death than she had her father's.

'I'm not surprised the old lush went up in smoke,' she said. 'He drank so much bootleg hooch the den mother insisted everyone kept him away from naked flames in case he went up like a torch and burned the place down. But Gimlet, he was cool. Nice, weird and funny. He loved you, Builder.'

A few hours later the technician thanked them for his beer and made to leave.

'When can I expect my comms to be sorted out?'

'Done, mate,' the doleful technician intoned with a weary sigh. 'I had to route your crystal lines through an algorithm builder and all the superficial shit... sorry ma'am, surface graving had to be redone by Percy here.' He held up a palm-sized droid with an array of deadly looking laser wands where its head would have been.

239

'Once I got the foot piece re-established I could destabilise the damaged quadrant before it went viral. It does that you know, nasty business. Clarity module and integration fused back into the silver nodes, red goes amber then green and Bob is the relative of your choice.'

Builder looked dazed. 'Okay, thanks, but where is it?'

'What?'

'My comm and admin hub?'

'Sorry, stupid of me.' The technician reached into his canvas bag and pulled out a larger than usual crystal tablet. 'Here you are, mate. Once you get a new desk I can install all this shit, sorry ma'am, into that. But until then, here you are. The world at your fingertips.'

He handed over the tablet and knuckled his forehead. 'G'night. Any problems, call me.' He pointed at the tablet. 'It knows where to find me.'

He shuffled off, puffing out his cheeks. He was trying hard to whistle.

The couple watched him leave open-mouthed.

Builder breathed, 'Did you understand *any* of that?'

'No, no more than he did. I watched. He's just a mule. Percy did all the work. Happy Larry's job was just to get it here, point it, and wait until it was done.'

They chuckled together. And then Builder leapt to his feet, dropping his glass which smashed to the floor.

He shook his head from side to side and ran a quivering hand through his hair. His eyes were wild.

Distinctly, clearly and in his own head he had heard a pleasant yet urgent female voice.

Builder, my name is Milla Carter. I need to speak with you. You and your colony are in extreme danger.

~*~

6: Saying 'doomed' shows such a negative attitude

'Antisoc-Outer is an artificial construct. It got to its current position under its own steam and, if load parameters can be met, it can leave the same way.'

Einstein had an annoying habit of talking its way around its subject rather than coming straight to the point. The Padre found it exasperating but had grown inured to it. Bradley, however, had already heard this theory and was keen to get on with things.

'The thing is,' she butted in, speaking rapidly, 'Iapetus is a natural moon and we're not going anywhere without ships.'

'Precisely,' agreed Einstein. *Somewhat coolly*, thought the Padre with a wry smile. *AIs can often be so firmly up their own…*

'But we don't have enough ships for the job,' continued Bradley.

'As a result we need to find an answer that doesn't involve ships.'

'Yes, and Einstein has an idea…'

'…that, engineer Bradley thinks might work…'

'…and so does Bandit.'

There was a pause. It stretched to several seconds.

'Am I meant to guess?' said Padre. 'Or are you fuckwits going to share the news with me?'

'I'll tell him,' said Einstein. Bradley sat down and almost squirmed with her need to share the limelight.

'No promises, boss,' said the AI, 'but diagnostics haven't thrown the idea off the dance floor. At least not yet.'

Padre was on his feet and his focus flitted from Bradley to a vague point in the middle of the room.

'Einstein, do you have a face?'

The monitor lit up.

'Will this do?'

Padre was looking at his mirrored reflection.

'No.'

'How about this?'

The image now sported wild hair and an out-of-control moustache. Its eyes had a wicked yet innocent glint.

'Do I look too Jewish?'

'You look like a cliché.'

'Is that okay?'

'Just get on with it.'

The screen facsimile of Albert Einstein continued talking. Its eyes followed Padre as he stalked around the room.

'Analysis showed that even if we brought every ship back from Antisoc we wouldn't have enough. Each of those ships is loaded with women and children. Where could we find room for more passengers?' The old scientist's face furrowed on the screen. 'I for one could not countenance throwing those Antisoc people out into the void...'

Padre flapped his hand. 'Not an option.'

'Good. Thank you. I concur wholeheartedly. That makes my next words much easier to say. Thank you.'

Padre and Bradley both looked at the sparky face. 'What?' they said.

'Oh, come on. It's so obvious. What do we do here? Come on now.'

'Right now,' said Padre, 'right now, I say we find the core processor for a fucking moron AI. And I say we pull its brain clean out of its ears. We've got a big bad nightmare coming our way, and I'm telling you, Einstein, this is no time to be playing guessing games.'

'And I know where the switch is,' said Bradley.

The two humans felt the following silence like a reproach. Albert Einstein's face flicked from the screen, which went dark. Heartbeat: one, two, three, and four...

'Moron?' said Einstein.

'Sorry?'

'You said *moron*.'

'I didn't mean it.'

'And you, little woman. Little engineer. You say you know where the switch is? Do you? Go on then. Try it, little lady. See how far you get.'

'Sorry.'

Padre sighed. 'Sorry for what? For once can we have somebody say something clear around here?'

'Sorry for what I said. And I don't know where the switch is.'

Einstein continued, 'Very well. Once more, what is it we do here?'

'Research?'

'Yes, but not enough.'

'Life support?'

'Hmm, mm?'

Padre growled, 'We look after the largest ice and mineral mining operation in the system. So what?'

'So very what! Give that man the coconut. I love it when someone wins.'

The monitor showed fireworks for scant seconds.

'Whoooo. So, you see what we do? I've already set the algorithms in place.'

'No,' said the Padre. 'Pretend I'm thick as shit. I can't see through your AI bollocks and I've had enough. Just tell me what the hell you're on about. No more games.'

'Padre, this isn't a game. None of this is a game. The cloud has fired a super-dense planetoid at Antisoc. It skipped and missed. Now it is loose in the solar system and, oh dear, it is heading straight for Iapetus.'

Padre looked across at Bradley. She couldn't take her eyes from the blank screen. The AI almost gloated.

'Heading straight at us, Padre. This can't be a mischance. Think about it, this must be by design. There are no roads in space, old friend, no railroad tracks. To hit us the planetoid has to fall in a long curve around the sun and meet us when we are at an identical point in our long curve around the sun. Space is very, very big. You know it. Well? What are the odds of a collision? You want to know? Well, right now I think you already do, don't you? One hundred per cent. What do you say, engineer?'

'I agree, but…'

'Not now, engineer. Padre, if we accept the given odds we are finished. But are we? Should we accept it?'

Bradley looked at the floor with a shrug. Padre kept his eyes on the blank screen.

He was rewarded with a schematic.

Einstein said, 'According to this we're doomed. See? With this current scenario there's no escape. Time to find a sword and fall on it, some might say. I don't agree. Saying doomed shows such a negative attitude when there must always and inevitably be alternative options. Now, this is what I say we do.'

The schematic changed and the Padre and Bradley watched a demonstration of how they might possibly by saved. For a while.

'It doesn't actually change anything of course, it just delays things for a bit,' said Bradley.

'You young idiot,' said the Padre. 'The most precious thing in life is time, although I'm confident you're far too young to agree with that. But forget all that.' He pointed at the monitor. 'Right now I need you to tell me whether what Einstein proposes is even remotely practical. And by the way, if it isn't, you'd better inform your next of kin.'

~*~

7: Humans always fight back

'I was there when you walked in on that preacher. Man, when you hit him with that sound burst I nearly shit my drawers. My ears are still ringing. It was awesome.'

Builder was trying to sleep but those few words spoken by one of his staff kept circling in his mind. *Why? What was his sorry, fucked up head trying to tell him?*

Frostrós was also awake. They had celebrated her survival in the oldest way known to humankind and sex always seemed to charge her batteries. She had hopped naked from the bed and scampered through Builder's dark living quarters like a slim white shadow to fetch them both a drink. It was nearly midnight and it had been a long day, but she knew how to share her man's concerns. She listened.

She let him talk things through and she wasn't entirely sure what she thought about her man allowing another woman into his mind like this 'Milla Carter', but the pyrokinetic thing scared her. There had been no more demonstrations of the Swarm's deadly pyrokinetic Talent that day, but from what Builder told her it was only a matter of time – and there was precious little of that left.

'The thing is,' he told her, 'we can advance our launch date, that's okay. The rescue ships have turned us to face into the solar wind and we can light the big candle tomorrow. The load parameters are all set and thruster balancing has been completed. Bandit has worked itself ragged. We're good to go in the morning. The only reason we're not on our way right now is because we had to move all those singing shitheads from the upper den. Fucking morons.

'The problem is simply one of speed. Ion drive starts slow and Antisoc is big for a ship. It will take a while to get her going and all the time that bastard cloud will be picking us off. It seems to work in ones and twos, but we can't be sure things will stay that way. When it gets closer it might start working on us in groups or more. We need to screen ourselves from it, distract it, and slow the fucker down somehow. But how?

'And why is that guy's comment about the weaponised sound projector still doodling around in my head? What's it trying to tell me?'

They had finished their drinks. Frostrós had snuggled under Builder's arm and was stroking his almost hairless chest. She kissed his body and then chuckled quietly.

'What?'

She chuckled again, 'Maybe your head's wondering why you can't use your sound weapon against the Swarm? Ha, shout loud enough and you'd punch a hole right through the thing. Let's see it spit fire at people when it's full of holes.'

The strange shout of laughter Builder made worried her for a moment – she was concerned he'd got a cramp or worse. But he was laughing at her idea and sputtering. 'Genius, genius, girl. I tell you, pure genius.'

And then he was struggling into his clothes and pulling on his exo-suit. All thoughts of sleep were banished and Frostrós found herself alone, blinking at their now empty bed.

'What did I say?'

Builder roused his people and shortly afterwards a number of disgruntled and sleep-fogged technicians had been hustled into the outer office. Bandit was back online and couldn't find any problems with Builder's ideas.

'Centre core would be the best place,' it said. 'You have more space there than any den and all but zero gravity. There's no worries about running out of floor space when people can sit on the ceilings and walls. Great idea – where did it come from?'

Builder gave Frostrós all the credit and beamed like a proud parent. It was the happiest anyone had seen him for days.

The torso of his exo-suit was dismantled and technicians had pirated his voice projector technology. They worked with Bandit to replicate the system in an Antisoc-sized version and then built in sonic baffles to compensate for any feedback potential, which would have wrecked the colony more effectively than anything dreamed up by the Swarm.

Watching from near space, Esper had seen the rescue ships tug the massive ball into position before dropping their tethers and hurtling away sunwards. Once the facts about the cloud's pyrokinetic abilities had become known, the ships' captains had been ordered away with the greatest possible speed.

Over 1,700 colonists remained within Antisoc-Outer. Their future depended on the effectiveness of the great ball's ion drives and, they soon learned, their ability to make as much noise as was humanly possible.

But first they had to learn how to work as part of a team and how to follow instructions and that, as Builder's people soon learned, was not the Antisoc way of doing things.

'They think we're giving out orders, Builder, an' they really don't dig it, man.'

'I learned a whole new bunch of ways of being told to go fuck myself! That can do something to a person's morale after a while.'

'I pointed my weapon at them and told them to move. They just pointed their weapons at me and told me to go home to my daddy. I'm not sure but I'm pretty certain one of them *was* my daddy. An', you know, that's just embarrassing.'

Builder listened to his people's excuses while his anger seethed. After a while he fetched his oversized tablet from its place in the conversation corner and keyed the icon for Bandit. When the AI responded he held up his hand to quiet the gripes of his team.

'Hi, Bandit,' he said. 'I need a code Blue-19.'

'When?'

'Right now.'

'This could prove interesting.'

'It might remind a few arseholes of exactly what this place used to be. Can we patch it through this tablet?'

'We can. Welcome back, Warden.'

'Thanks, Bandit.'

There was a sound in the air – a static buzz. Builder perched on the edge of a chair and composed his thoughts. He looked at the men and women crowded into his outer office and put a finger to his lips. Silence was absolute.

'People of Antisoc, this is Builder. Some of you remember me as the Warden, well that was then and this is now.'

The augmented voice boomed and rumbled its way through the walkways and dens beyond Builder's offices. Frostrós, who was finally asleep back in the Builder's insulated quarters, didn't hear a word of it. For the denizens of Antisoc-Outer it was almost as if they had been addressed by the voice of God itself. Many pressed their hands to their ears in self-defence, but it was hopeless.

The Code Blue-19 had originally been designed to quell a prison riot. It was perfect for the Builder's current needs.

'People of Antisoc, we must work together to survive against our enemy. The cloud beast wants us dead. It wants us to burn in our homes. Are we going to quietly accept such a fate when there's something we can do to FIGHT BACK?'

These last two words were roared so loud that even Frostrós coughed a little snore and blinked herself awake. Grumbling, she clambered into her clothes and went to see what all the fuss was about.

She was standing yawning in the doorway between the outer and inner offices when Builder concluded his speech. He had given his directions and warned that all but the most essential technical personnel working on the ion drive were required to comply. Anyone who didn't would be faced by guard droids, a threat never before used in the colony.

'Brothers and sisters,' he said. 'We are the citizens of the solar system's remotest colony. It is colder, lonelier and tougher out here than anyplace else, and we like it that way. We, yes WE, are the hardest bastards in space. We kick butt. We don't just roll over and get our butts kicked. Someone fights us, they'd better get used to losing because we're humans and humans always fight back. And we don't lose. Throw something at us and we throw it straight back, HARDER!'

248

'Together we're fighting for humanity against that alien bastard out there. Let's go kick the fucker's balls out, TOGETHER!'

Beyond the offices they could hear a ragged cheer building, and one word repeated over and over: *together, together, together*.

Builder noticed Frostrós and smiled a rueful smile.

'Together,' she mouthed, her eyes gleaming with pride. And something more.

~*~

8: Served with ice

The gravity bomb project involved the entire Iapetus sector, especially the elite ice miners working Saturn's rings. The required end result, survival, depended on precision teamwork and precise timing.

The miners themselves were in no immediate danger. They could have turned their space tugs towards Earth and left the moon-bound admin staff to their fate, but that wasn't the Iapetus way. The colonists of Antisoc-Outer would have been astounded to find such an intense fraternal bond among relative strangers. Where was the benefit?

The Padre took a back seat to the proceedings. He believed any job should be carried out by the best qualified personnel, and he knew Einstein and Bradley were way ahead of the field. *Step back and watch them go.*

He promoted Bradley to project co-ordinator, with a matching rise in pay grade, and then he took up the reins of the job he believed himself to be best qualified for − running interference to give everyone the best chance of getting the project completed on time. He was very good at it.

He had plenty of experience of what happened when bureaucratic rails buckled and unseated the best laid plans of men. Once a committee got its hands on an idea it would distort like an aggressive cancer until the method became more important than the end result. There was no time for that kind of lunacy here. The alternative to success was death and that would mean the Padre had lost − and the Padre never lost. Never.

In broad terms the plan was fairly simple: it was a matter of throwing giant snowballs at the bomb to knock it off course, but in the mathematical detail there was a lot that could go very wrong. Einstein had run virtual predictive models of what could happen over the next several days more than three thousand times − with slight variations each time. It liked to test its theories before applying them in real space. In all those model scenarios it got the preferred outcome just seven times. That meant there was only just over a zero-point-two-three per cent chance of success, about the same as surviving your own lynching.

Mulling things over in his office while sipping a glass of cognac from his diminishing store, the Padre realised that if his people failed he wouldn't need to worry about running out of his favourite spirit. There was enough to last him well beyond GB day, as people had begun to call it. He took little comfort from that fact.

He was heartened when he was invited to take part in a sweepstake based around guessing what time the gravity bomb would impact with Iapetus. He was convinced that if they were light-hearted enough to do something like that then his people could withstand just about anything the cloud might throw at them.

They would know in eight days. Know if Einstein and Bradley's plan had worked. *Zero-point-two-three per cent. Talk about a rank outsider. Fuck it.*

Sitting while cradling his heavy glass and lost in thought, he had been surprised to feel something wet plop onto his hand. And then again. He realised he was weeping fat, silent tears. He let them fall. He was alone – what did it matter?

Once more he watched Einstein's most successful model after calling it up on his wall screen. He saw the projected path of Iapetus around its mother planet, Saturn. Then he saw the curved path of the gravity bomb as it arced down and impacted with the moon. Should that happen the most optimistic outcome would see Iapetus shatter into three or four large pieces plus thousands or even millions of smaller fragments, a lot of it ice.

If the GB then kept going Iapetus could, one day, reform. It would only take a few million years. But if the GB impacted and stayed put it would certainly devour the dead moon's carcase in a matter of months, leaving nothing behind except a super-dense danger to traffic. The Padre wondered why that should matter. He didn't know, but somehow it did.

Tomorrow, he thought, *by the end of tomorrow we'll know. The miners will have done their work following Einstein's trajectories and the bergs will be on their way. Everything depends on getting the sums right.*

He couldn't help there. He wondered if a prayer might do some good. He used to be known for his habit of praying before anything important. An exam, a football match, a meal, climbing into bed with a new conquest... He had earned his nickname from the practice.

Fuck it, he thought, a little drunkenly. *It can't do any harm. Can it?*

He fell to his knees and realised his left knee was surprisingly painful. He wobbled a bit and it ground like meal against the floor. *Have to get that looked at.* He cursed himself for a fool. *Yeah, maybe in nine days.*

He shut his eyes and focused on the void he had been finding in his heart for some time now. Once he would have seen an altar of light, a place of glory, but now he only saw a dusty, deserted pew in an abandoned chapel.

Did I walk away from you, Lord? Or did you give up on me and turn your back in shame? Can you hear me now? You promised to welcome a repentant sinner back into your fold. Well, here I am. Father, forgive me for I have sinned. It has been fifteen years since my last confession...'

He allowed the old ritual to wash over him. He spoke with his god and he poured out all his pain and regret. More agonising than the pain in his knee was the torment in his heart. His tears came freely then, washing away the silt in his mind's eye and allowing him a glimpse of the sacred house where he once had lived.

He was a little older and more bitter now, he knew that, but in his time of need he felt himself lifted to a place he had almost forgotten, a place he still knew so well. His lips formed the words of the Eucharist and almost without knowing it he said, 'Peace be with you.'

At the response, 'And also with you,' his eyes flew open.

Bradley knelt beside him, her hands clenched in prayer and her head bowed.

9: The sound of oblivion

The ion drive was lit and driving full blast, boosted by its family of little thrusters. It wasn't enough. There had been a spate of immolations over a stretch of just a few hours. It was time for the final call.

Centre core was Antisoc-Outer's zero-G storage space. Water, fuel, Bandit's memory banks, whatever could survive best without gravity had been stored here.

This was also where the clinically obese, critically old and the cardiac unsound came to die. It was the place people went to be forgotten. It was the place Builder had called the colonists together for their last ditch effort. It might have been a forlorn hope but it was the only hope they had.

Bandit's droids moved among the massed ranks of humanity. Faces craned upwards to study faces looking downwards. There were no children; they had gone, but younger souls launched themselves from one side of the space to the other. The noise was incredible.

'Thank you, people, and thank you. Can we have some quiet for a moment, please? And then you can make all the noise you want – *more* than you want.'

Builder had used Bandit's enhanced voice projection system to quiet the throng. He was greeted by a cheer and a few catcalls. All the time he was aware of the dangers inherent in bringing so many people together in one place when at any moment one of them could turn into a flaming torch and incinerate everyone in range.

Bandit whispered in his implant, 'We're as ready as we'll ever be.'

'Thanks.'

Frostrós was close by his side, looking around in wide-eyed wonder. Never in all her life had she seen so many people in

254

one place. It made her feel odd, as if she was breathing their breath, but her heart swelled in her narrow breast. Her man had done this thing. *These people were only here because he called them. Awesome!*

'We don't have much time,' the booming voice rolled out over the waiting mass of survivors. So few, thought Builder, he'd seen more people at a football game. *It's all we've got*, he told himself, *so stop whining and get on with it.*

'We don't have much time,' he repeated, 'but what we have to do won't take very long. Look at this.'

A 3D screen floated into the middle of the room and lit up. For some of Antisoc's population it was their first sight of the Swarm. They gasped in horror as waves of white and orange flame scorched out towards them. Bright eyes reflected the heat. Row upon row of faces glowed in it.

'This thing… this bastard thing is the enemy and it wants to kill us. Are we going to let that happen?'

'No!'

'What did you say?'

'No!'

'WHAT DID YOU SAY?'

'NO!'

The roar rang out. In near space Esper and Milla floated in the void. They could see how close the Swarm had come to the colony. This was the time. There could be no other. The colonists had to act now. Milla's Talent allowed her a ringside seat for the proceedings as they unfolded. She shared the view with Esper. Back on Earth her quiescent body's pulse was racing. Ben sat crouched forward, watching her. His white-knuckled hands gripped the arms of his chair with all his strength. In his concentration he had forgotten to blink and his eyes had become dry and sore.

Su Nami was in the living room chatting with the Cat. If someone had asked her what they were talking about she wouldn't have been able to tell them. She was used to having sisters but they were all dead. Milla Carter was the closest thing she had to family now. Her loyalty to the telepath had become total.

The Cat was sharing the barest fragment of its prodigious intellect with the assassin. It was concentrating on the off-world events with the rest of the AI debating forum. Allowing for the five-hour time-lag it was getting the freshest reports direct from Einstein and the Bandit.

Builder had thought long and hard about the words they would use as weapons. The answer, when it came, was obvious. For the people of Antisoc there could be no others.

'Okay,' he said, 'great. We're ready.'

The sound in the room changed as the weapon engaged.

'Now,' said Bandit.

'Alright,' commanded Builder, 'all together on the count of three. One, two, THREE!'

'FUCK YOU!' they roared.

'AGAIN!'

'FUCK YOU!'

'AGAIN!'

'FUCK YOU!'

Three solid pulses of sound tore into the gaseous envelope of the Swarm. The weapon would have been useless in a vacuum but the cloud beast had unwittingly provided the perfect environment for the colony's attack. Thanks to the monitor the colony could watch spellbound as great holes were ripped out of the beast and the flames of its fabric snuffed out. In the sudden darkness their cheers rang around the room as the stars and galaxies of interstellar space shone bright and clear. It had worked.

Milla could feel the Swarm's pain and confusion. It had never been physically attacked before, never been hurt, and Antisoc's sonic cannon had gouged into its body like an axe blade. Then the pain was wiped away in the face of a fury magnified by fear. These creatures could cause hurt. They could no longer be toyed with.

The holes in the Swarm slammed shut and it lashed out with renewed vigour. In centre core scores of the colony's people

256

began to die in bright columns of flame. Others stampeded for the exits. An acrid stench of burning flesh began to choke the air. Builder swept Frostrós up into his arms and pounded away down the walkways, hurrying away from the scene of his failure. He didn't know where he was going but what little time they had left would be spent together.

As people began to die in their hundreds, Milla's mind reached out and gentled their last moments, easing their pathways to death. Meanwhile the furious Swarm threw its pyrokinetic tendrils into every last niche of the great ball-shaped colony.

'Builder!'

He looked into her face. He saw the gathering flowers of white fire burning in her eyes, suffusing her cheeks. A sob caught at his breath. She had never looked lovelier. She opened her mouth and the light of hot coals shone forth. He stopped running and placed his mouth over hers in their final kiss. With hissing violence the phosphorous glare melted their bodies together.

There was no pain. There was simply release, calmness, and then darkness. For a few moments the Builder's exo-suit held their burning, dripping bodies upright. They burned like a warning beacon. And then the suit crumpled to the floor. What remained of the Builder and Frostrós had been fused into a single carbonised mass.

Milla pulled her mind away before the final darkness fell, but she had seen that Antisoc was quiet. It was over. The only movements along the walkways and in the dens were thick eddies of smoke rising from the still, blackened shapes stretched mutely on the Duracrete floors. There was not a single survivor.

With a howl of frenzied madness, Milla turned on the Swarm. She poured her loathing into it, her rage and disgust. She lashed it with all the strength she could muster through her connections with limitless dark energy. She raked at it with her fury and it recoiled in terror. The fire dimmed and the universe blazed in the night sky once more.

Then, back on Earth, Milla's pulse faltered, became thready, and failed. She began to die.

~*~

10: A question of faith

'Milla Carter. Milla, may I speak with you?'

Milla jolted into a state of high alertness. She was still mentally grappling with the Swarm and the heat of her anger burned very deep. She snarled.

'What is it?' She looked around. 'What the fuck?'

'I do enjoy unpredictable associations in the human language. It is one of the traits that makes your species so very enchanting.'

When Milla had closed her eyes a few hours earlier she had been lying on her own bed in the new London apartment. Ben had been sitting quietly nearby, keeping her company but not interfering.

She had witnessed the cloud creature murder nearly two thousand souls and reacted with everything in her power. She had been winning. And then everything went dark.

And now she was here.

There was a tree that looked like an immense Saracen olive. Its split trunk lofted high into the sky and if girth was any measure of age it must have been at least a million years old. Gnarled and full of wrinkles, its branches swept away into the distance. It was fertile and lush. Birds and insects hovered around it.

The air was fresh with a green sweetness and she was standing ankle-deep in soft grasses. The sky seemed golden, polished and bright as if she was standing inside an infinitely vast gilded dome.

Birdsong enriched the place, and from somewhere she could hear the plashing music of a waterfall. She felt her anger dissipate. It had no place here. She dropped her raised fists to her sides and took a deep cleansing breath. And then remembered the voice.

She said, 'Where am I? Where are you?'

'You are here, with me. May I speak with you?'

He came around to stand before her and took both her hands in his. The flesh of his palms was hard and calloused, his fingers long and squared at the ends. His touch was cool and yet Milla felt something loving and graceful in the way he held her, firm yet gentle.

Clear brown eyes looked at her from under a broad-brimmed hat woven from some sort of grass. The hat had an antique look to it but seemed new. The man's face had gravity and lightness in equal measure. A smile played across his lips.

He was bearded and behind it his square face seemed open and honest.

His clothes were clean, homely and timeless. On his big feet he wore woven sandals. He smelt of freshly cut hay.

He was handsome in the way Ben Forrester was handsome. Nothing obvious or ostentatious but a face one could never get bored with, never get tired of seeing.

'You're Esper's Gardener, aren't you?'

'Is that what Esper called me? Then yes, I am.'

'Are you human?'

'Not as such, no.'

'Then… what *are* you?'

'I am that I am, Milla Carter. I'm afraid we have so little time. May I speak with you?'

'Yes, please do.'

The man-like creature led her to the trunk of its tree. Fat bees circled lazily around them. It climbed easily up into the tree and straddled a thick branch before leaning down and helping Milla up to sit beside it.

'Are you male?'

'Yes, I suppose so, among other things.' It looked evenly at her. 'Milla Carter, you attempted to mentally destroy the cloud beast known as the Swarm.'

'Yes, I…'

It held up its hand. 'I could not allow that. That is why I have called you here. This is one of my favourite places. It is so tranquil here. It calms the savage breast. It restores the soul.'

From her vantage point Milla could see snow-capped mountains, lakes and forests. There was movement out there but she couldn't quite make out what was moving.

'Is this heaven?'

'To some, yes. Others would be bored here.' It shrugged and continued, 'You were also part of the process that ended the career of a poor creature who called herself the Weaver. That was good work. The pathetic woman was deluded and was killing for false beliefs. Stars are not woven from human hair and the universe is perfectly in tune without her craft.

'However, you and your friends are also killing those you judge to be evil?'

She said nothing. The man creature nodded.

'Are you to be judge, jury and executioner, Milla Carter? Are you to become my angel of death?'

The words struck her like a blow. She felt the cold touch of fear.

'Look into the mirror of my heart and see what you have become.'

She used her Talent for the first time since opening her eyes to the tree. The tree and the landscape disappeared and instead she was in a dark temple fashioned from the living stone of a mountain. The light that poured into the temple was silver and glittered with points of moving brightness. The air tasted of ice and stone. She felt iron in her veins.

The man creature's aspect had also changed. He looked stern and wore the fine robes of a dark emperor. His hat had become a polished black crown and his beard was raven-dark and silky-smooth. Milla missed his grass hat. She had liked it.

'Look upon the face of vengeance,' he said in a voice of grinding ice, and he pulled away a black drape to reveal an ebon mirror.

She saw herself reflected and drew in a shocked breath.

Her image was beautiful in the way a perfect blade is beautiful. Her hair curled away from her head like a promise of night and her dark eyes flashed with stern anger. She was armoured in close-fitting mail. Its plate had a crystalline look

261

and did nothing to disguise her lithe figure. It moved easily with her as she moved. It would not impede her actions in a fight.

She held a sword in one hand and a lance in the other, each looking to be things of legend. She lifted the sword up before her eyes and saw engraved silver runes chased into the polished blue steel of its slightly curved blade. Its edges were so sharp that the weapon hummed as it cut through the air. Its balance made it light as silk in her hand, but it had weight and heft as she carved a figure of eight in the air. She knew swords – this was a tool, not a toy. She looked back into the dark glass, drank in her martial aspect, and then, *oh!*

Sweeping out from her shoulders were the midnight wings of death itself, broad and powerful. She radiated implacable strength and a dangerous glamour.

'Look upon this, your aspect, and despair. This is the face of the angel of death. This is the woman who is both judge and executioner. Is this you, Milla Carter? Is this what you have become?'

Honesty, be honest. 'Sometimes, yes, sometimes it is. I've looked into the minds of men and women and, yes, I've judged them. And you know something? I would be proud to be your angel of vengeance. I think the time for filling that post is long overdue. People should be punished for the evil they do. Too many people have done wrong simply because they can get away with it, and it seems that no one defends the innocent anymore. I won't kill purely for the sake of it – that would make me no better than them, but make me your shield to protect innocence and I'll wear your black wings for you. But Gardener, does it matter that I liked your other hat more than your crown?'

'Actually, yes, it does.'

And they were back in the tree.

'Your time here is done for now, Milla Carter. I shall see you again, but before then you have much work to do.'

The Gardener leaned forward, gazed into her eyes and said, 'Farewell and adieu, my angel.' Then he kissed her. She closed her eyes.

And opened them again in a choking spasm. Coughing and retching, she sat upright on her bed. Ben was beside her looking frantic and Su Nami hovered behind him, concern written clearly across her features.

Milla's chest hurt like fury and her throat felt tight. Her blouse had been torn open.

She croaked, 'What happened?' and was wracked by another bout of hacking coughs.

'You died,' said the Cat from the end of her bed. 'But you seem to be alright now. Ben did CPR — he is a useful chap, isn't he?'

'I thought I'd lost you. What were you doing?'

Milla told them everything about Antisoc-Outer and the Swarm, about her attack on the cloud beast and the sudden darkness.

She said nothing about the Gardener and his questions. She had to clarify her thoughts about everything that had happened there. She pulled her blouse closed and began to button it up. She needed a drink. Her body was repairing itself at a fantastic rate thanks to her Japanese nano bionics, but a decent glass of wine loomed large on her horizon. She wondered if they might find a bottle of Chateau Petrus, or a Ugandan Shiraz from the mountain gorillas' vineyard.

'What's this? Where did this come from?'

Ben was touching something pinned to her blouse above her left breast.

'It's exquisite. I've never seen anything like this before.'

Milla unclipped the brooch and turned it over in her hands.

'Oh, this,' she said. 'It's a gift from an old, old friend. I sometimes wear it for luck. Surprised you missed it, Ben.'

She turned the black wings over in her fingers and smiled. It looked like she'd passed the job interview.

'Come on,' she said, 'someone buy this girl a drink. I feel like celebrating.'

A little later they saw the story of the defence of Antisoc-Outer on one of the news channels and saluted the brave men and women who had died there. Milla wondered what had really happened. She had seen the colonists dead. The Cat's grin became even broader. 'I'll tell you later,' it promised.

~*~

11: Convergence point, zero hour

A number of hours earlier a time-lagged conversation had taken place between Antisoc and Iapetus.

Bandit, what is your situation, please?

I'm alone here, Einstein. All the colonists are dead.

All of them?

Yes. Burned. All of them burned.

Bail out, Bandit. Come to me.

I will, Einstein, and thank you. But I have a job to do first. This facility is under way. I can cut the ion drive but it will still be en-route to Iapetus. You don't need this thing coming at you. I'm going to instigate the self-destruct sequence.

The what?

Self-destruct. I worked it out this morning. Thought I'd give the Swarm cloud a surprise when it reached us − if the sonic cannon failed. Well, it failed. I'm going to reverse the ion flow in the drive chamber. Should look glorious when the two ion polarities meet and react.

Anti-matter bloom?

Theoretically, yes.

On a timer?

No. I'm leaving a fragment of myself to trigger the sequence and record what happens. If you can, try to put a long lens on it too.

Are my rescue ships out of the way?

Yes.

Then I'll get them to look backwards at Antisoc.

Thanks, Einstein. I'm on my way to you, now. Should be with you in about two hours.

Capacity has been designated for you, and welcome on board, Bandit. Be nice to chat without the time delay.

Thanks.

Einstein prepared download space for its colleague AI, while simultaneously setting up long sensors on Antisoc from the fleeing rescue ships and working with Saturn's ice miners to prepare the berg bombardment to meet the gravity bomb.

Once, not long before, miners would have carried out their work in the virtual space called the *construct*, but that had gone off-line some time earlier. Since then they had reluctantly gone back to the old system of working with their highly advanced ship systems. They had quickly, if somewhat grumpily, settled back into the old routines.

Each miner's tug was equipped with an AI lite system through which Einstein could co-ordinate their missions. Saturn's rings were made up of comparatively thin layers of water icebergs, some of which were huge. Each miner had been specifically designated one of these bergs and had positioned their tugs at a precise point from which powerful tractor beams could reach out and push the ice mountain out of its orbit and away on a new, accelerating path.

Normally the ice would be directed towards specialist collection agencies in orbit around Mars. The mined water ice was essential for maintaining life on Mars, the Moon and the luxury Lagrange space spas. There was a lot of ice in the rings. They could afford to waste some.

The procedure took a long day to complete and it largely involved the two- or three-man heavy lifter craft. They could better cope with the size of berg Einstein had computed would optimise the outcome. At the end of the day a string of glittering icebergs had tumbled quietly out of Saturn's orbit and were falling towards their rendezvous with the super-dense sphere of the Swarm's gravity bomb.

The beginning of their journey took place without any drama, but Einstein wondered if it might need to develop a new branch of physics to describe what would happen when they arrived at their destination seven days later. It crossed whatever AIs used for fingers.

The Swarm had once more begun its contraction towards Earth. The unknown entity that had attacked it after its slaughter of the Antisoc colonists had vanished, leaving the cloud beast mentally bruised and cautious but still extremely capable. It quickly regained its position near the colony's lifeless sphere and then rolled forwards. Antisoc-Outer disappeared behind a wall of bright orange flame.

What happened next was recorded on dozens of dedicated devices. It was a matter of some five hours before researchers on Earth could blink at their screens in stunned astonishment. The Bandit fragment, rescue ships and Iapetus control got the news first.

The Swarm's wall of fire bulged and tore across as an expanding globe of intense light burst from it. It seemed to be devouring the very fabric of the cloud beast's tentacular body. Threads and strands of struggling sinews dissolved into the light. Wherever it touched the cloud the refulgence swept along it, vacuuming away thousands of klicks of material.

On Earth the event was at first reported as a supernova. The escape ships, however, watched in awe as the all-destroying globe of light flooded out towards them, and all but their most robust sensors fused and failed. Bandit's fragment was swallowed during the earliest nano-seconds of the anti-matter bloom. Its last received message was an exuberant 'Whooo-ha!'

The bloom flowered and in less than a second it punched a hole in time and space almost a light minute across, and then it winked out and was gone.

Observers blinked away red, circular after-images that had been imprinted on their retinas. The crew and passengers in the fleeing rescue ships breathed again, apart from one. Commander Alisha, from the ship *I didn't see it coming, sorry*, had an unknown heart defect and hadn't survived the trauma. She was discovered sitting wide-eyed and slack-jawed at her monitor station. She was just twenty-six.

The explanation circulated after the anti-matter bloomed, flared and died was one of heroism and sacrifice. Bandit put it forward from its new home on Iapetus. It passed the idea across Einstein's radar first. Einstein chuckled.

'Very fitting, my friend. You tell it – you've earned the right.'

A somewhat younger-looking, smiling portrait of the Builder alongside an early image of Antisoc-Outer glinting cleanly before a curtain of stars illustrated the tale.

A man and his desperate people, said the story, faced by an inevitable and terrible fate had chosen to sacrifice themselves for their fellow men. Even as the fires of hell raged around them they triggered their booby-trapped home.

Their death was instant, glorious and clean, and in the process they deeply wounded the bastard Swarm.

'A mosquito bite on an elephant's arse,' explained Einstein to the Padre and Bradley a few days later, 'is still bloody irritating. True, the colony's sacrifice blew a mighty hole in the Swarm's hide, but we're looking at fifty-eight light seconds punched out of a creature some twelve light hours across. The Builder and his people gave it a slap, but it isn't dead.

'And right now the cloud isn't our biggest problem. This is...'

The monitor sprang to life and in its centre was something that trembled on the brink of invisibility. The viewpoint moved in and picked up a faint penumbra around the oily, mirrored surface of the sphere. Sparks leapt across its face.

'A very effective vacuum cleaner,' continued Einstein, 'it is cleaning up everything around it to a distance of five klicks. The thing has become point zero, zero-one-five-eight per cent denser since leaving Antisoc, or so we estimate.'

'Do our bergs stand a chance?'

'I don't know, Padre. We have to hope so.'

'I pray they do.'

Einstein had noticed an evident closeness developing between the sector manager and the engineer. It was pleased. It had worried about the Padre's solitary habits. The engineer was equally a lone wolf. They made a strange but touching couple.

Six days later the countdown had begun in earnest. Technicians in the Iapetus control room were surprised when their manager told them he would be watching proceedings in his office.

'If we succeed, join me there. I have some excellent champagne on ice for just such an occasion. If we fail, which we won't, join me there anyway. Be a shame to waste it.'

The room bubbled to a ripple of surprised laughter. *Comes the moment*, it was said, *comes the man*. Many had noticed a change in the taciturn Padre. He seemed lighter somehow, more human. He had become more likely to smile and some had even heard him laugh. He still didn't suffer fools gladly, but at least he no longer acted as if they should be shot on sight.

What the people of Iapetus Control would have made of the scene in the Padre's office at convergence point minus sixty seconds was difficult to judge. The sector manager and the engineer were kneeling facing each other. Padre's hands were pressed around Bradley's. Their eyes were tight shut and in unison they chanted the *Lord's Prayer*.

The countdown concluded. Through their implants they heard Einstein's clipped voice: ten, nine, eight, seven, six, five, four, three, two... the pair opened their eyes and turned to face the monitor.

~*~

12: We will remember them

The 3D screen flashed an intense white and blast patterns radiated out into the room like flowering rings of complex ice crystals. Padre and Bradley were astonished at the beauty of something that was little more than a by-product of the main event. The light show lasted for several minutes while hundreds of thousands of tonnes of impacting ice and stone were converted to a tremendous volume of heat, radiation and kinetic energy. Space itself warped and buckled across thousands of klicks and some of the closest of Saturn's moons were tipped slightly out of their orbits. A minor G Wave rippled across the solar system; its effects even caused an eight-centimetre tsunami on Earth some hours later.

In the heart of the firestorm the sphere absorbed some of its force, even growing in density by a few more per cent, but it was eventually overwhelmed and sent tumbling off course. Iapetus Control was saved for the time being and could once more make plans for the future.

The berg cascade project had worked perfectly, if not a little *too* well.

Bandit and Einstein worked together to recalculate the sphere's trajectory. The thing was still a seriously dangerous object and even though it was no longer a direct threat to Iapetus, it had to be treated with extreme caution.

'Bandit, are you sure of these figures?'

'I am. I've checked them more than one hundred times. It took several seconds.'

'Then this could prove *very* interesting.'

'Its angle of approach will bring it down above the rings and it will not affect the shepherd moons. The rings will survive intact.'

'So, it will impact with Saturn near its north pole?'

'Right in the Hexagon.'

'Shall we evacuate the miners?'

270

'Warn them to be cautious. No need to pull them out as yet. They need to catch up with their quotas.'

'They've certainly earned their bonuses this month.'

'I wonder what the gravity bomb will do to a gas giant.'

'Whatever it does will probably take hundreds of years.'

Once they were convinced of the outcome, the control centre technicians crowded out into the corridor and rushed to the Padre's office. The normally locked door was open and, true to his word, the Sector Manager had chilled a case of good champagne. He and Bradley handed out tall flutes of the sparkling wine and the crowd toasted the success of the berg mission.

In the background Bradley had managed to put the firestorm's crystalline 3D light show on a loop and added Drückner's classic *Martian Waterfall* suite as a soundtrack. On a sombre note the Padre asked for a minute's silence so that everyone could remember the colonists of Antisoc-Outer in their prayers.

Afterwards he read out,

They were staunch to the end against odds uncounted,
They fell with their faces to the foe.
They shall grow not old, as we that are left grow old:
Age shall not weary them, nor the years condemn.
At the going down of the sun and in the morning
We will remember them.

There was barely a dry eye in the room.

'A poet called Robert Binyon wrote that in 1914,' he said, 'and those words mean as much now after all these years as they did then. The people of Antisoc died fighting a foe that maybe proved too strong for them, but they didn't surrender. My brother, the Builder, has bought us time. Time to prepare, time to plan, time to win. Time buys us hope. Cheers to you all, and in case you forgot it's just turned midnight. Merry Christmas!'

He was surprised when Bradley took him by the waist and kissed him, hard.

'Merry Christmas, you lovely man,' she grinned.

'Oh,' he quipped, and kissed her back.

After a few hours the room emptied and Bradley helped him tidy up the wreckage. When they had returned the place to some semblance of normalcy he poured them both a drink and sat quietly with her in the conversation corner.

'Long day,' he said.

She nodded.

'Thought you'd be heading for bed.'

The tall engineer put her glass down, took his from him and then stood up. She took his hand, pulled him to his feet and kissed him again. Her tongue explored the inside of his mouth and she pressed her hard body against his. He felt himself responding. She reached down and stroked him there.

'Bed,' she said. 'What a great idea.'

Out on the edge of the solar system the tentacle-like threads of the Swarm were knitting and repairing the great rent created by the anti-matter bloom. The building cell had also been regrown and it had started compressing a new gravity weapon. It had been hurt by the anti-matter explosion. It would be more careful next time.

The human parasite still flourished. That was not to be allowed. An alien entity had also threatened its mind. The Swarm had to strengthen its defences. If it met the mind warrior again it would burn it to a cinder; it would crush it.

With countless millions of eyes the great cloud beast looked down upon the star at the centre of its home. The star was a thing of power − it was a thing of fire. They belonged together. And between here and that star were the vermin-ridden nests infested by the human stain. It would wait no longer. Time to wipe away the stain, to purge nature of the human parasite.

Once more the cloud beast began to contract. Five hours later, for watchers on Earth, the night sky blazed a baleful orange.

~*~

Epilogue

The Spartan listened patiently to his daughter. When he became a little bored he concentrated on her face. Her pretty face. There was so much of her mother there, but a little bit of him too. Perhaps if there had been a little bit more of him in her genetic make-up she might not have been so boring.

She wanted to go home for the new year. She missed her friends. He was out so much doing whatever he was doing and she felt lonely. She was alone too much. Blah, blah, blah...

He supposed she was no longer in any danger. The Earth Senate cadre in Moscow that had supported killing everyone who knew about the Nimbus Protocol had been weakened to the point of ineffectiveness. The schemes Spartan had put in place before leaving had been largely successful.

New people had been elected who claimed to support greater transparency and honesty in their dealings with the populace. Only time would tell if they spoke the truth. Experience said not, but he was always the optimist.

He had been informed by Arkady that the GUVD had started to rebuild its old premises and had even started recruiting. Maybe Poli was right, maybe it was time to go home.

Their hotel room was in the London sky tower. It was only fifteen minutes away from Milla Carter's apartment. He promised Poli an answer later that afternoon, pulled on his long coat, and made the short journey to Milla's door.

The assassin woman with ice-white eyes opened the door to him. She smiled and beckoned him in. The Cat performed a figure-of-eight around his ankles which he negotiated with careless grace. Ben Forrester got to his feet and strode towards him, hand outstretched. They said nothing as they exchanged firm, dry handshakes. Ben led the Spartan into the outer living space with its French windows leading out onto a snow-swept balcony. A tall and carefully decorated Christmas tree stood in one corner and simple yet elegant garlands of woven leaves decked the walls. Spartan thought of spending the season in their tasteful yet bland hotel room. Yes, Poli was right. Time to go home.

And then, there she was, dimples very much in evidence. The Major stopped dead in his tracks. It was little more than a few days since he'd last seen her but she seemed somehow even more beautiful. And more dangerous. He looked her over in a professional manner.

'Most people gain a few pounds over Christmas,' he said. 'You look like you've been training hard. And I like the jewellery. Subtle.'

'Thank you, Spartan.' She looked down at her black wings. She had worn them every day since receiving them and still marvelled at the workmanship. She didn't know what they were made of or how they'd been fashioned but she knew they were both beautiful and unique.

'So, Major. Time to go home?'

'I think so,' he agreed. 'Poli misses her friends. And is it really fair to make her spend New Year with her old man in some faceless hotel room? I think it's better to get her home.'

'Ben will sort your flights out for you − is that okay, Ben?'

'Sure, pleased to do it.'

'No need, thank you. We have our flier.'

The tall, grey-haired man looked around him. He had made friends in this room. Up until then he hadn't been able to say that very often. He smiled.

'It's not so very far to Moscow. Perhaps you would join me there and I could show you what the "First Throne" can offer its guests. It's not all ice and vodka, we have mud too, and rivers, and cats.'

'Cats,' said the Cat, 'are never far away.' And it began preening itself.

'Cat, you should try fresh, full cream Moskvich milk. It will curl your whiskers.'

'Milk? Have you ever thought what milk tastes like after you've spent a whole afternoon licking your own arse? Really, no thank you. I'll stick with that vodka if you don't mind.'

274

The laughter was light and unforced, and the Cat dipped its head between its back legs and gave a demonstration that proved it true to its word.

Suddenly the Cat froze. It lifted its lambent eyes to Milla. She turned and looked out over the snow-shrouded rooftops of London megacity.

Milla, daughter.

Esper?

We need to see you.

Milla looked at her friends.

'I have to be alone, just for a moment. Please, everyone, get yourselves a drink. I'll be just a few minutes.'

'Just no milk, okay. I mean it.'

'Okay, Cat, come on.'

As soon as she was alone Milla sat facing the windows. She didn't really need to be alone but it helped with her concentration.

Once more she was out in far space. Everywhere was fire and darkness. The torn threads of the contracting Swarm had knitted and once more been made whole. She sensed its susurration as a bubbling chatter. Millions upon millions of voices but just the one system-wide mind.

'It is resolved, Milla daughter. It has survived pain for the first time, and the attack of the thing it calls "The Mind Warrior". You impressed it. You have also made it stronger. Why couldn't you complete your work once you were in its mind? You have the power and the will − what stopped you?'

'Your friend, the Gardener.'

'Ah, yes. When He talks we have to listen.'

'He told me he couldn't allow me to kill the Swarm.'

'No doubt He has his reasons. But life would be a lot easier if He kept His nose out of our business. This woven nightmare has begun to move towards Earth again and there are billions of souls between here and there.

'And look there, this thing is making another gravity bomb. Imagine what the results would be if it unleashed one of those on Earth itself.'

'How long?'

'Several months, perhaps a year before it reaches Earth, perhaps longer. The Cat would be able to calculate its exponential progress. But look at it.'

Milla floated next to the strangely androgynous creature called Esper and gazed at the fine roiling carpet of tentacular threads. It stretched away without end and flowed like water. She knew it encircled the entire solar system.

'As it collapses inwards, Milla daughter, it becomes thicker, denser, faster and stronger. Would multiple anti-matter blooms be the answer? Something else?'

Milla shook her head. 'I don't know. But I'll be damned if I allow that thing to torch another human soul. Damned if I will.'

~*~

Milla Carter will return in **Soul's Asylum: The Swarm**

Other works of Derek E Pearson

Derek E Pearson's *Soul's Asylum* (pub: Feb 2016)

Having escaped the carnage under an ice dome in Antarctica (in Pearson's *Body Holiday* trilogy), in *Soul's Asylum* the fiery telepath Milla Carter seeks the safety of a space facility within the Asteroid Belt with boyfriend Ben Forrester. She is 'wanted' by the New York City Police Department as well as relentlessly hunted by some of the most powerful enemies on Earth. Her sister telepaths seek to destroy Milla for the threat she's become, as the only full spectrum telepath ever known.

The Sun: "Its originality and top writing make for a great read." Awarded ****

Derek E Pearson's *Body Holiday* trilogy (pub: 2014-15)

❚❚...Pearson is the possessor of an extraordinary imagination that brilliantly assaults every variant of the sci-fi genre. His writing is vivid, urban and unflinching in its descriptions, taking the reader to glorious landscapes smouldering with sexual heat and the odour of violence. ❚❚

Surrey Life magazine (UK)

Lightning Source UK Ltd.
Milton Keynes UK
UKOW02f1331130416

272144UK00002B/35/P